CERTAIN TRUTH

A CERTAIN TRUTH

JAMES SCOTT BELL

BETHANYHOUSE
MINNEAPOLIS, MINNESOTA 55438

Published by Bethany House Publishers
11400 Hampshire Avenue South
Bloomington, Minnesota 55438
www.bethanyhouse.com

Bethany House Publishers is a Division of
Baker Book House Company, Grand Rapids, Michigan.

Printed in the United States of America

Library of Congress Cataloging-in-Publication Data

Bell, James Scott.
    A certain truth / by James Scott Bell.
        p.   cm. — (The trials of Kit Shannon ; bk. 3)
    ISBN 0-7642-2647-9 (pbk.)
        1. Shannon, Kit (Fictitious character)—Fiction. 2. Los Angeles (Calif.)—Fiction.
3. Women lawyers—Fiction. I. Title II. Series: Bell, James Scott. Trials of Kit Shannon
; bk. 3.
    PS3552.E5158C47   2004
    813'.54—dc22   2004001024

JAMES SCOTT BELL is a Los Angeles native and former trial lawyer who's now a full-time writer and public speaker. He is the author of several legal thrillers; his novel *Final Witness* won the 2000 Christy Award as the top suspense novel of the year. He and his family still reside in the City of Angels.

Jim's Web site is *www.jamesscottbell.com.*

Books by James Scott Bell

Circumstantial Evidence
Final Witness
Blind Justice
The Nephilim Seed
The Darwin Conspiracy
Deadlock
Breach of Promise

THE TRIALS OF KIT SHANNON

A Greater Glory
A Higher Justice
A Certain Truth

Books by
Tracie Peterson & James Scott Bell

SHANNON SAGA

City of Angels
Angels Flight
Angel of Mercy

Bread of deceit is sweet to a man;
but afterwards his mouth shall be filled with gravel.

—PROVERBS 20:17

Part One

1

"LOVELY," TED FOX SAID.

Kit Shannon Fox, breathing in the bracing ocean air, leaned against her husband on the deck of the *Majestic*. On the eastern horizon, like the glow of an angelic fire, dawn was lapping at the sky. "Do you mean the sunrise?"

Ted looked at Kit's face, smiling. "There's a sunrise?"

"Silly. What are you talking about?"

"You, of course. You put the sun to shame."

Kit rested her head on Ted's shoulder. "Charmer. You should have been a lawyer."

"One in the family's enough."

"Then I am left with the charm," Kit said.

"That's why you married me, isn't it?"

"Of course not. I married you for your clothes."

Ted had on the flowered shirt he'd picked up on the big island of Hawaii. He looked like a pineapple advertisement. But Kit cared not a bit. They were together, husband and wife. That was all that mattered.

They were heading home after a belated honeymoon. Their wedding had been a glorious affair, but one with a twist ending. On the way out of the church, Kit had received a desperate message from a girl in trouble—one of Pearl Morton's ladies of the evening, thrown in jail on trumped-up charges in order to cover the tracks of a prominent politician.

Finally they had made it on a cruise to Hawaii, though six months after they'd anticipated. Even so, they soaked luxuriously in the island sun and in the wonders of each other. Time had raced by like the mahimahi in the waters of Waikiki Beach.

Now they were on their way home, aboard the cruise ship *Majestic,* and they had been given the honor of an invitation to the captain's table for tonight's dinner.

Six months married now, Kit mused, and it passed like six days. Indeed, it seemed as though only a week ago that they'd met, which was back in 1903. Nearly four years already! And in that four years they'd lived a lifetime together, their bond deepened due to the trials they had been through together. One was a court trial in which Ted had been framed for murder. The other was when Ted lost his leg in an accident with his plane. He even left Los Angeles for a time after that.

Here and now, however, in the glow of hope that was the new dawn, Kit dared to believe there was finally to be some equilibrium in her life.

Ted put his arm around Kit's shoulders. In the brisk morning air it felt to Kit like a soft blanket. Ted could always make her feel warm. Even on her darkest days.

"Sorry the cruise is almost over?" he asked.

"Only a little. I don't believe I could take more poi. I do believe they use it in Los Angeles to paste wallpaper."

"You're being charitable."

"I will be glad to get back to Angelita's shredded beef and tamales."

"At least I had you all to myself. For nearly two weeks I didn't have to share you with the criminal courts or the telephone or even Corazón. It was paradise."

"And it will continue to be, Ted."

He kissed the top of her head. It felt as if he were saying, "I hope so."

The waters splashed against the hull, reminding Kit of the Los

Angeles to which they were returning. A restless place, the City of Angels had become the 1907 incarnation of American agitation and energy, bursting out of its leisurely, hacienda ways with the ferociousness of a hungry mountain lion.

Local merchants and manufacturers and realtors all viewed the rapid industrialization as the key to the future of the city. Building was booming, to the point it became hard to tell whether this was the cause or effect of the continuing influx of cheap labor and quick-buck dreamers.

A recent cartoon in the *Los Angeles Times* had rendered a future city of crowded buildings, touting its vision of "balanced prosperity" with flags saying things such as: Building! More Building! Oil! Real Estate! Foreign Trade! More Factories! Agriculture! New Industry! One got breathless just looking at it.

Of course, all this led to some predictable troubles. The old collided with the new, and something had to give way. A month ago a stable boy driving a two-horse team for the Beeson Brothers down Fifth Street ran afoul of a Rio Light Touring Car. The screeching electric horn of the model was laid into by the autoist, spooking the horses. They tore down Fifth, the sandy-haired youth pulling on the reins with all his might, dodging trolleys, carriages, and pedestrians before finally coming to rest in Central Park. Unfortunately, the incident claimed one victim, a Mrs. Minerva Daly, who was unable to avoid the furious rush of the frightened horses.

Crime was on the increase as well, something which caused the telephone at the First Street office of Kathleen Shannon Fox, attorney-at-law, to ring constantly throughout the business day.

Kit sighed at the prospect of returning home as the refreshing spray of the Pacific created a mist around her and Ted. Then she noticed another early riser up top to catch the sunrise. She recognized his gait. It was the young man, Chilton Boswell, with whom they had become acquainted during the trip. Boswell was also newly married, to a waifish woman by the name of Wanda. It was not Kit's place to interfere, yet she could not help sizing up the newlyweds in the way they related to each other.

Which was not very well.

Perhaps it had been nervousness on the part of the young bride. Such was common. Marriage, as Mrs. Studdard had written in her column for the *Los Angeles Times,* can quickly become a trial for the wife, that is, if her husband does not continue the romance. "Many a man," Mrs. Studdard wrote, "has entranced an eager lass until vows are exchanged. Then he returns to his old ways, spending time at work and then the club, while his bride wonders whatever became of the man who had swept her off her feet."

Strong words, but ones that Kit sensed did apply in this matter. On two occasions at the Royal Hawaiian Hotel, Kit had walked by the gaming room and caught a glimpse of Mr. Boswell occupied with playing cards. His wife she had hardly seen at all.

"It appears we have company," Ted whispered, even though Boswell stood a good twenty yards away with his back to them. "I'll have to behave myself."

"I wish you wouldn't," Kit said.

"A scandal? We don't want the whole ship buzzing, now, do we?"

"Why not? The *Gazette* is in new hands and probably aching for material."

The *Gazette* was the scandal rag that Kit had tangled with during the Truman Harcourt murder trial.

"I can see it now." Ted waved his hand in front of him. "Kit Shannon Fox Falls to Temptation, Cannot Resist the Allure of Her Dashing Aviator Husband."

"What's so scandalous about that?"

"Nothing, but it certainly sounds good, doesn't it?"

A flicker of movement caught Kit's eye. Another figure emerged onto the main deck, wrapped in a cape and hood. This one moved like a woman, but with a mysterious grace, like a dancing shadow. Kit half-watched her, then turned her full attention back to Ted.

"When we get back to Los Angeles," she said, "what is the first thing we shall do?"

Ted shook his head in wonderment. "What a strange sound those words are. You have been buried in law books and court cases ever since I've known you. Suddenly you have asked me for a suggestion on how to apply ourselves to our time together. Is this a dream?"

Kit stroked Ted's cheek with her hand. "I am yours, fully and completely."

"At least until the next case comes up."

"I shall attempt to keep a low profile. In fact, let's extend our honeymoon, shall we? Two weeks was not enough."

"Let's. We will go to the beach at Venice and sample the canals. And how about a camping trip? We can ride horseback into Big Bear."

"What about the plane?"

Ted smiled. "There will be time enough. You give up a client or two; I'll give up Gus."

Gus Willingham was Ted's friend and chief mechanic on their monoplane project. Aviation in America had moved rapidly since the Wright brothers' triumph at Kitty Hawk the same year Kit met Ted. Virtually all the designs were biplanes, however. It was Ted's vision, fueled in no small way by Gus's mechanical acumen, that gave rise to the monoplane idea.

The woman who had come on deck was now speaking to Chilton Boswell. She used close and anxious gestures. Most likely this was his wife, for the way Chilton seemed to be ignoring her importunities was in keeping with Kit's assessment of their marriage.

Suddenly Chilton Boswell started shouting. Although Kit could not make out the words, clearly they were words filled with anger. His arms flailed for a moment, and then the woman in the hood turned and scurried away like a chastised dog.

After she left, Chilton Boswell glanced at Kit and Ted. Just as quickly he turned and walked on toward the bow.

"Are you ready?" Ted said.

"Hmm?"

"Are you ready?"

"For what, dear?"

"My rematch. Shuffleboard awaits."

Kit nodded. "And what shall the stakes be?"

"The usual. If I win, I get a long, lingering kiss from my wife."

"And if you lose?"

"You get a long, lingering kiss from me."

"Let's play."

2

THE CAPTAIN'S TABLE LOOKED as elegant as any at the finer restaurants one would find back in Los Angeles. Crisp white linen and exquisite silver. China that would have made her great-aunt Freddie proud.

Kit Shannon Fox nodded in silent tribute. She leaned over to Ted and whispered, "Not bad for a criminal defense lawyer, eh?"

Ted smiled, looking as happy as Kit had ever seen him.

Captain Wendell Raleigh seemed to delight in this privilege of his office. Genial and witty, he welcomed to the round table a curious mix. Kit had made passing acquaintance with a few of them back on the island. Now she saw them in a somewhat different light, as studies in social fusion.

There was Professor Aiden Aloysius Faire from the University of Chicago. A large man with a walrus mustache and pince-nez glasses, he was seen about the ship in a large flowing overcoat and floppy hat. He seemed a rather serious fellow, not one to crack jokes.

Unlike the first mate, Lowell Sanders, who was young and full of himself, a man whom Kit figured to be of an ambitious sort, a "go-getter" in the parlance of modern American slang.

Then there were the young newlyweds, Wanda and Chilton Boswell. There was a nervous strain between them. Was there something more to it than the newness and inevitable adjustments of wedded life?

Perhaps the cause of the tension was seated next to them, in the form of Chilton's mother, Glenna Boswell. A matriarchal and thin-lipped woman, she did not appear particularly fond of her daughter-in-law.

Rounding out this peculiar congress was the beautiful yet mysterious Delia Patton. Dark of hair and eye, she was unmarried and, Kit presumed, on the prowl. Certainly the way she made eyes at virtually all of the men aboard ship gave that distinct impression.

The dinner conversation flowed amiably, despite the undercurrents of tension. Besides the strain between the young Boswells, Professor Faire seemed to have something on his mind and kept quiet for the most part. And just what was Delia Patton up to, seated between the captain and Lowell Sanders? Wheels certainly were turning in her pretty head.

The meal was a masterpiece—roast beef cooked to perfection, julienne vegetables, Yorkshire pudding, and much to Kit's delight, fresh ice cream.

The latter was served with coffee, and as the guests began to repose, Captain Raleigh and First Mate Sanders shared seafaring stories. But others in the company—especially the Boswell party—grew less garrulous as the evening progressed.

Finally, during a lull, Professor Faire, who was seated directly across from Kit and Ted, made a pronouncement. "I understand, Mrs. Fox, that you are something of a biblical scholar."

This brought all at the table to rapt attention, looking at Kit for her answer.

"I would not go that far," Kit said, a bit embarrassed at being singled out.

"How far would you go, then?"

Again, the others waited for Kit's response. "I am a pastor's daughter. I do revere the Good Book and try to live by its principles."

"And it has some very lovely principles," the professor said. "Also some horrific ones."

Captain Raleigh smiled disarmingly. "I suspect Professor Faire is attempting to draw Mrs. Fox into dangerous waters."

"Nothing of the sort. I merely bring this up in the spirit of robust discussion. But perhaps Mrs. Fox would rather avoid the subject entirely."

"I'd be careful if I were you, bub," Ted said. "You might be getting into deep waters yourself."

Kit lightly jabbed Ted in the ribs. "Please don't mind my husband. He thinks rather highly of me."

"And well he should," Professor Faire said. "Nevertheless, if you wish to change the subject . . ."

"If the subject is the Bible I am always loath to change it. Still, I would not want the other guests to be bored."

This was met by a chorus of "No" and "Please." The group seemed to be interested in what was shaping up to be a lively debate. Kit understood, since people had spent the latter part of the afternoon looking for something to do, after the orchestra had canceled the afternoon concert due to bouts of dysentery in the strings section. Further, an unseasonable fog had taken away the sunset, rendering the view unremarkable. What better entertainment than to see an esteemed professor of philosophy going hammer and tongs with a lawyer?

The professor smiled. "I see that we have an assent to go forward. And so I shall repeat. The doctrines of the Bible contain what I call fool's gold principles to benefit mankind. It looks good on the surface, but for the most part the Christian religion has visited upon the world a dark record of bloodshed and violence. One need only look at the Crusades to see a record of killing that remains unmatched in the annals of our race."

The starkness of the charge seemed to catch the guests by surprise. Kit detected a bit of discomfort in their eyes yet something else in the expression of the professor. He seemed pleased to be the sort of man who enjoyed disturbing people, not by outrageous behavior but by the superiority of his thoughts. A man who liked to slay sacred cows.

Kit could imagine a classroom full of eager young minds

listening to this man as if he were a modern-day Moses, only one who carried tablets written by man's philosophy rather than by God. Her neck began to generate heat.

"I should think," Kit began, "that the real question is not how much evil has been done in the name of Christianity but how much evil Christianity has prevented."

Professor Faire, in the middle of lighting a cigar, paused for an instant. "Are you denying Christianity's record of bloodshed?"

"No one can deny that certain men have at certain times done evil in the name of Christianity. But much more evil has been done without the restraint of the church. Indeed, it was the influence of Christianity that abolished gladiatorial combat, human sacrifices, exposure of children, slavery. Are you willing to acknowledge this?"

The flame from the match burned Professor Faire's fingertips. He jolted with surprise. Recovering, he said, "Are you claiming all of that for Christianity?"

"I'm merely citing history," Kit replied.

"But the Bible specifically endorses slavery."

"The Bible recognized that slavery was a part of ancient society, and that's all. The movement to abolish slavery in the last century was almost exclusively a Christian one. I'm sure you know that Harriet Beecher Stowe, the author of *Uncle Tom's Cabin,* was the daughter of a Presbyterian minister and the wife of a professor of the Old Testament."

Professor Faire did not respond, though he did manage to successfully light his cigar with a new match and expel a puff of smoke over the table.

"The early American abolitionists," Kit continued, "were deeply religious. John Quincy Adams is but one example."

Captain Raleigh nodded. "The historical record seems pretty clear."

"The stifling of man's ego by religion," Faire added, "is the largest impediment to progress in the world."

Kit felt a familiar onrush inside her, which usually came before cross-examination. "It is quite true that men and women of good conscience can effect goodly changes. But the difference is that they are borrowing from Christianity without acknowledgment."

Faire furrowed his massive brow. "Explain."

"Where does a man get his knowledge of good? It can only be from above. For if man is free to define the good for himself, he ends up with only one conclusion—the stronger shall rule the weaker."

"Ah yes," Professor Faire said with a haughty air. "The argument of Polemarchus in Plato's *Republic*."

Kit gently cleared her throat. "Actually, I do not believe that was the argument."

Professor Faire reacted as if he had been slapped with a flounder. "I would remind you," he said stiffly, "that I hold a chair in philosophy at the University of Chicago, and my specialty is the ethics of ancient Greece."

"I have the read the Greeks as well. And I must say that in every way Christianity improves upon the ancient wisdom."

"How so?"

"Aristotle, for example. He did not believe a man born without certain benefits, including good looks, could be truly happy. He contended that fortune dealt such blows and there is nothing a man can do about it. Christianity, on the other hand, offers hope and happiness to all."

"Happiness is good," Delia Patton tossed in. "I like it so much better than unhappiness."

Lowell Sanders laughed. A bit too loudly in Kit's estimation.

"Your reading of Aristotle is cursory," Faire said, more weakly than his previous statements.

Kit was about to reply when she noticed the other guests in various stages of discomfort. Glenna Boswell was fanning herself; Wanda Boswell was listening but appeared to have other concerns on her mind. Chilton Boswell looked disgruntled and was downing what Kit estimated to be his sixth full glass of champagne. Kit did not think his agitation was solely because of her dialogue with the professor.

Lowell Sanders no longer seemed interested in the flow of the conversation. Perhaps that was because he was seated next to Delia

Patton, who acted as if her sole task for the evening was to bat her eyes as fetchingly as possible.

"Perhaps, Professor," Kit said, "we ought to hear from the others. There are sure to be plenty of opinions."

Faire exhaled a cloud of cigar smoke. "Your representations are rather specious in light of the fact—"

"Ah, put a cork in it, Professor." Chilton Boswell's voice rang out like shot. Everyone turned toward him. Chilton's face had reddened considerably.

"I beg your pardon," Faire spouted indignantly.

"You heard me, you high hat."

The tension was now as thick as the roast beef had been. Kit was appalled at Chilton Boswell's lack of manners. The professor was blustery, true. But that did not mean he deserved to be insulted. Even if Chilton's comment came under the impulse of alcohol, that did not excuse it.

"Now, why don't we all calm ourselves," the captain said.

Faire huffed. "If my presence here is such a distraction, I shall take my leave."

He got up from the table and, despite protests from the captain and Kit, slouched away.

"Oh, Chilton," Wanda uttered in soft rebuke.

That only made Chilton Boswell angrier. He glared at his wife. "And that's enough out of you!" He then stood up and threw his linen napkin on the table. "If you will excuse me," he said.

"Where are you going?" Wanda Boswell demanded.

"None of your affair."

"Not to the gaming room!"

"I'll go where I please, and don't you say another word about it." He staggered a little, and not from the listing of the ship. Kit felt badly for Wanda Boswell. A loud, drunken husband rebuking her in public, displaying for all to see the troubles in their marriage.

Chilton Boswell did not bother to comment further. He stormed out of the dining room, grabbing as he went another glass of champagne off a tray carried by a waiter.

An embarrassed silence fell over the table. Kit noticed Delia Patton trying to suppress a smile.

"Well!" Glenna Boswell said at last. "I cannot say as I blame Chilton." She looked hard at Wanda, who promptly burst into tears.

"Say," Lowell Sanders inserted with all the subtlety of a Clydesdale, "how about I tell a little joke?"

Wanda bolted up, knocking her chair backward, and ran from the table.

Glenna Boswell labored to her feet. Ted and the other men also stood, mouthing "Good evening."

"We hope all will be well," Captain Raleigh offered.

"I shall make it so," Glenna Boswell replied. With a final flit of her fan, she sauntered off, her dark blue evening gown swaying, the clacking of her pearls audible to the guests.

3

"DID YOU NOTICE ANYTHING strange at the captain's table tonight?" Kit asked Ted as she put the finishing touch on her braid. She sat in front of the mirror in their stateroom, still vexed by something she could not quite articulate.

Ted, reclining in bed, had his hands folded atop the covers. "Aside from the tears and women running from the room?"

"Besides the obvious. I would like your impressions overall, to see if they are in any way like my own." Kit looked at him by way of the mirror's reflection.

"Then I will tell you. My impression is that you are the loveliest woman in the world and I want you next to me right now."

Even from across the room Kit could see Ted's blue eyes waltzing. Her heart joined the dance. She was married to the man of her dreams, hopes, and prayers. Silently, as she had done over and over since their wedding, she thanked God.

Though it had taken them six months to get to their honeymoon, nothing had dampened the ardor Kit felt for her husband.

Kit fiddled a bit more with the tip of her braid, wanting to get rid of the odd feeling that something about the dinner scene was not right. Her mentor, the great trial lawyer Earl Rogers, had taught her the Rule of Human Probabilities. It was, in essence, an intense focus on behavior filtered through the hard sieve of common sense. People acted in predictable ways most of the time. If they didn't, usually it was because they were hiding something.

"Presently, darling," Kit said. "Think of the dinner for just a moment with me. Begin when the professor—"

"Professor Blowhard?"

"—when he decided he wanted to talk about religion."

"His mistake."

"What did you make of that?"

Ted shrugged. "He is one of the sophisticates who deem theology to be a dying enterprise. You read the series in the *Examiner*, didn't you?"

She had. The *Los Angeles Examiner*, owned by William Randolph Hearst and an upstart to the more stodgy *Times* of General Harrison Gray Otis, loved to stir up hornets' nests. So, in a city of abundant churches—both Catholic and Protestant—the *Examiner* ran a five-part series on the "crisis in theology," brought on by German higher criticism of the Bible, the works of a Viennese doctor named Sigmund Freud, Darwin's theory of natural selection, and the philosophy of the "humanist." The impression it left was that God might someday become an idea that was no longer useful.

"But why do you suppose," Kit asked, "Faire was so vehement in his arguments?"

"I do not think he enjoyed being bested by a young woman. Will you come to bed?"

Kit got up from the table, swept her rope of auburn hair over her shoulder, and glided toward the bed, wearing her silk nightgown. As she lifted the covers she said, "I believe it was more than that. The professor has been somewhat distracted this whole trip."

"The distracted one is that old battle-ax, Mrs. Boswell."

"Why, Theodore Fox, how you talk."

Kit slid in next to her husband, nestling her head on his chest. He put his arm around her, stroking her silken back with his hand.

"I feel sorry for Wanda Boswell," Kit said. "The poor girl is caught between the proverbial rock and a hard place."

"Her husband is, how shall I put it, a cad."

Kit raised her head a little. "Did you get that sense, too?"

"You smell like paradise."

"Perhaps that other woman, Miss Patton, is—"

Ted stopped her with a finger to her lips. "No more talking."

"I only want to—"

"No more." He kissed her.

"No." Kit surrendered with her next breath. "Let's not talk any-more."

———

Kit dreamt of warm places—beaches of white sand, of home with a fire blazing in the fireplace, dawdling under soft blankets with Ted's arms wrapped around her. Then she felt herself trans-ported suddenly to a lonely mountain, and it was cold. Not freez-ing, not snowy—simply lush green but with a chilly breeze.

It was a troublesome scene in her dream because it looked so beautiful, and yet the cold kept her from comfort. Something was wrong. She was alone, and she did not know where to turn.

Then, behind her, a chopping sound. Someone cutting into a tree. But she could not turn to see who it was. The chopping got closer, more insistent. . . .

Kit woke up as the sound of someone pounding on her door grew louder.

"What is it?" Ted mumbled, stirring beside her.

Kit quickly slipped on her nightgown and covered herself with the pink morning gown that had been a wedding present from Cor-azón. She glanced out the round window of the stateroom and saw only the tiniest hint of light over a dark ocean. Early morning.

The knocking came again, then Kit heard a woman's voice.

"Mrs. Fox." It was a low but desperate whisper. "Please, Mrs. Fox."

Wanda Boswell. Kit recognized the thin timbre of her voice. Also the fear. She opened the stateroom door. Wanda's face was par-tially silhouetted by the lights of the corridor.

"Please help me, you're the only one . . ."

"What is it?" Kit said.

"Please come . . . it's terrible . . . I don't know what to do." Wanda backed up a step, indicating with her head to her left.

Kit looked back into the room. "I must go for a moment, Ted."

"What's that?"

"Back soon."

Kit stepped out into the corridor and closed the door. Wanda, glancing around, hurried away. Kit nearly had to run to keep up. The spare lights in the corridor seemed like unforgiving eyes.

Wanda Boswell stopped at the end of the passageway, in front of a door. "I am so desperately frightened." Her hand trembled on the door handle.

"Let me." Kit opened the door and entered a stateroom very much like her own. It was a suite, and she had come into the receiving room. The chamber was illuminated by a small chandelier for the first-class cabins. The ornate wood paneling was also similar, as were the set of two wingback chairs and a divan of scarlet.

What was not the same was the body on the floor. Chilton Boswell, still in his evening clothes, lay motionless.

"He's dead." Wanda barely got the words out.

Kit reached behind Wanda and closed the door. "How did it happen?"

"I don't know, I don't know! I woke up. Chilton had not been to bed. I came out here and found him like this. I thought he was passed out from drink, but I could not rouse him, and then I knew he was—" Wanda choked back a sob.

Kit put her arm around the girl. "All right. We must summon the captain at once."

"The captain!"

"He is the law's representative here."

"Law?" Wanda stiffened. "What is going to happen?"

"You have nothing to fear."

"But I do." The girl took a step back, wide-eyed. "You don't know. His mother . . ."

"What about his mother?"

"She hates me. She will accuse me!"

"It is the facts that matter, not accusations."

"You don't know her. She is powerful. She wanted Chilton to leave me." She grabbed Kit's hand. "Please don't let them hurt me."

"No, no." Kit thought a moment. "Is there anything else you have not told me? Did you hear Chilton come in last night?"

"I did hear him. I did not speak, for fear of his anger. When he is drinking, he is so mean."

"But you heard him come in?"

"Yes, and I listened. He shuffled about for a moment, and then he went out again."

"Out?"

"Yes. I must have fallen back asleep after that. I woke up again when he returned."

"Do you know how much time passed before his return?"

"I do not."

"What happened next?"

"I could hear his breath; it was labored. That meant he had been drinking heavily."

"Did you hear anything else?" Kit said.

"I heard something like glass clinking. Like he was having more to drink."

A crucial bit of evidence. Kit glanced around the sitting room and spotted the bottle of champagne on a table by the window. A champagne flute sat empty next to it. "Where did that bottle of champagne come from?" she asked.

"Oh, that," Wanda said. "It was sent in yesterday."

"By whom?"

"Mr. Raffels."

"Who is that?"

"He is the one who runs the gambling room."

"Was the bottle sent to you, or to Chilton?"

"The card had both our names on it."

"Who delivered it?"

"A steward. I had him put it on that table."

"Did you open it?"

Wanda shook her head. "I was waiting for Chilton."

"All right," Kit said. "We must touch nothing in this room. Have you a dollar?"

Wanda looked confused. "Yes."

"Do nothing and say nothing until I tell you. Can you remember that?"

"I will do exactly as you say."

"THERE IS NO SIGN of a wound," Captain Raleigh said, standing up. "I will need the ship's doctor to take a look at him."

Raleigh's white uniform was impeccable. This was not a man to show up anywhere on his ship looking disheveled, even in the early morning hours in a stateroom that contained a dead body.

Next to him stood the first mate, Lowell Sanders. This was, Raleigh had explained to Kit, standard procedure for the investigation of wrongdoing aboard ship. Witnesses were vital, as the matter would be turned over to local authorities upon docking.

Wanda sat in one of the chairs. Kit looked on, feeling no concern about her morning garb, only that nothing was disturbed in the room and that Wanda should be comforted.

"I would like to be present when the doctor examines the body," Kit said.

Raleigh nodded. "But for the time being, we have a situation. So I would like to know exactly what Mrs. Boswell was doing from the time she left the dinner table until she discovered the body."

He turned toward Wanda, who was cowering in her chair. Kit immediately stepped in. "Captain, if you don't mind my saying, that sounds like an accusatorial request."

"Mrs. Fox, I am the captain of this vessel, and as such it is my duty to investigate any criminal wrongdoing."

"But how do we know it is criminal? Mr. Boswell might have died of purely natural causes."

Lowell Sanders smiled. He was a handsome young man, of the sort who knew it and who wore his uniform as a personal enhancement. The gold brocade around his shoulders appeared ostentatious yet at the same time jaunty. "She's got a point, Captain," he said.

Raleigh's reaction was swift. "I do not need insubordination added to my troubles, Sanders. I will decide the proper procedure here." He looked at Wanda once again, his face reflecting stern purpose. "Now, Mrs. Boswell, I must insist—"

"Captain, excuse me." Kit felt the full ire of Captain Raleigh rain down upon her. "The protections of an accused do not cease aboard an American ship. If you are treating Mrs. Boswell as the focus of a criminal investigation, she has the right to know it."

"Why don't you just stay out of this?" Raleigh said. "If she has nothing to hide, she shouldn't be reticent, should she?"

"I have represented innocent people whose words a zealous prosecutor has twisted beyond the truth."

"Hang it all, I am the captain here! I will not be hindered in my duty. Mrs. Fox, I will thank you to remove yourself from this room."

Kit nodded to Wanda. The girl reached into the pocket of her robe and pulled out a silver dollar. She placed it in Kit's hand.

"You have witnessed my retainer," Kit said to Lowell Sanders. "I am officially Mrs. Boswell's lawyer. I will remain with her for the duration of this trip and listen to all questioning."

A coolness swept over Raleigh's face. "Very well. Since you are officially Mrs. Boswell's lawyer, I will officially place Mrs. Boswell under arrest."

Wanda gasped.

"On what evidence?" Kit said.

"A corpse and a motive."

"Motive?"

"Everyone on this cruise knows that Mrs. Boswell and her husband were not getting along."

"Hardly a motive for murder. For all anyone knows, Chilton Boswell may have killed himself."

"Nevertheless, I am not going to take any chances here. If it turns out to be some sort of accident or suicide, there is nothing for Mrs. Boswell to worry about. Now I must ask First Mate Sanders to escort Mrs. Boswell to the room adjacent to my quarters, where she will be confined."

"It is your prerogative to do this, but I would request that you release Mrs. Boswell to me. She may stay in my room, and I will assume responsibility for this."

Raleigh did not look as if he wished to do Kit any favors. But after a moment's reflection he said, "Very well. Mrs. Boswell will remain in your stateroom until we pull into San Leandro. If there is no evidence of wrongdoing, she will have nothing to fear."

"Thank you, Captain."

"Sanders, fetch the doctor."

———————

"Two days left on our honeymoon," Ted whispered, "and we have a prisoner in our room?"

"Ted, please, she will hear you." Kit had closed the door to the bedchamber after helping Wanda Boswell move some of her things into the sitting room.

"What can possibly happen that she needs to be here?" Ted said.

"She's scared. I don't want her put in some room alone."

"And what about us?"

"I'm sorry. I know it is an inconvenience."

Ted shook his head. "I never thought your work could catch up to us on the open sea."

Kit stroked Ted's lips with her finger. "We will make up for it on the mainland. I promise."

"And I will hold you to that promise."

"Good. Now I must talk to as many of the witnesses as possible before we pull into—"

"Kit."

"Yes?"

"Just remember my name, all right?"

"Yes, Jack, I will."

Ted did not look amused. Kit kissed his cheek. "I am sorry this happened. Let's meet for breakfast, shall we?"

"I will put that down as an appointment—"

"Ted—"

"—and count myself lucky."

5

THE DOCTOR, A STAID MAN named Novak, went about his examination of Chilton Boswell's body with all the delicacy of a blacksmith. Kit watched his every ham-fisted move as he unceremoniously flipped, prodded, and poked Chilton's body with a selection of instruments he pulled from his black bag.

When she could stand it no longer, Kit said, "Sir, if you please. This body will be examined by the county coroner. If you could proceed with a bit more care, I would—"

"Who is the doctor here?" Novak looked up at her from his knees, his bushy eyebrows narrowed downward in irritation.

"Mrs. Fox," Captain Raleigh said, "may I remind you that you are not in charge here. I am."

"Would you kindly instruct the doctor to do his utmost not to disturb the body?"

"Can't very well examine 'im if I can't touch 'im," Novak protested.

"You go right ahead, Doctor." Raleigh faced Kit with military bearing. "Mrs. Fox, I assure you, I will see to it nothing is disturbed."

The doctor resumed his examination. Kit kept him in view from the corner of her eye as she addressed Captain Raleigh. "Then I should like to gather the rest of Mrs. Boswell's things while I am here and have them moved to my stateroom."

Raleigh shook his head. "I'm afraid I can't allow that at the moment."

"I beg your pardon?"

"What's in this room is evidence. I'll want to have a police detective analyze the contents."

"Do you have a subpoena?"

"No."

"Then I object."

"Do you have a judge around?"

Frustrated, Kit pursed her lips. If he was going to insist on ignoring the normal rules of procedure, there was nothing she could do, at least while they were at sea. There wasn't a courtroom out over the water, but there *was* a witness.

"Dr. Novak," Kit said. The examiner paused, again looking at Kit with a jaundiced eye. "I wish you to be a witness to the refusal of Captain Raleigh to turn over Mrs. Boswell's personal property to me."

"Now, be reasonable, Mrs. Fox," Captain Raleigh said. "Do you have to inject yourself so heavily into this?"

"Captain, I am a lawyer, retained by a woman you have put under arrest. The answer is yes, it is my job to inject myself."

With a heavy sigh, Captain Raleigh nodded. "All right, how about this? You may take Mrs. Boswell her clothes and sundries. But beyond that, I demand that this room be left as is."

"Then I would make a request as well. That we wire Detective Mike McGinty of the Los Angeles Police Department, for him to conduct the investigation when the ship docks in San Leandro."

"McGinty?"

"He's an honest cop. I've dealt with him before."

Raleigh reflected for a moment. "Does Los Angeles have jurisdiction over matters in San Leandro?"

"They share jurisdiction with San Leandro in criminal matters. And as a matter of maritime law, you have the discretion to refer this to the Los Angeles authorities."

Raleigh nodded. "Have it your way."

"Thank you."

"I apologize for having to take a hard line, Mrs. Fox. But I have been a sea captain for twenty-three years and never have had a hint of scandal or wrongdoing aboard one of my vessels. I do not intend to let that happen now."

"And I hope you understand that my job is to be certain the rights of my client are protected."

"I quite understand. In fact, I—"

"That's it," Dr. Novak said.

Kit and the captain looked at the doctor as he rose.

He removed a handkerchief from his coat pocket and commenced wiping his hands. "This boy's been poisoned."

"So it is indeed homicide?" Ted said.

Kit paced in their stateroom. Her usual method of cogitating about a case was to walk in circles in enclosed spaces, like her office back in Los Angeles. Usually, she did this as her assistant, Corazón Chavez, took notes and bounced around ideas with her. Corazón's perceptive mind was a perfect companion to Kit's own, and when they discussed cases together some new avenue, theretofore overlooked, was bound to appear.

She had not tried this method with her husband before. She'd somehow kept their life together apart from concerns with her work—an arrangement she was certain Ted preferred. But here they were, and she would try it.

"Yes," Kit remarked, "premeditated."

"First-degree murder, then?"

"Not necessarily." Kit stopped at the door and turned to face her husband, who was sitting comfortably in a chair. "It is possible that Chilton killed himself."

"I hadn't considered that."

"It is unlikely, but every theory must be considered to cast doubt upon the case to be made against Wanda Boswell."

"Do you believe she is innocent?"

Kit wondered about that herself. She had pledged to defend only those whom she was convinced were factually innocent of the crimes they were accused of. Sometimes, however, the reality of the situation and her professional obligations forced her to suspend judgment until more evidence surfaced.

"I do believe her," Kit answered.

"But you have been lied to before."

"Yes, by experts. But sooner or later such lies are exposed."

"What are you going to do until we hit land?"

"Question as many people as I—" She stopped, noting Ted's subtle but sudden look of concern. She went to him. "I am sorry, darling. This was not supposed to happen on our honeymoon."

With a smile, Ted said, "That's the duty I signed up for, isn't it? Kit Shannon Fox is a lawyer, not a socialite."

She kissed him. "I love you because you can tell the difference."

"You'd better get going, then, or I'm liable to persuade you to stay."

———

Kit had not been to the gaming room, not even to take a look inside. It held no interest for her. But now as she entered she was astonished to see the place was active even at this early hour. While most of the passengers were off finishing their breakfasts, a number of men were seated at the roulette wheel, standing around the crap table or at various stations where cards were being dealt—games of blackjack and poker. And all of it encased in a thick haze of cigar and cigarette smoke.

As she stepped into the fog, coughing a bit at the assault on her throat and lungs, Kit sensed several gamblers turning their heads toward her. She was dressed in a suit of brown wool with a tucked vest of crepe de chine—a simple, businesslike ensemble. Yet the men were as goggle-eyed as if she had cancanned in, dressed up in the latest French frills.

"Well, howdy do, missy," a burly man with a reddish nose said from the blackjack table. "Would you mind coming a little closer? I need my luck to change."

Ignoring the man, Kit approached the card dealer, whose skinny frame held a loose vest and in whose mouth a matchstick bobbed casually as he chewed on it.

Kit looked to the card dealer. "Is Mr. Raffels here?"

Before the dealer could answer, the burly man said, "Well now, Big Don's taste in women has gotten a little classier."

Kit waited for the dealer to answer her question. He seemed indifferent. "Is he expectin' ya?"

"Does one need an appointment?"

Burly man guffawed. "She's got a tongue on her, eh, Jackie? Say, missy, how 'bout I buy you a drink?"

The man then put his hand on Kit's waist. She slapped it away.

"Hey now!" Burly said.

"Sir, you are half drunk. Keep your hands—"

"Aw, come on, missy." He caught hold of Kit's wrist and squeezed it. Hard.

Kit did not hesitate to home in on the soft pressure point between the man's thumb and forefinger. Mr. Hancock, her jiu-jitsu instructor, had shown her several of these choice locations on the human body, should the need for self-protection arise.

One solid poke with her thumb and Burly cried out in pain as he slid off his stool. He grabbed his hand as if he had been burned by a hot iron. "Hey! You had no call to do that!" His eyes narrowed at her. "Why, I've got a good mind to—"

"To go get some food in your stomach." A dark-haired gentleman with almond-colored skin and an immaculate suit of continental design stepped between Kit and the man.

"What did you say?" Burly snapped at the gentleman.

"Please, Mr. Samuelson, I think it would be best all around, don't you? You need your full powers to—"

"I don't pay good money to get a lecture from a wop," Samuelson said, his face ruddy now with drink and anger. "I'll be reportin' this to the captain."

"You want to go of your own accord?" the gentleman said. "Or do you wish for me to escort you?"

The latter words were wrapped in a tone so unmistakably threatening that Kit gasped.

So did the man called Samuelson. Under the uncompromising stare of the dark-haired man, his rage was doused like a match under a hose. With a final, blustery attempt to salvage his dignity, Samuelson mouthed a flaccid *harrumph* before turning and walking out of the gaming room.

"I must apologize," the gentleman said to Kit. "I am Don Raffels. Did I understand that you came to speak with me?"

"Thank you, yes."

"Then why don't we step into the bar, eh?" He had a slight Italian accent that he worked very hard to hide.

Kit followed him through the smoky chamber, which was now back to its full activity after the slight diversion of Mr. Samuelson. The bar was on the opposite side of the gaming room. It was polished oak, and Kit could not help thinking of Carry Nation, who had recently been in Los Angeles smashing saloons with her hatchet. What she might have done to this place! Good thing Raffels was out at sea.

"May I offer you coffee?" Raffels said, motioning to the bartender.

"Thank you."

"You heard the lady." He turned to Kit. "What may I do for you, Miss. . . ?"

"Mrs. Fox. I am a lawyer and currently representing someone aboard this ship."

Raffels's eyebrows arched. "You are an intriguing lady. A lawyer? That is a rare thing, is it not?"

"Rare for a woman to practice law, but that is changing a little."

"And your husband?"

"Yes?"

"He does not object to this?"

Kit felt a little jolt of doubt about that. But she and Ted had talked about it thoroughly in the weeks before their marriage. "My husband is also rare, Mr. Raffels. He is—"

"A very lucky man," Raffels finished. His smile was no doubt one that caused many a woman's heart to flutter. He wore no gold band on his ring finger. He did sport a pinkie ring with a sparkling diamond set among a cluster of smaller stones.

"Thank you, Mr. Raffels. I wonder if I might ask you some questions about a situation that has come up."

With a rattle the bartender placed two cups of steaming coffee on the bar.

"You have my full attention," Raffels said.

"A man has died aboard this ship."

Without apparent concern Raffels took a sip of his coffee. "That would not be the first time. A man once fell over in this very room, his heart attacking him. It was very sad."

"I'm sure. A death is so often—"

"No, no," Raffels interjected. "The sad part was that he was holding a winning hand." He shook his head and took another sip of coffee. "Who is the dead man?"

"Chilton Boswell."

Raffels froze momentarily. "Mr. Boswell, eh? How did she happen?"

"She?"

"Death is a woman, Mrs. Fox."

Kit cleared her throat. "Well, we are not certain at this point, but I would like to know if you had contact with Mr. Boswell last night. I was seated with him at dinner, and he left with an expressed intention to come up here."

"Here?"

"To gamble."

Raffels smiled a white-toothed smile. "That is what we do here. And Mr. Boswell, he liked to gamble, sure."

"So he was up here last night?"

"Let me see. It was a busy night. Yes, I do think I saw him."

"Do you recall the time?"

"I do not keep track of the time, Mrs. Fox. My concern is only that people have a good time at my tables."

"Would you be able to estimate a time? Mr. Boswell left the dinner table at half past seven. Would it have been after that when you saw him?"

"Oh yes, I can safely say that much."

"Did you have occasion to speak with him?"

Raffels shrugged. "I speak with many who come here."

"Can you recall?"

The man took another lingering sip. "No, I do not recall that."

"Do you recall anyone who might have spoken to him?"

"Mrs. Fox, that would be very hard to tell. We were busy last night."

"Anyone."

"You know, that would not be good for me to tell. The men who gamble here, they come for the enjoyment. You know, I think many come to get away from the cares of the world. If they should think I told you some of their names, I think that would upset them."

Kit sensed a hardness in Raffels that was not going to budge on this point. "What kind of a gambler was Mr. Boswell?"

With another shrug Raffels said, "In the short time I knew him, he was not a man out of the ordinary. Sometimes win, sometimes lose."

"Did he wager a lot of money?"

Raffels shook his head. "He did not sit at the most expensive table."

"Can you think of anyone who may have held a grudge against him? Another gambler perhaps? Did you ever witness Mr. Boswell engaged in any long talks with anyone?"

"I am sorry, no. As you observed with Mr. Samuelson, I try to keep things pleasant in my place."

"I don't suppose you can tell me what time Mr. Boswell left here last night?"

"I am sorry if I am not able to help you. From the way you are asking questions, it appears that Mr. Boswell did not die of the natural cause. How did he die, if I may ask?"

"Until the coroner examines the body and it becomes public record, I would not venture to say."

Don Raffels narrowed his eyes, studying her. "You are a lawyer, and there has been a death, and I am thinking that you are on the side of someone who has been accused of this deed. I am thinking it is Mrs. Boswell, the man's pretty young wife."

"Very astute."

"Ah," Raffels said with a nod. "That is an old story."

"Old?"

"The wife of a gambler. It is not a good life for a woman to bear."

"But you told me Chilton Boswell was not a high-stakes gambler."

Raffels set his cup of coffee on the saucer with an adamant *clack*. "Perhaps Mrs. Boswell is a low-stakes wife."

"I'm not sure what you mean, Mr. Raffels."

"Every woman has a point at which she will lash out at her husband. For some, it will happen sooner than others. Maybe Mrs. Boswell is one of those kind of women."

"One more question, sir, and then I will leave you to your business," Kit said. "You sent a bottle of champagne to the Boswells last night. True?"

"As I say, Mr. Boswell liked to gamble. I like to show appreciation."

"So you admit to sending it."

"Why should I not?"

Kit nodded. "Who delivered the bottle to the room?"

Raffels shook his head. "I make the order and write the card. I do not know after that. Why do you ask?"

"I have a habit of asking," Kit said. "It goes with the profession."

6

THE STEWARD INFORMED KIT that Ted had finished his breakfast. It was late in the morning and Kit had been late in making it to the dining room.

"Shall I have a meal prepared for you?" the steward asked.

"No, thank you. I should like to ask you a question, if I may."

The steward bowed slightly.

"A bottle of champagne was delivered to the Chilton Boswell room yesterday."

"Yes, ma'am. I delivered it myself."

"Did you open the bottle?"

"No, ma'am. I offered to do so, but Mrs. Boswell said she preferred to wait for her husband."

"I see. Thank you. One more favor. I would like to have a breakfast prepared for Mrs. Boswell."

The steward's forehead wrinkled. "Mrs. Boswell? She is here, ma'am."

"I beg your pardon?"

"Allow me." He led Kit to the second chamber of the dining room. Only a few people remained, sipping coffee and conversing lightly. Then, in the far corner, Kit saw Glenna Boswell sitting alone with her back to her.

"I meant Mrs. *Wanda* Boswell," Kit told the steward. "Sent to my stateroom. Would you arrange the meal?"

"Of course." He bowed and left. Kit hesitated a moment and then slowly approached Glenna Boswell, observing the woman's posture. She had her head in her hand, and her shoulders sagged.

"Mrs. Boswell?"

Glenna Boswell jerked upward, turning in her chair. "What is it?"

Kit looked into red-rimmed eyes. "I wished to say I am sorry for your loss. I—"

"What are you doing here?" Glenna Boswell remonstrated, her features turning hard.

"I saw you from across the room, and I thought—"

"You thought you would try to manipulate me, is that it?"

Kit could hardly believe the words. "I assure you, Mrs. Boswell—"

"I am informed by Captain Raleigh that you have gone behind my back and held yourself out as Wanda's lawyer."

"It is true that Wanda wishes me to be her representative."

"This should be handled from within the family. I am, after all, her mother-in-law. Even though she would rather I not exist."

"Surely that is not true."

Glenna Boswell swung her imperious body toward Kit. "What do you know about it, young woman? Only what Wanda herself has said to you."

That much was true. On the other hand, Glenna Boswell was understandably upset. Yet the fact that she was up and about so soon after her son's murder was some testimony to her inner strength. This was a formidable woman, and Kit did not want her to be a hostile witness against Wanda.

"Perhaps if you gave Wanda a chance to explain . . ."

"Chance? What chance did she ever give me?" Sadness flooded into the woman's face. "She hated me from the start. She wanted to keep Chilton away from me. His mother!"

That did not seem like Wanda Boswell. Yet how much did Kit really know about her? Or anyone else on this ship?

"What right did she have to do that, Mrs. Fox?" Glenna Boswell sighed. "I come from a prominent family in Chicago. Chilton was my only son. I was widowed when he was but nine years old. I have dedicated my life to him, and—" Her voice choked on sobs. She put a linen napkin to her eyes and turned away from Kit.

Kit wanted to reach out and touch the woman's shoulder, to apologize for bringing her to this point. But she thought Mrs. Boswell would not want her to. Instead, she sat in an empty chair from the adjoining table and spoke softly. "Mrs. Boswell, I cannot tell you how sorry I am. I want you to know that my concern here is with the truth. I do not believe Wanda had anything to do with Chilton's death. I want to help everyone, including you, find the truth. I assure you that I will work diligently, for if a trial should become necessary I—"

"Necessary?" Glenna Boswell faced Kit once more. Her eyes were growing colder and firmer. "I shall insist upon a trial!"

"Mrs. Boswell, we must presume Wanda is not guilty unless and until convincing evidence comes forth."

"Convincing evidence? Is that what you are looking for?"

The harshness of Glenna Boswell's words startled her. "The D.A. will certainly be looking for evidence of guilt."

"And that includes a motive, does it not?"

"Yes."

Glenna Boswell dropped her napkin on the table and stood. "Then I suggest you ask your innocent client why she applied and paid for a life insurance policy on her husband three weeks before his death."

———

"Wanda, you must not ever hold information from me." Kit felt as if she were talking to a child. And Wanda did look childlike, dressed in a simple yellow dress with her blond hair worn down and unkempt, a wisp of it over her right eye. She might have been a neighborhood waif back in Los Angeles, waiting to play outside, being punished by restriction to the house.

"Please don't hate me." Wanda sat curled in one of the wingback chairs in Kit's stateroom. A tray of half-eaten breakfast lay on the table next to her.

"Of course I don't hate you." Kit sat in the other chair. "But you must understand that the one thing a lawyer needs from a client, above all else, is the truth. If I don't have that, I cannot be of help to you. And, believe me, the police will be searching for every detail that might connect you to the death."

"Will they put me in jail?"

"If they do, we will post bail."

Fear shot into Wanda's eyes. "Will they put me on trial?"

"It is too early to determine that. But I know Detective Mc-Ginty. If I can help him to rule you out as a suspect, I will. I will need your full cooperation. Understand?"

"Yes, I understand." Her head drooped. More hair fell across her face.

"What were you arguing with Chilton about yesterday morning, on deck?"

"You saw us?"

"It was difficult not to. Or to avoid hearing Chilton shouting."

"I was pleading with him to . . ."

"The truth now, Wanda."

Wanda Boswell looked at the floor. "Not to leave me."

"Did you ever plead with him in this way so that others heard you?"

"I do not believe so."

"You know, the troubles in your marriage were well-known."

"I suppose so."

"All right." Kit patted Wanda's hand. "Let's back up a little and start with the life insurance policy. When did that come about?"

"Chilton and I decided to do it right after we got married."

"Then you must have discussed it at some length before the wedding."

"Yes."

"Was there also a life insurance policy on you, or just one covering Chilton?"

"Just Chilton."

Kit nodded, placing herself as she always did in the role of juror. Though a trial might never take place, she always assessed the facts

with that end in mind. Earl Rogers always began his trial preparation with the closing argument, and now so did she. It made one
mindful of the incident from the layman's point of view.

"Tell me why Chilton agreed to this. If you don't mind my saying so, he did not seem the sort of man who was careful about
money or planning for a financial future."

"No, that much is true." Wanda sighed. "I was the practical one.
I hoped that I would be able to bring some of that practicality to
Chilton. A wife has such hopes for her husband."

Kit nodded.

Wanda went on, "I suppose I may have whined a bit about the
insurance policy. I told him I was frightened about something happening to him because of the people he knew."

"People?"

"Gamblers and the like. I knew Chilton had that side, but I
thought his love for me would have led him to reform. Perhaps I
was naïve."

"How did you meet Chilton?"

"At the theater."

"You were attending a play?"

Wanda brushed a few strands of hair behind her ear. "I was
performing. You see, I am a dancer."

"Oh? What style?"

"Have you heard of Isadora Duncan?"

Kit remembered reading something about her. "Rather scandalous, isn't she?"

"Some say so. I find her style liberating. I was performing a solo
dance to Ravel, and then I was part of a line at the Orpheum Theater."

"I know the Orpheum." It was here that Kit and Ted had seen
the young magician Harry Houdini, just before the Truman Harcourt murder case.

"Chilton came to the theater one night," Wanda continued. "He
was in the front row. Handsome, smiling. And looking right at me
during the entire performance. The next night he was there again,
and when I was dressing backstage after the show, three dozen red

roses were delivered to me. I suppose you could say I was swept off my feet."

"How long did he court you before he proposed?"

"Three months."

"Did Chilton's mother know about this?"

"Rather early. And from the start she did her best to keep us apart."

"Why was she against you?"

"Coming from the theater is not the best pedigree in Glenna Boswell's eyes. Perhaps she cannot be blamed."

"But Chilton defied her wishes."

"Not without much sound and fury from her."

"I can well understand. I have seen it myself."

"You have seen only the half of it. Watch her carefully, Mrs. Fox. I'm very much afraid of what she might do."

"I shall." Kit thought a moment. "Where is the life insurance policy now?"

"It is in a box at home." Wanda's eyes grew wide. "We are . . . were living with his mother."

"Does she know where you keep your important papers?"

"I wouldn't put it past her. She probably has done a lot of snooping around. She's that way."

"I'll want you to get me that document directly. I want to look it over. Now, can you tell me, while you've been on this cruise, have you observed anyone with your husband who might have had a disagreement with him? Any arguments?"

Wanda thought a moment. "He spent a lot of time in that gambling room."

"I've spoken to the boss up there. He does not remember anyone arguing with him. Anyone else?"

Wanda bit her upper lip. "There was one time, I think, on the island, when he may have had some words with that first mate."

"Sanders?"

"Yes. That's the one. I heard them arguing a bit one night outside our hotel room. I could not tell what it was about. Chilton would not tell me anything, of course. He just said it was about business. But what business could he have had with a man he barely knew?"

"That being said, what was Chilton's business? His line of work?"

"I don't believe Chilton knew what he wanted to be, unless getting by on one's charm can be considered a profession. He was desperate to make money, though. That was why he gambled so. He once said a man who does not get rich in America cannot be considered a real man."

"Was he involved in any enterprise besides gambling?"

"I was not aware of all that he did. I knew Chilton less than half a year. I think there may have been a real estate venture somewhere along the line. And he had some romantic notion about becoming a famous writer."

"Writer?" Chilton Boswell had not seemed the writerly type. But then again, neither did Jack London, whom Kit had met recently in connection with her campaign against children being employed in Los Angeles saloons. London seemed more like a pugilist than a writer. But his powerful prose was evidence of solid talent.

"He thought," Wanda explained, "that he might write a novel in the realistic style about the world of gambling." She added with a sardonic shake of her head, "He certainly was an expert in it."

"Did he ever produce any writing?"

"He had a manuscript that he was laboring on, but he never showed it to me."

"Do you know where it is? It might provide some helpful information."

"I suppose it is somewhere in his trunk."

"I'll see if I can get the captain to allow us access to it."

Wanda fanned herself with her right hand. "What's to become of me, Mrs. Fox?"

At the moment—considering there might be other information hidden, knowingly or unknowingly, by Wanda herself—Kit could not say.

7

Captain Raleigh said, "I would prefer that you leave matters alone."

"I know that may be convenient," Kit answered, "but I would remind you that the effects of the deceased belong to the widow—"

"Who is under my charge until—"

"Who still retains her property rights—"

"That detective, what's-his-name—"

"McGinty."

"Until he takes over."

They were just outside the captain's quarters. Raleigh did not look happy about being disturbed.

"Captain," Kit said, "I am not asking you for unbridled access. If you would accompany me, you may rest assured nothing will be amiss."

"I have other duties to attend to, Mrs. Fox."

"You also have a duty to the woman you have placed under ship's arrest."

Raleigh studied Kit a moment. "All right. But let's not make it all day."

They made their way to the room formerly occupied by Chilton and Wanda. Captain Raleigh took a key from his pocket and unlocked the door—and revealed the tremulous figure of Professor Aiden Aloysius Faire.

"What is the meaning of this?" Raleigh said.

The professor's face shone red. Behind him, strewn about, were clothes and pillows and other sundry items. His mouth dropped open, like a boy who'd been caught in the pantry by his stern mother.

"Speak up, Professor." Raleigh closed the door behind him.

Before uttering a word, Faire glanced at Kit and shifted his girth nervously. "Surely we can discuss this as rational people. . . ."

"I am waiting for an explanation."

"And I shall give you one. But why don't we do it in the civilized fashion, over a brandy?"

When Raleigh hesitated, Faire added, "But must we do it in her presence?"

Bristling, Kit folded her arms. "I should like to hear your explanation as well."

"I don't owe you any explanations." Faire thrust out his ample chest. "Captain, if you please . . ."

"Mrs. Fox is with me," Raleigh said. "She is representing Mrs. Boswell while she is under my jurisdiction. And you are where you should not be aboard my ship. I would like to know how you got in here. I have a key and so does my purser. So do the stewards. Who let you in?"

Faire blinked. "I do not wish to answer that question."

"And why not?"

"My ethics will not allow me to. I do not wish to land another person into any trouble."

"But your ethics allowed you to break in?" Kit blurted. She could hardly contain herself. Just like the little boy in the pantry, this man was concocting a wild justification.

"I did not break in!" Faire protested. "I entered here because my cause is just."

Captain Raleigh also folded his arms. "Please explain, Professor."

"All right. Have it your way. But may I at least sit down?" Without waiting for permission, Faire lowered himself into a chair. "That's better."

"Pray continue," Raleigh said.

"I am here because I was cheated out of money by Mr. Chilton Boswell. As he is dead, there is no way I can prove the debt—or at least not without great effort—nor can I confront him. But as it was a substantial sum, and as I am simply a poor professor of philosophy, I could not let the sum remain outstanding. When I learned that Mrs. Boswell was confined to Mrs. Fox's quarters, I took it upon myself to see that justice is done."

"Justice?" The word popped out of Kit's mouth.

"Yes, Mrs. Fox," Faire returned defiantly. "That is exactly what I mean. You are not the only one who believes in justice around here. Christianity has no monopoly on the concept."

"But you broke ... let yourself in here, to private quarters," Raleigh said.

"Precisely. To get what was due to me. That is the Greek concept of justice."

Kit shook her head. "Justice is to be administered through the government and the laws, sir."

"Lecturing me again, are you?" Faire jutted his jaw like a boxer. "My cause is just, with or without the state. The laws do not enforce gaming debts, so I am endeavoring to enforce them myself."

"When did this alleged cheating take place?" Kit asked.

Faire put his hands out toward Raleigh. "Must I be questioned by her?"

"She's doing just fine," Raleigh said. "I'd like to know myself."

"I would remind Mrs. Fox that the Greeks did not allow women into their discussions!" Faire's indignation seemed to disappear under Kit's stern glare. "Ah, very well. On the very first day aboard this ship, just after we'd left San Leandro harbor, I wandered into the gaming room for a look around. I'm not a gambling man, although I have played a few hands of poker in my time. I thought I could sit in on a friendly game. And Chilton Boswell was quite persuasive about it. So I sat down at the table with him."

"Was anyone else with you?" Kit wanted to know.

"A fellow named, I think, Edgar. Big fellow."

"Would the last name be Samuelson?"

"I believe so."

"Go on, please."

"It was the three of us, with Mr. Raffels dealing the cards."

"Raffels played?"

Captain Raleigh interjected, "No, he is the dealer for the house. He never plays with the guests. Continue, Professor."

"Well, as I say, I sat down for a friendly game. The stakes were affordable. And I was lucky early on. I won a couple of large pots. Mr. Raffels was called away and so passed the dealing to us. Presently, with Boswell dealing, I drew to an inside straight. Normally that is a fool's errand. But when I got the card I needed, I was filled with rather more exuberance than I should have had. I put everything I had into the pot. Boswell raised substantially. He had been drinking a good deal, and I judged that he was in his cups. That was my first mistake."

"How much was in this pot?" Captain Raleigh asked.

"I think it was on the order of five hundred dollars."

"You had that much money with you?"

"It was virtually all I had. I was certain I would win, however. But then, when Boswell showed his cards—I am sure he took one from his sleeve—he showed a full house. I was outraged."

"What did you do about it?" Raleigh said.

"I told the man what I had seen. He denied it, of course, and feigned anger. Then that big oaf, Samuelson, said he had not seen anything out of the ordinary. And since Mr. Raffels was not there as a witness, I knew I was lost."

"Did you say anything about this alleged cheating to Mr. Raffels?"

"No. I determined to use my rational faculties to seek justice for myself. So, you see, here I am."

Captain Raleigh pondered all this for a moment. As he did, Kit met Faire's irate glower with a sharp gaze of her own. Something told her this would not be the last time she would be in an adversarial situation with the professor.

"Have you removed anything from this room?" Raleigh said.

"I have not," Faire said.

"Will you give me your word that you will not attempt to enter this room again?"

Faire thought a moment. "Very well."

"Then I will forget this happened," Raleigh said. "I am afraid that your debt must remain uncollected. Who was it that said, 'He who steals my purse steals nothing'?"

"Iago," Faire muttered.

For once, Kit mused, he was right.

8

"KIT, LISTEN TO THIS."

Startled out of her thoughts, Kit turned toward Ted, who was sitting up in his deck chair, a pamphlet poised in his hand.

"This is the address of Alexander Graham Bell given at the New York Auto Show last spring. Do you know what he said?"

Kit shook her head.

"'We have entered the age of the aerodrome. The new science of aeronautics shall be the controlling enthusiasm of our finest inventors. I can see in the not too distant future an aircraft powered by man crossing the Atlantic. It may seem beyond our imaginations, but I assure you, gentlemen, that in our lifetimes we will be able to leave New York City in the morning and be in London that night.' Did you hear that, Kit?"

"New York?"

"Yes, these remarks were made in New York! But flying across the Atlantic—what do you make of that?"

"Remarkable."

"Remarkable?" Ted plopped the pamphlet on his lap. "Across the Atlantic! That's what Bell is saying is possible. And here I've been trying to fly from one end of a field to another. My sights have been set too low."

Kit nodded but couldn't keep her thoughts from Professor Faire's account. He seemed to Kit to be a fastidious and careful man, concerned with his outward appearance and reputation. That he should have been caught up in a poker game might be possible—more careful men than he had fallen into the gambling spell—but lurking about in another's stateroom? Where he likely would be caught? That didn't make—

"Kit, are you listening to me?"

"Yes?" She focused on Ted's eyes now.

"Bell is planning to begin an extensive experimentation in aeronautics with a man named Glenn Curtiss. The race is on! I've been thinking about the monoplane design. You know how unstable the whole thing has been? I wonder if my problem hasn't been the wing but the tail. You see . . . Kit?"

"Hmm?"

"Have you heard a word I've said?"

She searched her memory. "Bell. The Atlantic. Oh, Ted, I'm sorry. I have been preoccupied."

"That is not something I would have needed a detective to figure out."

"It's this case."

"No doubt."

"Do forgive me." Kit took Ted's hand.

Ted squeezed hers. "All I ask is that you share my dreams with me. And I will share yours."

"Of course."

"Why not tell me, then, about your case. If you are of a mind, when you are finished, I'll tell you my plans for the monoplane."

"It's a deal." Kit shook his hand as she would a professional colleague sealing an agreement. "I questioned Professor Faire earlier today, along with the captain. We came upon him rummaging about in Chilton's stateroom."

"Not very cricket, as the English might say. Especially for a man who teaches philosophy."

"That's just it. He justified it by making up a peculiar story about being cheated at cards by Chilton Boswell. For some reason I don't believe it."

A cool breeze carried with it not only the smell of the sea but a strong scent of perfume. Kit looked up to see the figure of Delia Patton, strolling alone by the ship's rail.

Kit was up in a second. "Ted, do you mind if I—"

He waved his hand resignedly. "Farewell, my love."

Kit joined Delia, who reacted to Kit's presence with coy bemusement. It was a look Kit thought fit the woman perfectly. With her dark, violet eyes and teasing manner, it was not a wonder that men could make fools of themselves over her. Certainly Lowell Sanders may have done so. But did Chilton Boswell?

"Why, Mrs. Fox," Delia said. She was dressed in blue crepe de chine with a fox fur around her shoulders. The gift, no doubt, of some admirer.

"Would you mind if I asked you a few questions, Miss Patton?"

Delia smiled playfully. "Oh, is this about the intrigue? The murder?"

"Word does travel fast, doesn't it?"

"One cannot keep something so juicy from becoming common knowledge."

"Juicy?"

"Oh yes." Delia adjusted her hat, which was flapping a bit in the wind. The black ostrich feather billowed on top. "You have an unhappy marriage, a young wife who could not take the, shall we say, demands of modern life. It is predictable."

"You seem to know a good deal about the Boswells' marriage."

"Only what I have observed. I am a student of human nature, you know."

Delia shifted so her back was to the rail, her arms resting on it, her body curved outward. Kit could see then another reason men would be drawn to Delia like moths to a flame.

"How well did you know Chilton Boswell?"

Delia Patton's eyebrows arched downward. "That seems to me an impertinent question."

"I seek only information."

"What is it that makes you tick, Mrs. Fox?" Delia glanced past Kit, toward where Ted was seated.

"Tick?"

"Your angle. Every woman has one."

"Miss Patton, I do not wish to—"

"Come along. You and I are birds of a feather, I'd wager. No woman becomes a lawyer without ambition and hope of reward. I should like my own school of beauty someday."

"Miss Patton—"

"Why else do you practice law?"

Kit took a short breath. "The practice of law is something I am called to do."

"Called? Oh yes, you and your God. Your dialogue with the professor at dinner was quite entertaining. Still, I wonder if you don't have some sort of ulterior motive." Delia's red lips parted in a grin. "Fame perhaps?"

"My only motive at the moment is to get the facts."

"Certainly." Delia's tone was less than believing.

"On the islands I observed you with Chilton Boswell on one occasion. Were there others?"

The sultry woman's eyes twinkled a bit in the sun. "Perhaps."

"When and where?"

"All right. Have it your way. Sure, I knew Chilton before the cruise, before he married . . . her. I know a lot of men, if you want to be strict about it."

"What was the nature of your relationship with Chilton Boswell, if I may ask?"

"I do not see that I should be compelled to reveal anything at all to you. I will say that I was quite surprised to find myself on a cruise with Chilton and his bride. I resolved to stay away from him, but he pursued me."

"He pursued *you*?"

"One night on the island, I was out walking on the sand. A man came up behind me and it was Chilton. I got the impression that he had followed me there and wished to get personal—very quickly, if you know what I mean."

"What gave you that idea?"

"It's what men do around me. Let's face it, Mrs. Fox, there are some of our sex who are gifted in that way. You, with a little more attention to facial makeup and hair, would have them lined up."

"I have a husband."

"How provincial."

"What did you and Chilton Boswell talk about?"

"Oh, this and that. You know how it is."

"I'm afraid I don't, Miss Patton."

Delia flashed a look of consternation, clearly a woman used to being shown great deference by virtue of her being Delia Patton. "He asked me how I had been getting along, how I liked the islands, what interests I had, if I ever thought of trying the sport of surfing—the sort of small talk men like to make."

"How long did this conversation go on?"

"I don't know. Perhaps an hour."

"Did you talk about anything pertaining to his marriage?"

"I certainly did not. Chilton may have offered some information of his own accord."

"Such as?"

"I feel like such a gossip telling you this." Delia Patton looked eager to continue.

"What you tell me may be helpful to my client."

"In that case, Chilton was distressed, I think, by his marriage. I believe he thought he had made a mistake marrying that girl."

"Did he explain?"

"Do you know what a gold digger is, Mrs. Fox?"

"Yes," Kit said, thinking that the term would fit Delia like the form-flattering dress she wore.

"Chilton wondered if his young wife saw him as a way to get in the chips, so to speak. She is some kind of performer, a chorus girl. Not exactly made of money. Landing a husband with a rich mother, who might someday come into a fortune, that's perfectly understandable, isn't it?"

This suggested to Kit another tack. "Why is it that you have never wed, Miss Patton?"

Delia looked at her nails, painted red in what Aunt Freddy would have called the "fast style."

"Just waiting for the right offer to come along," she replied.

Kit imagined Miss Delia Patton had many an offer, and not just for marriage.

"What prompted you to take this cruise?" Kit asked.

"I had not been to the islands, I had just come into some money, and I thought it would be fun. I thought I might meet a handsome adventurer of some kind."

"Lowell Sanders seems to have taken a liking to you."

With a wave of her hand, Delia said, "I should not be surprised. As I said, that is the lot for some of us women. Men flock our way."

"Would you mind telling me, Miss Patton, where you went after dinner last night?"

The woman's body stiffened in the breeze. "You cannot be serious!"

"I beg your pardon?"

"Accusing me of poisoning Chilton?"

"I don't recall mentioning poison."

Delia Patton's eyes darkened. "Do not try to be clever with me, Mrs. Fox. You will find yourself out of your element."

"Would you like to answer my question now, or under oath before a jury?"

"I have nothing to hide from you or a jury or anyone else," Delia said. "And it was Lowell who told me about the poison, just so you know. Last night after dinner I went for a walk on the deck."

"Did you speak to anyone?"

"I may have said hello to a passenger or two."

"Anyone you can identify?"

"I did not pause to study faces."

"How long did you stay out on deck?"

"I don't recall."

"An hour? Two?"

"I told you, I don't know."

"Was it more like all night or more like one hour?"

Delia sighed. "What does it matter?"

"It is going to matter to the police, Miss Patton. I am going to make it matter."

"You are quite unpleasant."

"You have not yet seen me unpleasant," Kit said.

The two women glared at each other. The chill between them was not due to the Pacific breeze. Kit wondered what Delia might have done had they not been in public.

After several seconds passed, Delia blinked and said, "I think I shall let you call me to the stand. I have nothing to say to you, nothing to hide, and would therefore request that you do not talk to me again." She then turned and walked away, her hips swaying defiantly.

Kit watched her for a moment then returned to her deck chair.

"Quite a package, that one," Ted remarked.

Kit shook her head.

"But then," Ted said, taking her hand, "you are quite a package yourself."

9

"WELCOME TO THE BRIDGE, Mrs. Fox." Captain Wendell Raleigh gave a bow. He looked like a man who reveled in his office, and this was his throne room. "You know," Raleigh said, "in the old days, a woman was not allowed anywhere near the bridge. Aren't we much more civilized today?"

Kit smiled, looking around at the map desk and large compass near the wheel. A man Kit did not recognize manned the helm. "Thank you for the privilege," she said. "I was informed you wished to speak with me further on the Boswell matter."

"Yes. And I thought it best we meet here. This is my domain, so to speak. The sea is my enterprise. The *Majestic* is a quadruple screw ship driven by direct-drive steam turbines. Service speed twenty-five knots."

"How long have you been a ship's captain?"

Raleigh cleared his throat in mock embarrassment. "Longer than I care to admit to one so young. Many, many years."

"Where is it that you make your home when on land?"

"I have a home right in San Leandro. It is convenient for me and for the line."

"I see. And what was it you wished to speak with me about?"

Raleigh took a quick look out of the bridge window, then walked Kit to the rear of the bridge, out of the hearing of the mate at the wheel. "We are one day from port, Mrs. Fox. My job is to see to it that everyone onboard has a pleasant journey, despite the recent unpleasantness."

"I quite understand."

"I am not merely the captain of a ship. I am the host of those who have booked a relaxing trip. We have 463 first-class, 364 second-class, and 1,038 third-class passengers onboard. Suffice to say a murder is not the most relaxing of developments."

"No, I readily admit—"

"I well understand your duty to your client. However, I have received some complaints about your conduct."

Kit stiffened. "Conduct?"

"Rather aggressive questioning, shall we say."

"Did that come from Delia Patton or Mrs. Boswell? Or Professor Faire?"

"Rather than linger on the names, perhaps we can simply agree that you will not conduct your investigations further, until we reach port."

Kit frowned slightly. "But, Captain, there are people aboard now that I might not have the opportunity to question once we reach land. As it is, they are here—"

"As a captive audience?"

"I was not thinking in those terms."

"But that is the fact, which is why I must insist upon your cooperation."

Kit folded her arms. "Captain Raleigh, I don't wish to make waves, as it were. But I must remind you that maritime law, that which gives you certain authority, still does not supersede the guarantees of the federal constitution."

"What guarantees are you referring to?"

"The rights of free association, speech, to a fair trial, to representation by counsel—"

Raleigh put up his hand. "I will take your word for it. But you must appreciate my position as well."

"Captain, I do appreciate it. With your help, I am sure all parties could be satisfied."

"Tell me what you have in mind, Mrs. Fox."

"I would like to speak to the guests who have staterooms on either side of the Boswell room. One is, I believe, an elderly woman. The other contains a couple. That's all my client knows."

"You are asking for my help in questioning these people?"

"If you were with me, it might give them reassurance."

Raleigh thought about it a moment. "Very well. Give me an hour and I will get back to you. And please, during the interim, do not interview anyone. I would appreciate that."

———

"Well, Mrs. Fox, I suppose this is the last time we shall be speaking together." Professor Aiden Aloysious Faire had on his flowing overcoat and wide-brimmed hat.

Kit turned from the rail where she had been observing the ocean. "Where will you be going after this?"

"I will be in Los Angeles for a series of lectures. Then it is back to my duties at the university." He paused, clearing his throat. "I do hope you will not hold any hard feelings for the freewheeling spirit in which we have engaged."

"No hard feelings, Professor. You will, however, likely be called as a witness if this case should proceed to trial."

He shook his head. "No, that would not do. I have important business to attend to."

"A murder trial is important business, too."

"I have a book to write, classes to prepare for."

"You teach a full schedule?"

"Oh my, yes. The life of an academic, you see."

"If I am ever out in Chicago, perhaps you would like to have a guest in one of your classes. For a debate, I mean."

Faire raised his eyebrows. "You are a curious woman, Mrs. Fox."

"Oh?"

"Most women of your age and marital status are not so interested in the minutiae of philosophical thought."

"I have always considered ideas to be the most important commodity in society. From bad ideas flow bad consequences."

"And in your mind, Christianity is a good thing?"

"With the best consequences."

"That, of course, is where we differ."

"Tell me, Professor, what do you think happens to our souls when we die?"

"I would challenge the premise of your question, Mrs. Fox. The idea of a soul is an antiquated notion, in view of the work of Mr. Darwin."

"Mr. Darwin might be wrong. Even if one should entertain the notion that we are descended from lower forms of life—which I do not—that does not logically rule out the intervention of God."

"Yet there is not any evidence to that effect either."

"But there is evidence, I would submit, of a soul."

"And what would that be?" the professor asked skeptically.

"The fact that we sense it," Kit explained, sensing the stirring of her soul even now. "We all know deep down that the world makes no sense without our having a soul."

"I do not believe the world makes any sense other than what we give it. We must all live as courageously as possible in light of the futility of it all."

"But, Professor, if one truly believed that, what is to stop us from performing acts of terrible evil? If there is no immortality of the soul, no judgment after death, it seems to me that anything I do, whether for good or ill, is permissible."

"A society can choose its own moral codes."

"Yes, but there is nothing that distinguishes one code from another. In Germany at the moment there is a massive building up of arms. What if that country should decide to attack its neighbor, without provocation, believing, let us say, that it is the only model for civilization?"

"That will not happen, Mrs. Fox. War has been outlawed, and men, by rational thought, have discovered that it does not lead to anything. Thought alone, you see, is what will make the peace. Religion has only led to bloodshed in the past."

"And so we have come full circle, back to our original discussion over dinner."

"Quite so. And with the same result. Let us call it a tie for the moment. When my book comes out, I will send you a copy."

"I promise you I will read it."

As Professor Faire extended his hand to Kit, Captain Raleigh approached from the starboard side. "I trust, Professor, that Mrs. Fox is behaving herself."

"Quite so." Faire shook Kit's hand and bowed slightly. "And now I am off for my constitutional around the deck. The life of the mind requires a fit body!"

The professor trundled toward the bow of the ship.

"I have spoken to the guests you wish to contact," Raleigh said.

"Thank you. May I—"

"I'm afraid that one of them, Mrs. Dimble, the older woman, does not wish to speak with you. She is very distressed by the turn of events."

"What, exactly, did she say?"

"I am sure you will understand if I do not reveal anything more, at her request. Once the ship has docked, of course you are free to proceed as you wish. In the meantime I must insist that no contact be made until you are off the ship."

"Can you at least tell me if she might have anything relevant to say? Did she hear anything that night?"

"I cannot answer that because I don't know. I'm sorry."

"What about the couple on the other side?"

"Yes, Mr. and Mrs. Barton Ferrell. They are willing to speak to you, but I don't think they can be of any great help."

Kit sighed. "At this point, any help, great or small, would be of benefit."

———

Mr. and Mrs. Barton Ferrell were a young couple, well dressed and disposed. Kit had seen them once in Hawaii and once on the ship and each time thought they looked to be of good social stock.

Now, seated in their first class stateroom, they appeared cooperative, even serene. The fact of a murder aboard ship did not seem to disturb them in the least. Were they the sort of people for whom self-interest trumped all other concerns?

Kit thanked them for their time. "May I ask about your activities on the night of Sunday, January the sixth?"

Barton looked at his wife, who nodded to him in deference. "Let me see, I believe we had dinner sometime around seven. As I recall we dined rather leisurely with several other couples."

"Four other couples, dear," Mrs. Ferrell added.

"I know that, dear. I am perfectly able to count the number of guests. But as that is not relevant to Mrs. Fox's inquiry, I did not feel the need to go into detail."

Mrs. Ferrell, pretty in her way with dark brown hair, folded her hands in her lap. "I was only trying to help."

"Of course you were, dear. Why don't you let me answer Mrs. Fox in my own way?"

If this went on too long, Kit thought, the ship would likely be in port before her questions were answered.

"What I should like to know," Kit said quickly, "is where you were between the hours of ten and midnight, if you recall."

Barton Ferrell furrowed his brow and nodded. "Yes, yes. I believe we took a stroll around the deck after dinner and sat under blankets in deck chairs for an hour or so."

"An hour and a half, dear."

"Yes, I know, dear."

"Time is very important to—"

"Thank you, dear. If I may continue? And then we came down to the parlor and played cribbage until roughly eleven o'clock."

"Closer to eleven-thirty, dear. I remember distinctly because I was winning and you said—"

"Thank you, dear, but I am certain Mrs. Fox is not interested in our leisure activities. She has a murder case to investigate, and we must keep to the point—"

"I believe I am keeping to the point, dear. Perhaps if you ask Mrs. Fox—"

"What hour did you retire to your room?" Kit asked.

"I remember now," said Barton Ferrell. "It was exactly eleven forty-five." He shot a rebuking look at his wife. "I remember because I looked at my watch."

"Is that the watch that runs slow, dear?" Mrs. Ferrell said.

"No, it is not the watch that runs slow." Barton Ferrell looked at Kit sheepishly as if apologizing for his wife. He seemed to Kit to be the type of man who could not brook any correction from anyone, especially a woman, especially a woman who was his wife.

"As I say, Mrs. Fox, we were in our room at eleven forty-five and retired shortly thereafter."

"Not exactly, dear. You went out for a moment, I believe."

Balling his fists, Barton Ferrell said, "Please, Mavis! If you continue to interrupt, I think I shall be cross with you."

"Really, dear, there is no need—"

"For you to speak further. Mrs. Fox, we retired around midnight, and that is all you need to know about our evening."

"Did you happen to hear anything in the Boswell stateroom, next to your own?"

"Not a thing."

"I thought perhaps we might have, dear." Mrs. Ferrell's voice had an extra note of sharpness about it.

Kit turned to the young wife. "What is it that you think you may have heard, Mrs. Ferrell?"

"Mavis!" Barton Ferrell stood up. "I thought I made it perfectly plain that I do not want you butting into my colloquy with Mrs. Fox."

"I only wish to help."

"Leave the helping to me. Mrs. Fox, my wife and I may have heard a door closing or some such thing, but we have no way of knowing where that came from. For all we know it could have been across from us or on the other side from the Boswells. There is simply no certainty in this matter. Which leads me to conclude that this interview has reached its conclusion."

Kit was not at all certain of that. She wanted to talk to Mavis Ferrell alone now. But in view of what that might do to the already frayed ends of this marital knot, she chose not to proceed further.

"If anything occurs to you," Kit said, rising, "please call my office in Los Angeles."

"We will not need to call you," Barton Ferrell said as he opened the stateroom door. "What I have told you is all we know."

10

TWO LOCAL DEPUTY SHERIFFS were planted, like glowering statues, at the bottom of the gangplank. Kit held Wanda's arm as they began their descent from the ship. The girl was trembling, even though Kit had tried to prepare her for her arrest. But it was one thing to imagine, quite another to see lawmen actually waiting to take one to jail.

"I'm with you every step of the way," Kit assured her.

Lowell Sanders, walking just behind the pair, said, "I'm sorry to have to do this, Mrs. Boswell. It's a rotten deal."

"It's all right," Wanda said. "Let us get this over with."

The harbor at San Leandro was advertised as a major port to the world in the brochures the boosters of Los Angeles prepared for distribution. The City of Angels, being well inland, did not have the capacity to entertain ships or even smaller craft. The Los Angeles River was too capricious for boats, even the occasional rowboat. It was, much like the civic life of the city, unpredictable—sometimes swollen with the pride of rainwater, at other times humbled to a trickle during the hot summer months.

As Kit guided Wanda down, the smell of fish grew potent. In San Leandro, the fishing trade, tourist ships, and merchant vessels all competed for the precious docks. A flock of sea gulls hovered nearby, though they made Kit think of vultures.

Also vulture-like was Glenna Boswell, whom Kit saw disembarking behind her. The woman perched at the top of the gang-plank, looking all too satisfied. What was behind her satisfaction with the arrest of her own daughter-in-law?

When they reached the bottom of the plank, Lowell Sanders spoke to one of the deputies, who then stepped toward Kit and Wanda.

"Wanda Boswell?" he asked with official purpose. He wore the brown uniform of the Los Angeles County Sheriff's office, a silver star for a badge pinned to his left breast pocket.

Squeezing Kit's arm, Wanda said, "I am she."

"I got a warrant for your arrest." He held up a folded paper and then lowered it as he reached for Wanda's free arm.

Kit stepped between them. "One moment. I would like to see that warrant, if you please."

The deputy's face creased with annoyance. "How's that? Who are you?"

"I am Mrs. Boswell's attorney."

"Attorney?" His look grew into astonished confusion.

The other deputy, an older man, moved alongside his partner. "You must be Kit Shannon."

"Kathleen Shannon Fox," Kit said with a nod.

A familiar voice sounded from behind. "You best show her the warrant if you know what's good for you."

It was Mike McGinty, the Los Angeles police detective.

The older deputy said, "Kit Shannon! She's trouble on the half shell."

"Only if you mess with the law." Mike had his ever-present cigar stub planted firmly in one corner of his mouth. By this time there was quite a bit of commotion around the small drama being played out at the bottom of the gangplank. Ted, who had been directly behind them, watched. Kit glanced at him once, and his wan smile appeared enigmatic.

The reluctant deputy handed Kit the arrest warrant. She unfolded the document and scanned it. "I will accompany Mrs. Boswell to the jail." She handed the warrant back to the deputy. "Mike, I requested you conduct the investigation into the killing."

McGinty nodded. "I brought two of my boys with me. We'll let you know."

"Let her know?" the young deputy protested. "Whose side are you on?"

Mike McGinty poked him once in the chest. "That of the truth. And I'd advise you to do the same with Miss Shannon on the case."

"Mrs. Fox," Kit corrected. Then she saw Ted behind the deputies, looking none too pleased.

The ride to the San Leandro jail turned out to be short yet extremely uncomfortable. The horse-drawn paddy wagon was completely unnecessary, but the sheriffs had insisted. The wagon might have been built in 1817. The wood benches were worn and laden with splinters.

Wanda rested her head on Kit's shoulder the entire way. At one point she whispered, "It wasn't supposed to be like this."

Kit stroked her hair as if this woman were her younger sister.

"What will happen to me? Are they going to hang me?"

The words sent a chill through Kit's body. This could very well be a hanging offense. And so far it was not the strongest case she had ever taken on.

Earl Rogers had never lost a murder trial; nor had she. But there was always a first time. She was not infallible.

"I am going to fight for your freedom," Kit said.

"But will they hang me?"

"Wanda, don't allow yourself to think of such things. They will do you no good."

Wanda sat up, stiff. "But will they? If they find me guilty, will they?"

"I cannot tell you that it is not possible. But we are a long way from that possibility, and I am going to do everything in my power to keep it from happening."

"What if you thought I did do it, Mrs. Fox?" Wanda Boswell's voice grew high and desperate. "What if you really and truly did?"

What would she do? She knew what Earl Rogers would say. He would say fight with all his might to keep anyone from going to the gallows, guilty or not. And if you engage a client, you are obligated to fight the prosecution, within ethical bounds, and hold them to their burden of proof.

Had Kit been naïve in thinking that she could represent only those she was *convinced* were innocent?

"Wanda," Kit said finally, "I am your lawyer. I am not going to abandon you."

And with that Wanda allowed her head to rest again on Kit's shoulder.

———

"We do things a little differently down here, Mrs. Fox."

The district attorney, Fielding Hardy, was Falstaffian in mass, with coils of gray hair springing from the sides of his shiny bald pate. His gray suit seemed the size of a circus tent.

Kit stepped around the brass spittoon in the middle of the spare, wood-frame office. "I am quite sure your procedures will conform to the requirements of the law."

"Now, there's no need to go threatening me with the law, Mrs. Fox."

"I mean no threat, Mr. Hardy. Perhaps I misunderstood you."

"Then I'll make it real plain. We don't do anything with frills flying in my town. We've got a little courthouse and two judges, and as long as we make 'em happy, things move along nice and easy. You been down to our fair city before?"

"Only to begin the cruise. Other than that—"

"San Leandro is a city with a port. That's our bread and butter. It makes people come on down here and provides most of the jobs. So I pretty much keep the place neat and tidy so there won't be any interruption to our quiet little life. Now, we'll just let things take their course and see where we are."

"I would remind you that my client has the right to go before a judge within forty-eight hours."

"And we'll do that."

"Also, I would like her to be released to me, as she was aboard the ship. You may check with Captain Raleigh to see that I cooperated."

"What's your hurry with all that?"

"All what, sir?"

"You and your client are the talk of the town. Already had a story in the paper about it."

"How did the paper get the information?"

"I don't rightly know." Hardy laughed, causing his stomach to jiggle. "News travels fast these days."

"I would like to see that story."

"You can go on over to the *San Leandro Clarion* and take a look for yourself. What I'm trying to tell you, Mrs. Fox, is that we can make things easy on ourselves. Doesn't matter that it's a murder case."

"But you have hardly had the chance to investigate. You haven't considered all the evidence."

"I've heard enough to say there's a good chance your client killed her husband."

"I just left Detective McGinty at the dock. He has not completed his investigation."

"Mrs. Fox, please sit down."

Reluctantly Kit took a chair. She knew nothing about this man Hardy, save what she managed to get out of McGinty—that he was once a deputy of the District Attorney of Los Angeles County. But that was before she arrived in the City of Angels in 1903.

"Now, I don't mind that you had the captain wire for a fancy-dan detective from Los Angeles. But we do our own investigations around here. He doesn't have jurisdiction, is what I'm trying to say."

"But you've had police help before."

"When I've asked for it. This time I didn't ask. You did." His forehead wrinkled amply, all the way up to the top of his dome. "In a lesser man, that might cause an offense."

"No offense intended, Mr. Hardy. I was simply looking out for my client."

"And I shall do the same."

"Then I would like my client released this afternoon."

Hardy pinched the folds of skin under his chin. "I don't rightly know if I can do that."

"Mr. Hardy, let me put this as directly as I can. Your sheriff has my client incarcerated for a crime for which there is no evidence."

"Poison in the champagne?"

"That's your theory?"

"Consistent with the evidence."

Kit folded her arms. "Poison which came from an unknown source."

"In her stateroom?"

"Late at night, when she was in bed."

"So you say."

"A woman with no criminal past."

"So you say."

"If you have other information, produce it."

"We've just started our investigation."

"As she sits in a jail cell. I want to know if you are going to oppose a motion for bail."

"I hadn't really thought that far ahead, Mrs. Fox."

"Would you mind terribly thinking about it now?"

Hardy took this moment to sit down at his desk. It was covered with random bits of paper, ink stains, open law books, and what looked like scattered ash. Kit was of the opinion that a person's desk was a reflection of one's inner life. From the looks of it, Fielding Hardy had a bit of a jumble in his soul.

The prosecutor laced his fingers across his belly. "Mrs. Fox, I know your reputation for being, shall we say, persistent in the cause of your clients. I read the Los Angeles papers, you know."

"Didn't you used to work for the Los Angeles District Attorney's Office?"

Hardy's demeanor darkened. "That was a long time ago."

"What prompted your departure, if I may ask?"

"I believe we were talking about you, Mrs. Fox. You are in my neck of the woods at the present time. Should I venture up to Los Angeles someday, we can talk about me. What I want you to know is that I am well aware of your methods, even down to what you've pulled in court."

"Pulled, sir?"

"Like firing a gun in the middle of a trial, with the jury present."

"That was a piece of demonstrative evidence, Mr. Hardy. The gun held a blank. It was an essential element of proving my case. I was not held in contempt."

"What about the time you got a judge to allow you to take a jury to the scene of the crime and had a stage magician put on an act?"

"Again, that was a way of showing the jury what really happened and could not have been done in any other way as effectively. All within the code of procedure, I might add."

"What I'm trying to tell you, Mrs. Fox, is that you won't find us as loose with the reins down here in San Leandro. We have standards and ways of doing things. The judges and myself have worked out a nice, efficient system of justice. You will find that if you don't try to push things too hard, you'll get a lot further along."

"Mr. Hardy, I am not interested in getting along. While you will find me cooperative if treated fairly, if I believe my client's interests are in jeopardy, I am not going to sit idly by."

"The interests of your client may be tied up with your own behavior. I am trying to tell you, in a friendly and professional way, that you'll do more good for Wanda Boswell if you operate with a light hand."

"I believe we understand each other now, Mr. Hardy."

"I certainly hope so, Mrs. Fox."

"Then let us return to the matter at hand. In the spirit of the cooperation you seek, will you tell me what you intend to do about a bail hearing?"

Hardy wheezed out a tired breath. "Tell you what I will do. I'll walk across the street to the courthouse and have a sit-down with Judge Tenny. See what he has on his calendar. He likes to go fishing in the afternoons."

"Fishing? When there is pending business?"

"Keeps his mind alert."

"I would like to go with you."

Hardy shook his head. "Don't think that'd be such a good idea. The judge may not understand you the way I do. Just meet me at the courthouse around three-thirty. I'll give you an answer then."

11

THE JAIL, AN OLD BRICK building that might have held a man of Jesse James's era, had been built downwind from the harbor. It was nothing like the newer jail in Los Angeles County but was more in keeping with a quaint, quiet burgh.

The older deputy from earlier at the dock sat at a wooden desk, his worn boots propped up on a corner. He raised his eyebrows when Kit entered.

"Been expectin' you," he said, making no move to stand. He held a dime novel in his big hands, one with a cowboy-and-Indian picture on its cover. Kit saw the words *Buffalo Bill* between the deputy's fingers.

"May I see Mrs. Boswell, please?"

"You got anything in that handbag of yours?"

Kit glanced down at the simple bag in her hand. "Of course I do, but only personal items."

"Got to see 'em."

"Do you really think I am going to try to pass illicit items to my client?"

"Never can tell."

"I do not intend to be searched."

"Then I do not intend to let you inside."

Kit's jaw clenched. "Do you have a written set of procedures for this? Or do you make decisions arbitrarily?"

The deputy dropped his feet to the floor. His swivel chair creaked as he loomed forward. "Now, you listen here, I don't care what that detective has to say. You aren't gonna push us around down here. We may be a little town, but that doesn't mean you can walk in with your highfalutin ways."

Kit felt like yanking her hat off and whipping the deputy with it. In Los Angeles she would have known who to see, who to pressure, which judge she could count on to get a writ if she needed it. But here she was in someone else's yard, and she knew her Irish temper might not be the most persuasive tool.

"Fine," she said. She opened her purse and dumped its contents onto the startled deputy's desk.

The surprised lawman looked down at a pair of white gloves, two pencils, folded blank papers, a comb, a small hand mirror, three hairpins, a strand of shoelace, and two items in print—a small, leather-bound book and a pamphlet. The deputy picked up these latter two items.

"The book is the New Testament," Kit explained. "The pamphlet is the Constitution of the United States."

With widening eyes the deputy clutched them in his hands.

"Do you have any further questions?" Kit asked him.

"Pack away your things," the deputy said, letting drop to the desk the book and pamphlet. "Clear my desk."

Kit did just that while the deputy grabbed a ring of keys from a peg behind his chair and motioned for her to follow him. He unlocked a heavy door with a barred window and led Kit into a room that held four cells. Wanda was the room's sole occupant.

"Mrs. Fox!" Wanda said, her face red from crying. "Why are they doing this to me?"

"You may leave us now," Kit said to the deputy. The man grunted and exited through the door, mumbling to himself.

Kit took Wanda Boswell's hands through the bars of the cell. "I am trying to get you before a judge so we can have you bailed out."

"But I have no money."

"I don't want you to worry about that."

"But—"

"Not to worry. I will have you put up at a hotel until we get to the bottom of this. I have an assistant, Corazón Chavez, who will be helping us."

Wanda paused. "What has become of my things?"

"A detective I know is going through them, no doubt at this very moment."

"I am much concerned about . . ." Wanda looked at the floor.

"Tell me."

"You will think me frivolous."

"Not at all. Something personal perhaps?"

"My jewelry box. It is quite valuable to me."

"I trust Detective McGinty."

"Will you make sure my jewels are taken care of?"

"Exactly what do you have in that box?"

"Two rings, a bracelet, a necklace, a pin, and a brooch."

"I never saw you wearing any of that."

"Chilton objected to them. They were given to me by admirers of my dancing."

Kit squeezed Wanda's hands. "You must tell me who gave you the jewelry."

She looked at Kit with alarm. "But why?"

"A man does not give such things to a woman without the intention of getting something in return. If you were being wooed by someone, this could come out should we go to trial. Is there something you have not told me?"

When Wanda's face turned crimson, Kit had the beginnings of an answer.

"We have much more to talk about, Wanda. As I told you before, you must not keep anything—*anything*—from me. You must trust me."

Wanda took a deep breath. "I do trust you, Mrs. Fox."

"I will see to your things, all of them. What McGinty does not determine to be evidence I will secure. Don't you worry."

"It is so difficult not to worry."

"Talking will help. Tell me about the jewelry and the men who gave these to you. Did Chilton know who they were?"

"No, nor did he want to know."

"Who were they?"

Wanda looked up toward the ceiling. "One of them said he was a count or something from Russia. I don't even remember his name. I saw him only twice."

"And yet you accepted jewelry from him?"

"Do you think me bad?"

"No. Tell me, do you know where this man is now?"

Shaking her head, Wanda said, "He may have gone back to Russia. I have not seen him since."

"What about the other men?"

"Only one other man."

"His name?"

"For . . . Fortas or something like that."

"You don't remember his name?"

"Forbus. That was it."

"First name?"

"Vernon?"

Kit sighed. "Either you remember or you do not."

"Is it absolutely necessary to bring out my past like this? I would just like to get all this behind me."

"Did you love Chilton?"

The question seemed to explode inside Wanda. She snatched her hands away from Kit and took a step back from the bars. "How can you ask me that?"

Kit did not wish to confront Wanda with Delia's accusation that she was a gold digger, but she hoped Wanda would trust her enough to let her know how she really felt. There would be no safe way to build her defense unless she knew all the details.

Something in Wanda's protestation struck Kit as theatrical, and she decided to remain direct. "I am asking you to tell me the complete truth about your feelings for Chilton. I know his murder is a shocking thing. Still, please describe your affections for your late husband."

Wanda looked at Kit for a long moment. Finally she dropped her gaze to the floor. "I did love Chilton. I did. He became somewhat difficult after our wedding. The gambling, his mother—these were points of contention between us. But I so wanted the best for him and for our life together." Tears formed in her eyes.

"That's enough for now," Kit said. "Try to bear up for a few hours more. I am going to get you released from here."

"Thank you for not abandoning me, Mrs. Fox. I am all alone."

"Never alone." Kit removed the New Testament from her purse and handed it to Wanda through the bars. "Something to read while you wait."

"The smell of fish is lovely this time of year, isn't it?" Ted turned from the window that looked down across the ocean.

"We will be here only one night, and at least we will be together."

"Is that a promise this time?"

Kit went to him and threw her arms around his neck. "A promise sealed with a kiss."

She sealed it.

"Don't be long at the courthouse," Ted said.

"Only long enough to get Wanda out on bail. I have secured a room for her here at the hotel."

"Not our room I hope."

"Silly."

"Seal that promise again, will you?"

"Once more." She kissed him again, then set about preparing her suit for the meeting with Hardy, scheduled for three-thirty that afternoon. To get the judge to entertain a bail motion, Kit knew she needed to look as professional as possible. Perhaps Wanda would be out of jail by the close of business today.

As she laid the suit out on the bed, she saw Ted looking out the window. He was quieter than usual. "Are you feeling well?" she asked.

"Never better." Ted's voice held little conviction.

Kit walked around the bed to the window, placing a hand on his shoulder. "Really, what is it?"

"Nothing."

"Theodore Fox." She waited until he looked at her. "We have known each other quite a while now. I think I know when something is on your mind."

"Mind reader, eh? Like that fellow Kajar." Ted was referring to the fraudulent medium who had tried to pull psychic wool over Kit's eyes during the Harcourt murder trial.

"Please, do not mention Kajar and me in the same breath." Kit stroked his hair. "I should like to be a wife you can confide in, Ted. If there is anything concerning you, I want to know about it."

He stood up and took several steps away, then turned to face her. "You are so good to . . ." He paused, searching for words. "Just plain good, I suppose. It's all so . . ."

"Tell me."

"So intimidating."

That was not the word she expected to hear. "What do you mean, Ted?"

"I look at you and then I look at myself and I don't feel I measure up. Your faith is strong, and you don't seem to have any hesitation about what you are doing."

"You mean the law?"

"That and everything else you do. It's as if God has touched you in some special way."

"I don't know if that's so. I merely—"

"It is so. Am I able to be a good husband to you?"

Kit threw her arms around his shoulders and pulled him close. "Did you ever stop to think that God is the one who brought us together in the first place? We were meant for each other, Theodore Fox."

He looked at her with a half smile. "And what God has joined, let nothing separate, is that it?"

"That's it."

"Except your court appointment." He shook his head, laughing. "You'd better hurry."

12

IT WAS FOUR O'CLOCK when the judge entered the courtroom.

Kit thought for a minute that she was seeing double. The judge—what was his name again? Penny? Tenny?—was built very much like Fielding Hardy. His head was the same shape. His hair, though there was substantially more of it than on the district attorney, looked to be nearly the same color. The judge's curls were only slightly darker.

She could not help looking across the courtroom at Fielding Hardy, who sat chewing tobacco at the other counsel table. The resemblance was uncanny.

A young clerk in a suit and high-collared shirt intoned, "All rise! Court is now in session! The honorable Clarence Q. Hardy presiding."

Hardy?

The judge dropped into his chair behind the bench. "Be seated," the judge said. He even sounded like the D.A. "Hello to you, Mrs. Fox. Welcome to our courthouse."

Kit stammered, "Thank you, Your Honor."

"Not like those big courtrooms in Los Angeles, is it?"

Kit tried to smile good-naturedly. "The law does not take note of the size of the chamber."

The judge threw back his head and laughed. "Well said, young woman. You know, I've never seen with my own eyes a woman lawyer before."

Feeling a bit like an exhibit, Kit kept smiling. "It shan't be the last time, I should think."

"Let us hope not."

"Your Honor?"

"Yes?"

"If the court please, I could not help noting that you are not Judge Penny."

"Tenny," the judge corrected. "I've taken his calendar for the day."

"I see. Nor could I help noting the similarity in your name and that of the district attorney."

"Didn't Fielding tell you I am his brother?" The judge shot a sour look at the prosecutor, although it was with obvious humor. "Why'd you go and hide that small fact from the defense, Mr. Hardy?"

Barely concealing a laugh the prosecutor said, "I assure the court it only slipped my mind. Of course, the defense did not ask me about either of our judges. I figured she's from Los Angeles and so didn't need to bother with small details like that."

Now Kit was feeling like a mouse batted between two cats.

"I assure Your Honor I have the utmost respect for the court," Kit said, "as I do any court of law. And I am sure that Your Honor recognizes the inherent conflict of interest here presented and would gladly consider recusing himself."

There was almost an audible gasp from Fielding Hardy. But it stuck just behind his lips, puffing his cheeks out a little. To Kit he looked like a consternated chipmunk.

When she looked back at Judge Clarence Q. Hardy, however, he did not seem such a benign creature. More like a raging bull.

Trouble. Kit had stepped over some invisible line of small town courthouse propriety, and the recipient of the consequences was likely to be her client.

"Your Honor, I—"

"Are you questioning the honesty of this court, Mrs. Fox?"

"Not in the slightest."

"My reputation for judicial integrity is unquestioned!"

"No doubt, Your Honor. I was only trying to—"

"Force your hand upon me?"

"Allow me to explain, please."

For a moment the judge was silent.

"Any defense attorney," Kit said carefully, "would want to note for the record an instance of a judge's relationship with any party in a case. Conflicts of interest are—"

"That's the second time you've used that term, young woman. I'll not have it. I am telling you that there is no conflict here. I have presided over numerous cases prosecuted by my brother without the least hint of misconduct."

"And no defense lawyer has appealed?"

"There was one, but the verdict of this court was affirmed."

"The federal courts have held—"

"I do not care what the federal courts have held, Mrs. Fox. This is California, sovereign and independent. Save for the long arm of the United States Supreme Court, we have our own constitution and precedents. And that is how I am going to run this court. If you have an objection, you can note it for the record."

Kit was about to so note but then thought better of it. Her immediate concern was for her client's welfare. If this case ever got to trial—which it shouldn't—there would be plenty of time to object.

"I am prepared to go forward," Kit said.

"That's more like it," Judge Hardy said. "You may proceed."

"I am here to request that my client be released to me on her own recognizance. She is a woman without a criminal past, a young woman for whom I will take full responsibility."

Judge Clarence Hardy traced a finger along his chin. "But this is a case of murder, isn't that right, Fielding?"

"Oh yes," the judge's double said.

Kit stole a glance at the court clerk, jotting this down for the record. She hoped he'd gotten that last part right—the judge using his brother's first name.

"Again I emphasize the lack of a criminal past," Kit said, "and the lack of motive. There is not a shred of evidence to suggest Wanda Boswell is a danger to the community. I also have a reputation to uphold, Your Honor. I give you my full assurance I will see to it that—"

"But murder, Mrs. Fox, is a serious charge."

"It is merely a charge, and the evidence is marginal at best."

"Now, Fielding," said the judge, "are you bringing me a marginal case?"

The prosecutor snorted. "Would I do that, Your Honor?"

"I dunno. You remember that horse thief you brought in, oh, four years ago?"

"That man was guilty as sin."

"Had to throw that out, as I recall."

"You always were a stickler."

Kit was incredulous. "If the court please."

The two men stopped their colloquy and looked at her.

"I wonder if we might return to the issue at hand, which is Mrs. Boswell's release to me." Kit was certain now that the judge would not grant it, yet by making this her opening position she hoped he would at least set a bail amount.

Judge Hardy cleared his throat and looked at his brother. "What is your view on this, counsel?"

Counsel. It was good to see the judge was returning to professional appropriateness. If this case actually proceeded to preliminary hearing—and Kit was determined to get the prosecutor to consider other suspects—she would make a formal written motion for the judge to be recused. At the moment she wanted his good graces.

Fielding Hardy had that look about him, the one Kit used to see on the face of her Los Angeles rival, Clara Dalton Price. Mrs. Price had been the toughest prosecutor Kit had ever faced, until the deputy D.A.'s ambitions got the better of her and she was implicated in witness tampering and murder. But when she was trying cases, Mrs. Price was adept at holding back crucial information and looking smug about it.

"The facts," Fielding Hardy said, "are these. That on the night of January sixth, or the early morning hours of January seventh, the deceased, Chilton Boswell, husband of the accused, was found dead in the stateroom of the couple on the cruise ship *Majestic*. Examination by the ship's doctor revealed the cause of death to be poisoning. Mrs. Boswell immediately retained Mrs. Fox as her lawyer."

"Of what relevance is that?" Kit said.

"It's evidence she was awful worried about what she'd done."

"Your Honor, if you please. The retention of legal counsel is not evidence of anything but the exercise of a constitutional right. To have that considered—"

"Mrs. Fox, this court understands the law." The judge looked down at the prosecutor. "You tell me just what your position is, Mr. Prosecutor."

"The position of this office," Fielding Hardy replied, "is that this is a case of cold-blooded, premeditated murder, and at the preliminary hearing we will present evidence that not only establishes probable cause but is proof beyond a reasonable doubt."

"What proof?" Kit demanded.

"Not so fast, Mrs. Fox," the judge said. "This is a bail hearing only, and the prosecutor does not have to reveal that evidence if he does not wish to. The fact that the two of you agree upon is that the victim, Mr. Boswell, was found dead in the couple's stateroom, is that right?"

"But that is not nearly enough for—"

"Is that right?"

"Yes," Kit said. "A victim who may have been poisoned anywhere on the ship."

"Anything else from the defense?"

"Nothing, Your Honor. We will vigorously defend this case, and question whether the prosecution has such proof."

"Well, until we get to the preliminary, I'm not going to take a chance. I will not release Mrs. Boswell to you."

"Then we would request a reasonable bail based upon—"

"Bail is denied."

"On what grounds?"

"I do not have to explain my reasons, Mrs. Fox."

"Oh, but you do, because I am going to take this up to the Court of Appeal, and if there is no ground in the record, you shall be summarily reversed."

Fuming now, the judge said through clenched teeth, "Your client has no ties to our community. If we release her, even to you, there is a possibility she would not return. I assure you she will be well treated."

Kit got a sudden feeling and looked into the gallery. "Or is it that a murder suspect in your jail is good publicity?"

That brought red to the cheeks of Judge Hardy. "Mrs. Fox, you are close to contempt."

"I will petition the Court of Appeal tomorrow."

"You have not heard me out," the judge said, his tone a touch more deferential. "I will entertain another bail motion after the preliminary hearing. I will assess the state of the evidence at that time. Shall we say one week from today?"

"One week with my client in jail?"

"It would take that long for you to get an answer on your petition."

"But—"

"This court is adjourned," the judge said.

Kit almost charged right through the uniformed man. She was seeing white lights behind her eyes. This small town, which seemed so quaint when she and Ted had arrived for their cruise, was wearing on her. Judges with prosecutor brothers!

"Whoa there," the man in the white uniform said, his hands in front of him. He stood at the foot of the gangplank to the *Majestic*.

"Beg pardon," Kit said. "I need to go aboard."

"I'm sorry, ma'am. There's been some trouble, and the police are—"

"I know all about that. I am a lawyer representing the woman accused."

"Lawyer? Oh yes, Kit Shannon Fox, isn't it? I saw the manifest."

"May I?"

The man shook his head. "Sorry, my orders are to keep anyone from boarding while the investigation is taking place."

"Who gave you those orders?"

"The captain."

"May I speak with him please?"

"Not possible. The captain ain't here."

"If Captain Raleigh is not here, from whom then are you taking orders?"

He squinted, like a schoolboy stumped by a teacher's exam.

"From me." Lowell Sanders, first mate, stood at the top of the gangplank. "Let her aboard."

Stiffening, the uniformed man said, "But I was told—"

"I'm telling you now," Sanders said. "I am in charge at the moment, and I say she can come up. Now move aside."

He did, albeit with reluctance. Kit made her way up to Sanders. "Thank you."

"A pleasure." Lowell Sanders gave her the smile that might have enraptured any number of women. With his crisp whites, square chin, and easy manner he would no doubt have many a conquest behind him. He might also be the kind to use his magnetism to control women should they stray off his narrowly defined path. She'd have to keep her wits about her.

"Is Detective McGinty still on the ship?" Kit asked.

"I imagine. I suppose you'd like to talk to him."

"Yes."

"Do you know why I supposed that?"

Kit waited for his explanation, which came out as smooth as maple syrup. "Because you're the kind of woman who can't be stopped when she's got her mind made up."

"McGinty—is he still in the stateroom?"

"You know, Mrs. Fox, you fascinate me."

This was not why she came aboard. What was he trying to do? Casual conversation? Or something more? She had no interest in either, but she did see an opportunity.

"You fascinate me as well," Kit said.

The first mate frowned for a moment. Then his easy smile returned. "Tell me why."

She had been right in her assessment of him. There is nothing a masher likes more than speaking or hearing about himself. Perhaps she could turn this to her advantage.

"I noticed the way you tried to bring the shipboard dinner conversation to a happy close, after Chilton Boswell bolted from the table. You seem to be a man of action, perhaps captain material someday."

"Captain material right now if experience counts for anything."

"Oh? What is holding you back?"

His smile dropped behind a tense jaw. "Nothing is holding me back. The opening just hasn't come yet."

"I am quite sure with Captain Raleigh's recommendation, you could take command of a ship of this line, or another."

A chill silence passed between them, interrupted by the shriek of an angry sea gull that split the air.

"I don't need his help," Sanders said.

"Don't you and the captain get along?"

"I do my job. The captain knows how competent I am."

"What does he think of you flirting with the passengers?"

Sanders sniffed. "Just what is your insinuation?"

"You were none too subtle about your interest in Miss Delia Patton."

"Ha. She is the one who made her interest known."

"To which you willingly responded."

"What does it matter? No harm was done."

"But then there was the other matter Captain Raleigh might be justifiably upset about."

"Oh? And what might that be?"

"Your argument with Chilton Boswell."

Kit watched his eyes closely to see if they betrayed anything. As with a witness in court, she always watched the eyes.

Sanders's eyes seemed to want to tell a story, but then he hauled them in like a catch of fish. "Argument? I assure you I never had cross words with Mr. Boswell."

"You were heard one night in what was described as an argument."

"By whom?"

"Mrs. Boswell."

"The old battle . . . the older woman?"

"No, my client. She had the impression it was over some item of business. Do you recall raising your voice during the conversation?" It was a trick question, the sort she had used in court before. By assuming the important fact—a conversation—and asking about a relatively unimportant point—the voice—she hoped to catch Sanders in something resembling the truth.

But the first mate only shook his head. "I do not recall any private conversation with Chilton Boswell."

They were then interrupted by the heavy steps of Mike McGinty, followed by two younger men in suits. She recognized them as Los Angeles cops. They were carrying a trunk between them.

"Got to turn this in to the D.A.," McGinty said around his cigar.

"What'd you find?" Kit asked.

McGinty smiled. "Now, Kit, our friendship goes only so far."

"Just thought I'd give it the old college try."

"D.A. wouldn't like it if I told you what I found."

"Mike, may I have a word with you?" Kit walked away from the two assisting detectives and Sanders.

"You're not going to put the strong arm on me, are you?" McGinty seemed slightly amused.

"I certainly don't want you in Dutch with the local prosecutor, Mike. Just remember, I requested that you be put on this case."

"And it was approved from upstairs." He was referring to the new chief of police of Los Angeles. Horace Allen, the previous chief, was currently in jail for the murder of a key witness in a trial Kit had won the year before.

"Sure it was, Mike. We can't have you violate the trust of police and district attorney. It's a longstanding rule of protocol that the police cannot be telling the lowly defense lawyers what evidence they've found."

McGinty squinted at her suspiciously.

"But there is nothing that prevents you from telling me what you *didn't* find, is there?"

"What?"

"I can properly ask you about an item of evidence and whether you uncovered it. You will be revealing nothing about the evidence you *did* find."

"There is a reason you are a lawyer, Kit Shannon."

"Fox."

"Why didn't I marry you myself?" McGinty shook his head. "All right, I'll give you two minutes."

"A jewelry box. Did you find one?"

"No jewelry box."

"Any type of small container that might hold jewels or other like items?"

"Now wait just a minute. If I say yes to that, then I'm telling you about the evidence I did find."

"Maybe you should have been a lawyer after all. Just one more question."

"Kit—"

"A manuscript. A written manuscript of some kind."

"Nothing like that. Now can I go?"

"She's not guilty, Mike. You did not find any evidence to suggest otherwise, did you?"

"That's enough, Mrs. Fox. I've given you what I don't know. But I'll leave you with a small word of advice." He finally removed his cold cigar. "Watch out for this guy Hardy."

"Do you mean the prosecutor or the judge?"

"Judge?"

She explained that Fielding Hardy's brother sat on the bench.

"Then I suggest you watch out for them both," McGinty said.

13

KIT WALKED BACK THROUGH the little town, along the main street where tidy shops with the flavor of both western expansion and native tradition sold their wares. Parts of it reminded Kit of the Old Plaza in Los Angeles, a place that still offered a taste of Los Angeles before it became a fast-paced city on the move.

As she strolled she felt the eyes of the townspeople casting her examining looks. It was likely that an unescorted woman was not as common a sight here as in Los Angeles, and perhaps for good reason. As a port city, San Leandro was known to be rougher, not only around the edges but right in the heart of things, than its sister city to the north.

With the sun about to set, the gas streetlamps were being illumined. Full electric power had not yet come to this municipality. Come to think of it, Kit had seen only two automobiles on the avenue, one of them a rickety piece of homemade parts. She thought of Gus Willingham, Ted's friend and partner in the monoplane project. Was he even grumpier than usual as he waited for Ted to get back to work?

Across the street she saw a two-story building with a sign on the window: *San Leandro Clarion*. Lights burned inside, and she could see a few men rushing around as if some news were breaking. A fire perhaps? Or, Kit shuddered, a murder?

She crossed the street. Two young boys played mumblety-peg in the dirt. They didn't look up upon her approach.

"You boys newsies?" she asked.

The two squinted up at her. The bigger of the pair said, "That's right. Me and Sam own this town. Right, Sam?"

"Right, Al," the other boy said.

Kit smiled at the youthful bravado, which gave her an immediate idea. "I suppose you know as much about what goes on around here as anyone."

"More," Al said.

"Lots more," said Sam.

"I wager you can keep secrets, too."

"Nobody can make us talk," Al boasted.

"And enterprising, aren't you? Men of business?"

Both boys nodded.

"How would you like to do a little job for me?"

Al looked skeptical. "What kinda job?"

"How much does it pay?" Sam asked.

"You cut right to the chase, don't you?"

"That's the way it's done," Sam said.

"Surely. Then I'll tell you this. I will be staying here in town for a while, and I may need some information from time to time. If you can keep this to yourselves, there's ten dollars in it for you."

Sam, the smaller one, gasped. "Ten dollars?"

"Each," Kit added.

Al smiled and, with his partner, jumped to his feet. "You got yourself a deal, lady." He stuck out his hand.

Kit shook it. "My name is Mrs. Fox. I'm staying at the San Leandro Hotel. Come around and see me tomorrow, say at noon."

Al scratched his chin. "Your name sounds familiar. Where're you from?"

"Los Angeles."

"That's it!" Al snapped his fingers. "You're that lady lawyer."

"Guilty," Kit said.

"That murder case. It's in the paper."

"And how did the paper happen to get the story, do you know?"

Al grinned. "I expect it came direct to Bob Barry. He's the city reporter."

"Shh!" Sam said. "You shouldn't tell!"

"Why not?" Al waved a dismissive hand at his partner. "She's paying us, ain't she?"

The logic appeared to work on Sam, who nodded his agreement.

Before Kit could inquire further, the door to the office swung open. A mean-looking man with huge arms motioned with his thumb behind the building.

"Hey!" he called to the boys. "The evening edition's out. Hop to it!" He gave Kit a quick once-over, decided she was not newsworthy, and slammed the door.

"Gotta go," Al declared.

"Wait." Kit fished out two dimes from her purse and handed one to each of the boys. Then she gave Al a nickel. "The dimes are for your trouble if you'll please fetch me a copy."

MURDER ON THE HIGH SEAS!
Wife under arrest for poisoning husband while on honeymoon!
Noted Los Angeles attorney Kit Shannon takes over defense!

Kit let out a huge sigh. How many times was she going to have to repeat her married name before people started getting it right? But this was the local paper, and her maiden name was news. Accuracy in reporting was not so important, apparently.

She turned up the lamp in the hotel room. Ted had left a note that he was out at a bookseller and would be returning shortly.

> *As she sits in the San Leandro jail awaiting her preliminary hearing on the charge of murder, Mrs. Wanda Boswell has ample time to contemplate how a life of seeming promise and hope turned into one of disaster and despair.*

Kit shook her head. This was a reporter whose florid prose was more indicative of a bad novelist in the making than a competent newspaperman. Was it Bob Barry, the one Al had mentioned? The story carried no by-line.

> *Wed a scant five days before the deadly cruise, Mr. Chilton Boswell of Los Angeles was found dead in his first-class stateroom aboard the* Majestic *on the morning of January 7, victim of a lethal dose of poison. For Mr. Boswell, an enjoyable evening of cards and conviviality on what was supposed to be a pleasant honeymoon trip ended in his death.*
>
> *Also aboard the doomed cruise to the Hawaiian Islands was the noted Los Angeles defense lawyer Kit Shannon, the winner of several stunning verdicts in recent years. In an example of being Josephine-on-the-Spot, Miss Shannon was retained by Wanda Boswell almost before the body of her late husband had started to cool.*

Florid prose indeed, with a dash of melodramatic theater! What brand of journalism were they practicing in San Leandro?

> *According to the San Leandro District Attorney, Fielding Hardy, this is a case of cold-blooded murder. "We have on our hands a woman whose plan to marry into wealth ran into reality. She took matters into her own hands to see that she got what she thought she deserved. A life insurance policy was taken out on her husband just before the cruise. That is the motive."*

And a fine opening statement for a jury. This was the most blatant attempt to infect the jury pool that Kit had ever seen. In Los Angeles there was enough of a population that a single newspaper could not reach everyone. The *Times* and the *Examiner* each had subscribers, but there were plenty of citizens who didn't read either of them.

But here in a small town, even the ones who did not read would be sure to hear the story at the barbershop or in the local saloon.

What could she do about it? Move for a change of venue? Not likely granted by the prosecutor's brother. This newspaper would be a prime exhibit on appeal, should such a thing become necessary.

Trials for murder are rare in San Leandro, one of the garden spots of the West. The last time a murder took place within the city limits was in 1904 when a sailor named Nathaniel Turner was found guilty of murdering a fellow sailor. The prosecutor was Fielding Hardy.

Now we will see what our intrepid D.A. can do against the famous lawyer from the City of Angels. "I look forward to the challenge," Mr. Hardy says.

It will be a hearty challenge. Miss Shannon is the protégé of Earl Rogers, perhaps the most famous lawyer in America. Also one of the trickiest. His courtroom antics have apparently been passed along to Miss Shannon.

In one famous case, Miss Shannon convened a jury at the scene of the crime, the home of the wealthy Angeleno who was murdered. There she reenacted the murder with the help of a stage magician named Harry Houdini, and earned what some have called a magical acquittal of her client.

Another trial found Miss Shannon firing a pistol in open court. Luckily for the prosecutor and judge, it was a blank. Will there be such fireworks in our modest courthouse? We shall have to see.

If anything is certain, it is that Kit Shannon is news, and so is murder. Putting those two together is going to make for entertaining days ahead.

That was when Ted walked in.

"I see you've got the evening paper." He said it as if he meant she'd contracted a sickness.

She got up and went to him just as he closed the door, and hugged him. "I am so outraged."

Ted took her shoulders in his hands and looked into her eyes. "You'd think they could get your name right."

"No one talked to me about this story."

"I was not implying anyone did." He walked to the window and leaned his cane against a chair. There was no mistaking the coolness in his voice.

"Dear, I am so sorry for all this mess." She moved toward him again. He spun around and sat on the window seat. His expression stopped her.

"I think we've both been distracted," he said. "I from my monoplane and you from your work. And both of us from the Bible Institute." Ted paused. "What is the status of Wanda Boswell?"

Kit sat on the edge of the bed. "She has been denied bail and will remain in jail until the preliminary hearing, in a week."

"Which means that you will be hard at work in preparation."

"I am afraid so." She added with a smile, "But she is my only client at the moment."

Ted did not smile. "When will we be going home?"

"I thought that if we keep the room for at least another week, we might go back and forth. You must admit it is cozy here."

"Too fishy for my taste." He stood up. "Kit, why don't you stay here until your work is finished? I'll go home and get back to work on the plane, see to the Institute's books. Then we'll be able to see just how far this case is going to go."

For some reason his words sent a chill through her. She suddenly felt like pleading with him to stay, but that might have caused more distress, caused Ted to think things perhaps not on his mind right now.

Nevertheless, she was troubled by the proposition. "I don't want us to be apart," she stated. "I will take the train tomorrow—after I have had the chance to speak to some witnesses."

"More witnesses?"

"And then home."

At last Ted smiled again. "Very well, my wife. Will we be having dinner together tonight?"

"Of course we will, as soon as—" She stopped herself, feeling her face flush.

"As soon as you question someone?"

14

CAPTAIN RALEIGH'S SEASIDE HOME had to be the largest structure in San Leandro. It rose up out of the wooded hills like a ship breaking through fog. Especially this evening, in the onrushing darkness, as Kit approached in a rented horse-drawn carriage. The lights were beginning to glow in the windows, reminding her of the way Raleigh's ship, the *Majestic,* looked in the harbor at night.

In comparison to the mansions of Angeleno Heights, including Kit's own—passed down to her from her aunt Freddy—the Raleigh home was modest in appearance. But in the context of this harbor town, situated as it was high above the bay, it appeared stylish and imposing.

Raleigh would no doubt be a prosecution witness. Kit wanted to make sure she knew, as the sailors put it, the cut of his jib.

"Good evening, Captain," Kit said when he answered the door. "I wonder if I might have a word with you."

Captain Wendell Raleigh wore a red smoking jacket and white cotton pants, as well as a look of abject surprise. "What are you doing up here?"

"If you are entertaining, I can come back in the morning."

He paused. "Will this take long?"

"No, sir."

"Come in then."

His home had been done up in all things oceanic—coral sculptures, seascapes in frames made of rope, a mounted swordfish in the foyer. A stairway wound upward in the fashion of a ship, as if one would be passing between decks. A large ship's wheel from an old clipper dominated one wall.

Raleigh led Kit into a library where a fire crackled in the fire-place, under a mantel that held several varieties of bells. No doubt from various ships he had captained. Raleigh removed a pipe from a holder between two of the bells and lit it as Kit looked around at all the seafaring decor. Only the tea set on the table near the window seemed conventional and dainty. All else was masculine, straight out of Richard Henry Dana's *Two Years Before the Mast*.

"The sea has been my life, Mrs. Fox," the captain said. "No doubt you can see that for yourself."

"The theme is quite evident." She noted the shelves of leather-bound books, perfectly matched by the color of their spines. In fact, everything in the library was what a sailor would have called *ship-shape*.

"I got my papers when I was sixteen years old. I've been around the world twice. I am what they call an old salt. Please, sit."

Kit took a soft chair by the fire, opposite Raleigh.

"I wanted to have a house that reminded me of the sea. Bought this one when I moved up from San Diego, about four years ago now. Up here, looking out at the sea, well, it makes things a little less lonely."

"Lonely?"

"The sea life doesn't leave much time for family. But I have had a life of adventure and good work. I am a member of the ancient Order of the Deep three times over."

"I am not familiar with that order."

Raleigh laughed. "It is for those who've been over the equator, who have crossed the line. It's all in fun, really. You're a pollywog until you've crossed. Once you do, Davy Jones, in the name of Neptunus Rex, Ruler of the Raging Main, initiates you into the order—all in jest, presided over on the ship by those who've crossed before you. I first crossed the line four hundred miles south of Palmyra, on course to Pago Pago. Have you ever been in the South Seas?"

"I cannot say that I have."

"Quite a place. The islands are volcanic in origin. Sheer walls of igneous rock with smooth coats of green foliage. The native men are thick and muscular. I daresay those Samoans would make a fearsome line for Yale's football team."

He was charming, though Kit felt that his talk of things like the South Seas was an effort to keep from talking about other things, such as the murder aboard his ship.

"Captain, I do not wish to take any more of your time than is necessary. If I may ask you some questions."

"About the killing of Chilton Boswell?"

"Yes."

"Hasn't the case been turned over to the district attorney?"

"Yes, but you may be called upon to testify."

Raleigh puffed on his pipe. "I suppose that cannot be helped. Well, you know everything I do. You were there when the doctor examined the body."

"And when we found Professor Faire in the stateroom."

"I was not pleased about that."

"There were some items from the stateroom that seem to have disappeared."

"Such as?"

"A jewelry box and a manuscript. I am afraid that someone else may have entered the room and taken them."

"Who might that be?"

"I was hoping you would have some idea."

Raleigh, veiled by a plume of smoke, shook his head. "Do you think Professor Faire might have taken them?"

"I really can't say. I don't know the man. Do you think he was telling us the truth about the gambling debt?"

"I have my doubts."

"As do I."

"Then he would be the one to question, would he not?"

"I hope to do that soon. Who else would have access to the stateroom—besides yourself, of course?"

"Anyone with access to a key."

"You issued an order that the stateroom was off-limits, did you not?"

"Yes. The stewards and the crew."

"Is there anyone among them who you might suspect would be interested in sneaking around in the stateroom?"

Raleigh thought a moment. "I do not think so. I know the staff."

"What about your first mate?"

"Sanders? An ambitious young man. I don't think he would do anything to hurt his career. If he'd been caught where he was not authorized to be, that would be a black mark against him."

"Can you tell me anything about the passengers, anyone who might have had some connection with Chilton Boswell?"

"Other than Faire?"

"Yes."

"Can't say that I can. Faire purchased his ticket at the last moment, I know that."

"Curious. What about Don Raffels, the gambling overseer?"

"You don't have to worry about Big Don. He plays it close, stays out of trouble. He has to, or he knows he'll be thrown off."

"Where does he reside when he is not aboard ship?"

"You might find him aboard one of the gambling ships. There are a few out of San Leandro and Long Beach harbor. He's in demand, you might say."

"Then there is Delia Patton."

Raleigh frowned. "Yes, Miss Patton."

"What do you know of her?"

"Trouble. I smell trouble with Miss Delia Patton."

"Why is that?"

"Mrs. Fox, must we go over everything? I cannot be of much help to you. What I know the prosecutor knows. I spoke with that detective."

"McGinty?"

"For half an hour. Do you want to know what I think?"

"Please."

"I think your client did him in, but she had good reason. Oh, I don't mean one can justify murder. But I should think that a jury might look upon her sympathetically if you bring out the facts surrounding Chilton Boswell. The man was no good."

"Do you possess some evidence of that fact?"

"When you captain long enough, you get so you can tell what a man's made of from less than complete examination. Boswell was not the sort of man, how shall I put it, I would want for a son. Goodness knows what your client had to put up with."

Kit shook her head. "That's just it. She and Chilton had not been married for very long. One does not develop a murderous heart in such a short time."

"Have you thought about the possibility that your client may have a heart she has not fully exposed to you?"

Kit did not have a ready answer.

"Mrs. Fox, you are a Christian, are you not?"

"I am."

"Are you one of the modern Christians? The ones who think the Bible is just a book of ancient stories? Or do you favor the old-time religion?"

"I am firmly in the camp of the Bible as God's holy Word, inspired and without error."

"And I salute you for that. I don't see how one can be a Christian of any consequence without such a belief." Raleigh strode to his bookshelf and removed a large leather-bound Bible, one that had seen considerable use. Kit smiled inwardly at that. She loved a worn-out Bible. She'd seen too many of late, in fine homes, looking new save for the thin layer of dust over them.

Raleigh opened the Bible and flipped several pages. Then he read: "'The heart is deceitful above all things, and desperately wicked: who can know it?' The prophet Jeremiah, chapter seventeen, verse nine. Are you certain, Mrs. Fox, that you know anything about the heart of your client?"

"Your point is well taken, Captain. Thank you. If anything else should occur to you that you think I should know, please contact me."

"You can be certain that I will," the captain said.

Kit said good-night and soon was back in the carriage, on her way down the hill.

When she entered her and Ted's hotel room, she saw that Ted was already in bed, asleep.

15

TED LEFT THE NEXT MORNING. Kit told him she would join him the following day, to attend to business and to bring Corazón into the case.

"And see your husband?" Ted had remarked. He was half joking, but she wondered about the other half.

For an hour after he was gone, Kit prayed and read her father's Bible, the legacy he had left to her after his death. She could almost hear his preacher's voice still, expounding the Scriptures, showing his love for sinners and saints alike. His numerous interlineations, his comments on Scripture in his own hand, were like his own private whisperings to her alone. *Do you see, Kit darlin'? Do you hear the Master?*

She thought of her mother, too—her quiet strength, which had been a comfort to her father all the days of their marriage. Kit turned to the thirty-first chapter of Proverbs, where her father had inscribed, next to the chapter number, *This is Mary*. Her mother.

Kit began with the tenth verse: *"Who can find a virtuous woman? for her price is far above rubies. The heart of her husband doth safely trust in her, so that he shall have no need of spoil. She will do him good and not evil all the days of her life."*

Yes, she thought. Let that be me. She ended with the last verse: *"Give her of the fruit of her hands; and let her own works praise her in the gates."* She remembered then that she had one task left before traveling home to Los Angeles. That was when a knock sounded at her door.

Kit answered the door. It was the desk clerk.

"I am terribly sorry to disturb you, Mrs. Fox, but there is something of a commotion going on downstairs. It seems two boys, ragamuffins really, wish to see you. I told them to get out, but they insisted they had an appointment with you. When I attempted to usher them from the premises, one of them kicked me in the shin and wailed like a stuck pig. Surely this cannot be."

"I am sorry about your shin. I will give them a good talking-to about that."

"Then it's true? They are here to see you?"

"Tell them I will be down presently."

The clerk looked terribly embarrassed. "I never would have thought—"

"And if you would, have the kitchen prepare two cups of hot cocoa. Thank you."

Al and Sam stood in the lobby, their arms folded, their resolve as strong as two Spartans.

"Hello, boys," Kit said.

"They tried to give us the bum's rush!" Al said indignantly. "But Sam here gave 'em what for."

Sam smiled with evident satisfaction.

"Kicking someone is not permitted," Kit explained. "If you work for me, you need to remember that."

Al frowned. "A man's got to defend himself."

"That's right," said Sam.

Kit tousled Sam's hair. "Our Savior taught us that we should turn the other cheek when struck. That's the way we're going to do things."

"Are you crazy, lady?" Al seemed genuinely perplexed.

"Do you boys go to Sunday school?"

"That's for sissies," Sam said.

"My old man don't want me in church," Al added.

"What about your mother?"

"Don't got no mother."

"And you, Sam?"

"I live with my aunt."

"Where are your folks?"

Sam raised his shoulders, and that gesture saddened Kit more than anything in a long time. "Come along, you two. Let's talk some business."

In the dining room, the boys seemed ecstatic with their cocoa, as if it were the treat of a lifetime.

A cup of coffee had been prepared for Kit. "What do you boys want to do when you grow up?" she asked.

"We *are* grown up," Al said.

"Ah yes, of course. Then tell me, what do you wish to do with the rest of your lives?"

Sam and Al exchanged looks, befuddled. Al took a thoughtful sip of his cocoa. "We're part of the newspaper game. Old Man Erskine says we'll make good reporters someday."

"Mr. Erskine?"

"He runs the *Clarion*."

"And what manner of man is he?"

"He's a good sort, I guess, as much as any editor can be."

Sam and Al laughed.

"What about the reporter, Bob Barry? What can you tell me about him?"

"The best reporter there is," Sam said.

"Tough as they come," Al agreed. "That's who I want to be like."

"Tough?" Kit inquired.

"You bet."

"As tough as Samson?"

The boys looked at Kit with bemusement.

"Hasn't anyone ever told you the story of Samson?"

"He was a strong man, wasn't he?" Al said.

"The strongest. You know what he once did? He took an old jawbone from a dead donkey and went out against an army and killed a thousand men with it."

Al's chin dropped. "A thousand?"

"Right."

"Hoowee. How could he do that?"

"He had special strength from God. God made a deal with Samson, that as long as he didn't cut his hair, he would have great strength. And then his enemies, the Philistines, got to him and tricked him and cut his hair, and he lost his strength. Then the Philistines put his eyes out."

Al and Sam were now silent and intent upon Kit's words.

"And they made him a slave. But while he was a slave his hair grew back. And then one day the Philistines were in their temple, thousands of them, and they brought Samson up so they could make fun of him."

"That's a mean thing to do," Sam said.

"What happened next?" Al said.

"Samson asked the young man who had brought him to let him lean on the pillars that held up the place. He then prayed to God for his strength to return. Afterward, he pushed those two pillars down, and the whole temple fell, killing everybody."

"What about Samson?" Al said.

"Samson died too. He knew he would. But he wanted vengeance on the enemies of God."

"That *is* tough," said Al.

"It really happened. It's in the Bible. And what's in the Bible is true. You boys want to hear more about it?"

As if joined together, they nodded.

"Then we will have our own Sunday school from time to time. Would you like that?"

"I dunno," Al said. "My old man and all."

"Would you like it if I had a talk with your father? Maybe I could persuade—"

"Oh no! He wouldn't like that one bit. He can get awful mean."

"Well then, no matter. You boys still want to earn a little extra money, don't you?"

The two nodded eagerly.

"Do you know what *confidential* means?"

Sam whispered something to Al, who said, "No."

"It means that when people do business together, they agree to keep some things to themselves."

"We can keep our mouths shut," Sam said proudly.

"Grand. Then this will be our secret. What I'd like for you boys to do is try to keep track of who comes and goes at the *Clarion,* anybody who seems a little, oh, out of the ordinary."

"We can do that," Al said. "We know places to hide, too."

The *San Leandro Clarion* office was up and running when Kit walked through the door and introduced herself to the receptionist, an older woman who seemed in keeping with the small town pulse. At the mention of Kit's name, however, she took on a respectful air. And went to summon the editor.

"Well, it is indeed a pleasure to welcome such a famous personage to our humble offices." A short man waddled forward to greet her. "My name is Sanford Erskine."

Kit shook his hand. "Kathleen Fox."

"No need to introduce yourself. You are well-known already."

Kit looked around at the tiny, cramped office and could not help but compare it to the giant fortress that housed the *Los Angeles Times,* or the nearly equal opulence of its rival, the *Los Angeles Examiner.* Neither Otis of the *Times* nor Hearst of the *Examiner* were shrinking violets when it came to their cherished papers. This man Erskine, on the other hand, was a throwback to a different era. His high collar struggled to hold back the folds of his neck in men's fashion of the 1880s. Erskine's hair, grayish black, was parted in the middle.

"How long has your paper been serving the community?" Kit asked.

"Oh my, lo these many years. I have been the editor for fifteen of those years, and the paper was begun ten years prior to my tenure."

"And you have no rival?"

"There is an upstart weekly that has aspirations for more, but we are the beacon of truth for the people of San Leandro."

"That is what I would like to talk to you about."

Erskine nodded, reached for a little bell on his desk and jingled it. An eager boy of fifteen or so appeared at his door. "Tea, Millard."

The boy nodded after giving Kit a wondering gaze, then disappeared.

"Now what is it I can do for you, Mrs. Fox?"

"You are the beacon of truth for the people?"

"The people. Yes."

"I should like to ask you about the beacon aspect."

"I'm not sure I follow you."

"Your story about my case seemed to have a slant. That is, toward the sensational."

Erskine frowned. "My paper is dedicated to the reporting of the news. If it is exciting for us, so much the better. Circulation, you know."

"You employ a reporter named Bob Barry?"

"Yes. He's one of the younger ones on the paper. Very ambitious, very good."

"Might I have a word with him?"

"I am afraid he is out pursuing a story."

"Then perhaps he might contact me at the San Leandro Hotel, at his convenience."

"In what regard?"

"My regard, if you please. I should like, when he writes a story that mentions me, that he hear from me first."

Erskine puffed his cheeks and expurgated a stream of air. "Why, I . . ."

"That is only fair, is it not?"

"Yes, but . . ."

"But what, sir?"

"We have to sell papers and—"

"I am news?"

Erskine spread his hands. "There you are."

"Why such interest in this case, Mr. Erskine? The prosecutor, Mr. Hardy, and his brother the judge, they are quite anxious to keep this case in San Leandro as well."

"And why not? Law and order, you know. We can't have murders going unpunished here. What would that do to the—" Erskine stopped himself.

"Do to the what, Mr. Erskine?"

"Nothing, nothing." He grabbed his handkerchief and dabbed at his forehead.

Kit studied the man's face, which was growing flush. In court, that would have been the signal to strike. "Might it be bad for the good name of this town? And might that hurt the prospect of . . . a harbor?"

Erskine puffed his cheeks again.

"That's it, isn't it?" Kit felt the pieces shuffling in her mind. "Los Angeles is looking to annex a city for a port. San Pedro to the north is the leading contender. You don't want to hurt your chances here. Indeed, a highly publicized trial that ends in a victory for the prosecution could be a boon."

"Mrs. Fox, I believe you have a fevered imagination."

"I wonder what the *Times* and *Examiner* might think of this little intrigue?"

"That you imagined all this, I am certain."

"And I shall continue to imagine, as I read your paper. Thank you for your time, Mr. Erskine."

16

"BEEN THINKIN'," GUS SAID. "We gotta keep her from rolling out of control when you bank on a turn."

Ted nodded.

"Flaps."

"What's that?"

"Are you listening to me?"

They were back on the bluffs, where Ted owned a parcel of raw land. He'd constructed a hangar to house the monoplane, a workshop for the science of aeronautics.

It was the place he wanted to be, needed to be, and yet he found himself unable to concentrate. Since his leaving San Leandro the day before, thoughts of Kit swirled in his mind like dust kicked up by a spinning propeller. Nothing substantial, but enough to obscure his thinking and choke his contentment.

He shook his head. "Sorry, Gus. What were you saying?"

"At the tips of the wings, see?" Gus held his scarecrow arms out from his body and moved his hands up and down, like some stiff albatross. "Flaps."

"What for?"

"For stability. Control in the turns."

"But how would we control these flaps?"

"I'd put together a harness," said Gus. "So that when you lean left or right, you work the flaps. It gives another level of support."

Ted smiled at his mechanic and said, "You really have been thinking. You may be a genius."

Gus cast him a sour glance. "Don't try and butter me up. You been moping around like a boy who lost his dog."

Ted sighed.

Gus spit a stream of tobacco juice into the sand. "While you were out lollygagging in Hawaii, I was working. One of us had to."

"Lollygagging? I was on my honeymoon."

"Ah, anybody can go on one of them. Not everybody can fly."

Ted pondered Gus's point a moment. Certainly the honeymoon had ended oddly, and Ted found a certain solace in resuming work on the plane. This was the diversion that excited him most. What about Kit? She was so wrapped up in her defense of this woman, Wanda Boswell. Was that going to be a constant in their marriage? He'd gone into this with his eyes wide open, encouraging Kit to continue her law practice. Maybe it would just take some time to get used to things.

"All right, enough complaining," Ted said. "Are we ready to go?"

"I been ready for a week."

"Come on then."

As far as the weather, the day could not have been better, with the skies blue and clear, the air barely a whisper over the bluffs. The sea was calm. If they were going to get their monoplane to fly, now was the time.

Gus demonstrated the harness mechanism to Ted. According to Gus's theory, the outward flaps would lend tremendous stability to the plane. Brilliant with all things mechanical, he had designed the harness to work almost effortlessly.

After nearly an hour of practice and demonstrations, Ted felt ready to give it a try. He slipped on leather gauntlets, climbed up the stepladder and into the cockpit. Gus helped him with the harness while Ted tested the rudder pedal that Gus had designed so he could work it with his good leg. The rudder dutifully swept back and forth.

He nodded to Gus. "Let's go."

The mechanic walked around to the front of the monoplane

and placed both hands on the propeller. "Ready for contact?"

"Ready."

With one mighty crank, Gus thrust the prop downward. Ted felt the entire plane vibrate with the roar of the three-cylinder engine Gus had built for the plane. He could sense the urge of the machine to take off, as if it were some huge bird preparing to escape an open cage.

Next Gus moved behind him, cut loose the mooring, and gave the monoplane a push down the wooden tracks. While increasing the pressure on the throttle, Ted released the brake and eased the plane forward. The *Kathleen II* was on its way.

Soon the wind was coursing past his ears, and a bit of sand kicked up and skittered across his goggles.

This was it! The next hundred feet would make all the difference. Would he get the lift he needed? If not, the monoplane would end up grinding to an ignominious halt. That wouldn't be so bad, as they were not yet flying for the press or investors. It would simply mean more work.

But Ted remained confident. Gus had added to the engine, which meant more weight but also more power. He was sure getting up in the air wouldn't be a problem.

It was staying there, controlling the plane, bringing her down smoothly so that both ship and pilot would be able to fly again—that was the challenge.

Fifty feet to go. There was still great risk, Ted knew, because the monoplane was not as inherently stable as the biplane design of Wilbur and Orville Wright. Two sets of curved wings made their planes look like flying parentheses. Not that Ted and Gus were interested in pursuing that design. The word was that the Wright brothers were not shy about lawsuits to protect their patents.

Twenty-five feet.

The row of eucalyptus trees some three hundred yards away looked like confused townspeople, wondering what the strange monstrosity was that charged toward them. Some had their leafy arms outstretched, waving in warning to Ted.

Ten feet.

The last time Ted had been in the air he'd had two legs and all the hope in the world. Then everything had come crashing down. The accident cost him his left leg and nearly his life—both physical and eternal. He'd left Los Angeles a lost man, leaving behind the woman he knew he loved but could not bring himself to burden. He'd wanted to find a way to die.

Five feet.

But God had a different plan, and that was to find new hope in His Son and also a life with Kit Shannon.

Now! The *Kathleen II* tilted upward, lifting. The sound of the tracks abruptly ended, with no scraping sound replacing it.

Ted was airborne.

And the exhilaration, the freedom, the adventure came rushing in. Ted remembered a time when, as a boy, he'd watched a gull with his father and thought he heard God's voice telling him this was what he'd be doing someday. It was finally happening.

Climbing slowly, he brought the plane to ten feet off the ground, then fifteen, then twenty. Twenty! And the plane was holding steady. Just keep it that way until the trees, he told himself, and then one leisurely turn. That would be the test.

Would the wing flaps actually work? Would Gus's innovation stand up to the challenge? If the plane started to wobble or list, would he be able to right it? The specter of another crash landing was always present. Nevertheless, he'd always felt he would be able to keep from disaster; it was an inner faith that God's hands were under the wings.

Forty feet up now and all seemed stable. The townspeople-trees were awestruck. As Ted approached, the waving of their leafy arms turned respectful, honorific. Then the plane flew over the tops. Ted smiled down at them and gave a salute.

"Now watch this!" he shouted.

It was time for the turn. But which way?

Gus had said on the inland side, to keep away from the bluffs. That was where Ted had gone down the first time.

Something told him he shouldn't play it so safe, that he needed to go back into the teeth of the previous danger. Aviation meant taking risks, and a flier wasn't going to get anywhere by fearing failure.

Ted also felt the utmost confidence that he could make the turn.

He worked the rudder and banked slightly to the right, skimming the tops of the trees. And then he caught sight of a breathtaking view—the placid glass of the Pacific Ocean.

It was glorious.

Gus, of course, would be screaming. But up here Ted could not hear him. He could hear only the rush of the wind, the roar of the plane's engine, and the beating of his heart.

"What's your name?" he shouted to the plane. "Kathleen? Then show me your spirit, girl."

Righting the plane, he began a descent toward the ocean.

He made the quick decision to bring the plane down on the sand in front of a small crowd of witnesses. The sand would provide the best landing area, since it was softer than the harder sand and rocks up on top of the bluffs.

Then, suddenly, he was flying a hundred feet aboveground as the bluffs dropped off behind him. Higher than any manned flight before, he allowed himself to suggest.

Was he crazy? If the plane did not hold steady, if any of a number of things did not remain consistent, this would not be an ordinary crash landing. It would be certain death.

His nerves stayed intact. Other than the pleasant sensation of all his energy being sharply focused, his mind fully engaged, he felt supremely calm.

He guided the plane out toward the ocean.

Ted wished Kit were here to see this. The design was working! The plane held steady. He felt as if he could make it dance if so desired, or play leapfrog with the sea gulls.

The weight of the engine set the nose in a downward angle but not so steep that Ted worried about it. Everything was going to work out just as he had hoped.

As the plane continued its descent he could see people below scattered along the beach at Santa Monica. Some children began running and pointing, followed by a bevy of excited adults, looking up at him and waving their arms. He was perhaps fifty yards from them when he waved back and banked the plane left. He glided over their heads as smoothly as a hungry pelican.

Down, down, down in a graceful line Ted anticipated where he would land. A long stretch of sand about a hundred yards before him. It was perfect. All he would have to do was land and then come to a stop before reaching the rocks that jutted out from the cliffs to the sea.

Ted cut the engine. He pulled on the stick. The wings vibrated but held firm. He was going to make it.

Just then the nose shot skyward. Was it the wind? Ted didn't know; he only knew he had to fight the stick to compensate. Now the wings did not vibrate. Instead, they shuddered, the stress on them suddenly becoming too great. He had to pull up again quickly to keep from a nose dive.

The plane tilted upward only slightly. Was it enough? Ted did not know, could not be sure.

It took him several more seconds to steady the plane. The wind from the ocean subsided. But now Ted's careful calculation of the landing area had been thrown off. Keeping the same line, he would now land directly on the rocks! He had ocean to his right, the cliffs to his left. And with the engine cut, he was losing altitude fast.

———————

Kit thought she saw a giant bird out of the window of the train. A bird out over the ocean, miles away. But perhaps it was only her imagination. No bird could be that large. She blinked and looked more closely and then saw nothing but blue sky.

Up ahead, she saw the crowd of buildings that was downtown Los Angeles. The short trip from San Leandro had taken under an hour, even with stops in Wilmington and Whittier.

As she looked at the view it seemed to Kit her adopted city had almost grown up in the short time she had been away. Or maybe it was simply that she'd never come in from this direction before.

The buildings extended up like arms reaching for a piece of sky, some as high as ten stories. Incredible, even reminiscent of New

York, where she'd spent many of her formative years.

However, there was something quite different about the City of Angels, something that distinguished it from America's more famous cousin to the east. As she approached from the eastern side, Kit had the sensation of sunny optimism. Whereas the sky in New York could grow dark with soot and dirt, the sun over Los Angeles always seemed to be shining.

She remembered the words of Jesus: *"For he maketh His sun to rise on the evil and on the good, and sendeth rain on the just and on the unjust."* Los Angeles had its share of both evil and good, just and unjust. Yet that was why she had her calling, to play her small part in the often messy enterprise of sorting out the just from the unjust.

The train whistle sounded, signaling the approach to the depot. It jolted Kit to attentiveness and to a question. She wondered if Ted would be there to meet her at the station.

As it turned out, it was Corazón who was waiting for her, dressed in a blue cheviot walking suit. With her soft brown skin and luminous, intelligent eyes, Corazón was a comforting sight after all the turmoil aboard the ship and in San Leandro. The two embraced immediately as Kit alighted from the train.

"I have missed you," Kit said. "I felt as if I'd lost my right arm while down in San Leandro. I will need to be back there in two days. We must get right to work."

"Yes, and I am more than ready," Corazón replied.

With a quick glance around the depot, Kit said, "And Ted. Do you know where he is?"

Corazón shook her head. "I tried to call him on the telephone to tell him you are arriving. I think maybe he had some business?"

Kit nodded. "I am sure that's it. I will telephone him from the office. Perhaps he's at home or at the Institute."

Within minutes they were sitting in an Owl cab on their way to Kit's law office. The ride to 238 West First Street was eventful for the mix of horse and automobile. The restless city seemed to be embracing the gas-powered engine with a passion. In less than a year the character of the streets had changed greatly. Metallic conveyances chugged all around them, not without a bit of unpleasantness. Angry pedestrians cursed as autoists, some unable to completely control their contraptions, nearly hit them. Horses neighed in protest as their trodden paths were overtaken by tin and sputter.

In fact, the smell of exhaust fumes seemed stronger to Kit now than even a month ago. It was probably just her imagination, but still, she wondered what might happen to the air people breathed if the roads became overrun with autos, all driving at the same time.

"Now tell me what you are up to," Kit said as the horse-drawn cab bounced along. "You have a smile on your face that intrigues me."

Corazón looked down, the smile sticking to her face.

"Ah," Kit said. "Raul Montoya."

Corazón laughed. "I cannot hide it from you. I think he will ask me soon."

"It's about time."

Raul Montoya was the man who had rescued Corazón from a goon who had meant to do her harm during the Truman Harcourt murder case. That they would someday marry was, in Kit's mind, as inevitable as the orange blossoms budding in the southern California spring.

"He waits, I think, because he is still looking for work. He does not wish to go in with his father in the saloon."

"That is a good thing, Corazón." She took her hand and held it firmly. "I am very happy for you both."

"We will be the happy couple, no? Like you and Mr. Fox?"

"Yes." Kit felt a tugging in her heart. "Well now, enough of our talk of domestic bliss. Shall we begin with the business of getting a client a fair trial?"

Corazón took a pad and pencil from her purse. "I am at the ready."

With that, Kit began to think out loud. It was how they worked together. Kit offering her thoughts; Corazón recording them in shorthand and, when the spirit moved, adding thoughts of her own. Almost always it was an incisive comment that helped Kit to formulate a theory of the case—the legal and factual basis for any successful defense.

"I am troubled by some of the testimony I've gathered," Kit said. "Several people appear to be hiding things, keeping secrets."

"Because you are a lawyer?" Corazón said with a twinkle.

Kit smiled. "Only partly. It seems to me there is another story lurking beneath the surface. Let's start with Professor Aiden Aloysius Faire." Kit recounted the infamous shipboard dinner conversation, also their finding Faire rooting around the crime scene. "We must question him again, and I want you with me to observe him."

"I will be there," Corazón promised.

"Next is Delia Patton, an attractive woman who uses her looks like a weapon. She was alone on this cruise and told me she had known Chilton before he was married."

"Is true?"

"I'm not sure that it is," said Kit. "She indicated that Chilton had been a romantic interest of hers at that time. But when I questioned her aboard the ship and asked what they conversed about on the islands, she recounted only small talk from him. Now, is that the way a man would talk to a woman he had once known romantically? I do not think so."

"This Patton woman, she is maybe a suspect?"

Kit waved her hand around. "Everyone is a suspect, or else they have some reason to want Wanda to take the blame. Which brings us to Glenna Boswell, Wanda's mother-in-law."

"I have followed her."

"Already?"

"*Sí.* From the wire you sent to me. She has gone on a trip."

"Another trip?"

"To Santa Barbara. I follow her to the train, and that is where the train was to go."

"Curious. Why would she be heading up there, so soon after the loss of her son?"

Corazón scribbled something on her pad. "And she has closed up her house."

"No servants?"

"No."

"As if she is not expecting Wanda to return."

The cab pulled over next to the building that housed Kit's law office. She was glad to be back. It was familiar and friendly, unlike the odd little setup in San Leandro. Kit knew most of the lawyers and judges around here and had gained their respect. She felt as if she could move in and around the legal system of Los Angeles with increasing confidence.

And Earl Rogers was just down the hall from her. He was always ready to offer advice from his vast store of legal knowledge and trial experience. He was still the finest trial lawyer in the country, although his drinking had started up again. Kit, as always, was concerned for him, and for his daughter, Adela, too. Her prayers for him had grown more fervent in the last several months.

Once inside the office, with hats off and the dust shaken off, the two were ready to begin in earnest.

Just one more concern remained. Kit picked up the telephone and asked the operator to connect her with the Los Angeles Bible Institute, which Kit had helped to found. It was her aunt Freddy's legacy. But it was not where Ted was at the moment.

Then she called home. Angelita—Corazón's mother and Kit's housekeeper—answered. She did not know the whereabouts of Ted. Kit replaced the telephone earpiece.

"All is well?" Corazón asked.

"I pray that it is. Ted has a way of getting into, shall we say, interesting situations."

17

TED WAS GOING TO CRASH. There was no doubt about
that now. Instinct told him to bank the plane toward the ocean and
hope for the best. Perhaps he would catch just a little more of the
breeze and be able to complete the turn and then land on the sand
going the opposite direction.

Either that or he'd be swimming to shore. With a plane and
engine left behind to the depths, unsalvageable.

He silently prayed for a miracle.

Then, suddenly, a man rose up from the sea. Ted was so close
to him he could almost reach down and touch his head. And an
odd head it was, too. A long gray beard, and scraggly hair hanging
down about the man's shoulders like kelp.

When the man saw Ted in the plane above him, he screamed.

Ted jerked backward and felt the harness engage. The plane
seemed to jerk with him. He lost control.

His mind became a jumble of thought and desperate prayer.
Images of Kit seeing his broken body mixed with wild speculations
about the man in the water below.

The plane banked hard to the left, its left wing skimming the
shoreline. A foot lower, Ted figured, and the wing would hit the
sand, sending the plane into a tumble.

With no time to think, operating on little experience and the
few lessons Gus had given him, Ted threw his body to the right.

For a split second he thought the plane would break apart, the stress on the wing being too much.

But it did not break up. Incredibly, the left wing lifted, righting the plane, sending it once more to the right.

Ted was now just above the rocks that would mean certain destruction. And yet the plane held steady. Whether it was a breeze or the hand of God, Ted had no idea. Perhaps they were one and the same.

The plane made contact with soft sand only a few yards past the last boulder. The rails under the plane dug into the surface and brought the plane to an almost instantaneous stop.

Ted felt his body thrust forward. The harness, tethered to each wing, pulled him backward like a fish on a grappling hook. His head snapped back.

Everything faded to black.

———————

"We need to do a little digging around in her house."

"House? Digging? What do you mean?"

Kit bobbed her eyebrows. "Do you like baseball, Corazón?"

With a slightly confused expression, Corazón said, "Sí. The Angels of this town, they are good, yes?"

"Yes, the Angels of the Pacific League. Well, they play with a hard ball. And that is what we are going to do now with Mrs. Glenna Boswell."

In five minutes' time the women were in Kit's Ford runabout, chugging toward Glenna Boswell's home. Corazón said, "But she is not home. No one is in the house."

"Precisely. A perfect time to take a look inside."

"But that is trespassing, no?"

"No."

Corazón blinked at her. Kit kept the Ford to the right side of the road, aware that some people were gawking at the sight of two women, alone, in a gas-powered automobile.

"Let us review the law," Kit said. "To enter a dwelling house without the consent of the owner or a person in the lawful possession thereof, is trespass. We're going to enter with consent."

"Of Mrs. Boswell?"

"Yes, only it is Mrs. *Wanda* Boswell's consent that we have. She is also in lawful possession of the dwelling. She lives here."

"But she does not own the whole house, is that not true?"

"And we are not going to search the whole house. Only Wanda's room. To get there we will have to enter through a common door and walk through a common area, but since Wanda has joint control of those areas, she has the right to give her consent to those as well."

Corazón wrinkled her brow. "I do not think Mrs. Boswell, the older Mrs. Boswell, is going to be happy about this."

"I'm not concerned with her happiness. I'm concerned with Wanda's innocence."

"But how do we get inside? Not the window, I am hoping."

Kit smiled. Corazón was no doubt remembering the time Kit had entered a crime scene through a window, much to the consternation of the Los Angeles Police Department, Mike McGinty in particular.

"You remember when Mr. Houdini gave me his skeleton key after the Truman Harcourt case? He assured me it would open almost any lock I could find. It is time to test his theory."

Presently, Kit guided the Ford down the quiet street where many of the more wealthy residents of Los Angeles lived. The auto sputtered along a tree-lined avenue. A few blocks more and she cut the engine in front of the Boswell home. It was just as Wanda had described it—Victorian in style, slate gray with blue trim. A bougainvillea with brilliant red flowers twisted and turned through enormous trellises like pretty tentacles.

The two women got out of the Ford and walked briskly to the front door of the house. Just to be sure the home was vacant, Kit gave a quick couple of knocks. When no one answered she took out Harry Houdini's skeleton key, inserted it into the keyhole, and turned it back and forth.

"Mr. Houdini told me to feel for the spaces delicately, as if I were holding a wounded bird."

Corazón nodded. "I am hoping we do not have to escape like Mr. Houdini."

"You worry too much." The door unlatched. "See?"

Kit pushed the door open and found herself staring into the barrel of a gun.

———————

"Hey, are you hurt?"

The voice came from the darkness. The light then streamed back in, and Ted blinked. He saw stars behind his eyes.

"Answer me, man!"

Someone in a white suit and white beret appeared in front of him. Ted thought for a moment he was some oddly dressed angel. Was he in heaven?

"Who?" Ted heard his own voice.

"Sensational!" the white-suited man said. "Stupendous! Can you do it again?"

"Again?" Ted's vision slowly came back into focus. The odd man seemed less angelic now and more like one of those hucksters one saw on Los Angeles street corners, selling the latest nostrum promising hair growth.

"I want to get it!"

"I'm afraid I—" Ted stopped when he saw the bearded man, the one who had risen out of the sea, gawking at him.

"Oh, don't mind him," said the man in white. "He's just an actor. You, sir, are a marvel. Coming out of the sky like that! I thought you were a goner for certain."

"Help me out."

This strange pair—the man in white and the sea beast—came to Ted's aid. Ted felt all his parts were still in working order, although his neck felt somewhat out of place. But once he was upright he felt a return to normalcy.

"Please tell me your name, young man."

"Fox. Theodore Fox. Please, tell me yours."

"Francis Boggs, my fine fellow." He clapped Ted on the shoulder. "And this is Ignatz Pine, the psychic reader."

"At your service," Pine said with a bow. Part of his beard fell off. It was false.

Ted shook his head. "I don't understand what is happening. Why are you dressed like that . . . and coming out of the water like you did?"

Boggs laughed. "Don't you recognize Edmond Dantes, the Count of Monte Cristo?"

Pine bowed again.

"I make motion pictures," Boggs explained, "and I want to put *you* on film! I want to make you famous."

Ted looked over Boggs's shoulder and saw a small group of men, women, and children running toward them.

"Mr. Boggs, I would greatly appreciate your help in getting my plane off the beach."

"Why don't you two just sit down?"

The gun-toting man was of average height. He wore a brown woolen suit and a brown derby cocked slightly to one side. He did not have the look of a common burglar.

Kit gently took Corazón's arm and led her to a chair, sitting her down. Kit remained standing and faced the man. "What is it you are doing here?" she asked.

His face betrayed a look of anger, almost as if he had been insulted. He held the gun out farther. "I want you to sit down."

"I do not think you want to shoot me for remaining on my feet. Nor do you strike me as a murderer."

The man's eyes widened.

"You are not going to kill two women. What is it you came in here for?"

"Look here! I have a gun in my hand." He shook it in the air. "I ask the questions!"

"Be careful with that."

The man almost spat. "Tell me what you are doing here and tell me now."

"I do not see as yet that it is any of your affair. By what

authority, besides that gun, are you asking me?"

"I won't have any more of this! I am in control here!"

"It appears we are at a standstill, sir."

The man's hand began to shake. Kit wondered whether it would be a good idea to anger him further, seeing as how the gun was pointed at her.

"You know what I have a mind to do?" the man said. "Call the police, that's what. You are intruders."

"We are guests," Kit said.

"Guests? Mrs. Boswell didn't say—" He stopped himself.

"What is your connection with Glenna Boswell?"

"I didn't . . . I'm not . . ."

"Are you her employee? Who do you work for? What do you want?"

"Cease!"

"I will not. And as for the police, I think it might be a very good idea to have them here. I will just ring them."

"Don't you move."

Kit turned toward the telephone, which was mounted on the wall near a large mirror.

The gun fired.

————

"Kit Shannon?" Francis Boggs's eyes almost popped out of his head.

"Kit Shannon Fox," Ted responded dryly. They were still on the shore, surrounded now by curious onlookers who stood staring at the monoplane as if it were a beached whale, waiting for Gus to return with tools and a hitch to get the plane back to the hangar.

Boggs now seemed less interested in the plane than in the mention of Ted's wife's name. "Why, she is a sensation! The woman who beat the railroad trust in court, who won a murder trial with the help of that magician, Houdini."

"Has that news reached Chicago?"

"Reached it? Young man, I clip the newspaper. I look for the odd bit, the story that may deserve recording in my camera. Your wife, sir, is a curio. How can a woman do what she has done? I must record her. I must get her on celluloid!"

"Boggs, listen to me. All I want is to lead a quiet life and do my work. My wife is the same way."

"Do you know what you're saying? Are you against fame?"

"I do not care one way or the other."

"But think of the publicity! Ted Fox, the daring young man of the skies, and his wife, Kit Shannon . . . er, Fox, the ideal of young women everywhere, the bane of dishonest men! Do you know what people will pay to see that? Twice a nickel, sir, twice a nickel. And they will return, over and over, along with their friends and family members. Imagine if we had been at Gettysburg to record Lincoln, or at San Juan Hill with Teddy! And now here's our chance to get the greatest American couple!"

Ted had to laugh. "I don't know, Boggs. Our colorful days may be behind us. It's true Kit got into her share of scrapes some time ago, but that's behind her now. Her life is going to be rather dull if I have anything to say about it."

18

"THAT SHOT WAS A WARNING," the man said.

Kit glanced up at the ceiling to where the bullet hole was. Spider-leg cracks spread out from it. "Mrs. Boswell is not going to appreciate what you have done to her home. As her employee, in whatever regard—"

"That's enough." The man's face grew crimson. "You don't know nothin'. And if you don't do what I say, next time it won't be the ceiling I shoot."

"I don't believe you will shoot me." Kit was less sure of that than she sounded, but as she studied his face she did not see the look of a killer.

"No, I won't shoot you. I'll shoot the Mex." He swung his arm and aimed the gun at Corazón.

"Sir, you are crazed."

"You want to take that chance with me? Go ahead."

Kit looked at the business end of the handgun and at the man's eyes. Perhaps not a killer, but still a man who was capable of pulling the trigger if pushed too far.

Kit was not going to put Corazón in danger. "What do you want with us?"

"I want you in the library. Now."

Kit took Corazón's hand, which was trembling, and led her into the library as ordered.

The man instructed Kit to place two wooden armchairs back to back and then for both of them to sit down. From a bureau he secured a length of rope, all the while keeping the gun pointed at Kit and Corazón. Kit considered her jiu-jitsu and thought she might attempt to take the gun from him. She had once done this to the corrupt chief of the Los Angeles Police Department and had been shot for her trouble.

With Corazón, however, she was not going to take that chance.

The man made a loop of the rope and tossed it around the women as if they were calves. He pulled it tight, pinning their arms, then began to wrap the cord around them.

"Now, don't you go making any noise," he said when he was finished, "or I'll put gags in your mouths."

After checking the restraint once more, the man left the library. Kit heard him going up the stairs.

"Who is this man?" Corazón whispered.

"I have no idea."

"But why did he not stay?"

"I suspect he is merely trying to intimidate us."

"How is it you knew he would not shoot you?"

"I did not know for certain, but his eyes told me he wants something that he hasn't yet found. I think he is looking for the same thing we are—the life insurance policy."

"Why is that?"

"Maybe he was sent by Fielding Hardy. He's an operative, hired by someone. He is not working alone, otherwise he may well have shot us instead of the ceiling."

"What are we to do now?"

"The only thing we can do. Wait."

———

"Yes, film has become quite popular," Ted said to Francis Boggs. They were sitting in Schneider's eatery, where Ted had brought the enthusiastic filmmaker. They sat at a wooden table enjoying the lunch special, 35 cents, which today consisted of boiled corned beef and cabbage and cauliflower in cream sauce. Gus, however, was not eating. He had his arms folded and barely seemed to be listening to the conversation.

"Both for telling stories and recording images of history," Boggs added. "The possibilities are without limit. And I want you to be a part of it."

"I told you before I don't seek fame, Mr. Boggs."

"Are you against success? That is not an American attitude, I must say."

"No. I will take the success of my venture. But my name need not be glorified."

Boggs pounded the table with his fist. "That is the most confounded thing I have ever heard."

"Are you a religious man, Mr. Boggs?"

"Ah. I see. But I do not see that there need be any conflict there. I want to chronicle your efforts to conquer the air. I saw what your machine can do. We will preserve this for all mankind to see. A record of achievement unlike most others in our memories."

Gus shook his head. "Just another distraction."

Boggs looked at the mechanic. "And you, my good man, the genius behind the genius. Think of it! The name of Hoss Willoughby across the—"

"Gus Willingham!"

"—across the nation. All you have to do is smile and nod, my friend. Can you do that?"

Gus unlocked his arm. "I can take a poke at you, that's what I can do."

"Steady, Gus." Ted put a hand on Gus's shoulder.

"We don't need this," said Gus. "Just more distraction from our work. You just got married, and now that's gone and blown up all to—"

"Gus!" Ted squeezed the mechanic's shoulder so hard Gus shouted. "That will do."

"You don't have to get violent on me."

"You'll have to excuse my partner, Mr. Boggs," Ted said. "He is rather closed-minded when it comes to anything but the aeroplane."

"He's perfect," Boggs said.

Gus squinted, showing some interest now.

"The faithful sidekick," Boggs explained. "The comedy relief. I can see it now!"

———————

"Do you recall what Mr. Hancock taught us about taking down an attacker with our feet?" Kit whispered so the man upstairs would not hear. The two were still sitting back to back, tied to chairs. Mr. Hancock taught the ancient art of jiu-jitsu, which had become all the rage in Los Angeles. Kit and Corazón were among his first students, still attending his class once a week.

"*Sí*," Corazón replied. "With the foot behind a leg, and push with the other."

"When he comes back down, I'll get him to face me, close enough to reach his legs with mine. When I say *Now*, I want you to push with your legs."

"Push?"

"Yes, with all your might. That will send me forward and you in the air. And we will both land on top of him."

"And then what?"

"I don't really know."

Corazón paused. "You think this is a good thing?"

"Once we are down, we may be able to get our hands free of the rope. I will keep a lock on his legs with mine. What I want you to do is try to get free, run to the phone and call McGinty."

"What about the gun?"

"He is not going to shoot us. He is going to try to scare us. But we will scare him instead. If he has the gun in his hand, though, we won't do it. There's too much chance it will go off."

"I understand. If you would like me to scream at the time you are putting him to the floor, I will do it."

"I think that would be a nice touch."

More waiting. Kit heard the sounds of the man opening and closing doors, seemingly searching through the entire upstairs. Finally, after fifteen minutes or so, he came down the stairs.

He did not have the gun in his hands. What he did have was a determined, angry look.

"All right, where is it?" he said as he got to the foot of the stairs.

"I beg your pardon?" Kit said quietly, hoping he would move toward her.

He did, but only a few steps. "You know what I'm talking about. The life insurance policy. The one on Chilton Boswell. Where did you put it?"

"You work for the insurance company, don't you?"

The man's cheeks reddened. "I am getting impatient with you." He was also standing too far away for Kit to reach him.

"If you get the insurance policy, will you let us go?"

"Maybe."

"Take a look in my coat pocket."

He frowned, then started toward her. From behind, Kit felt Corazón tensing. Kit watched the man's shoes.

He then reached her chair and stuck out his hand to pull back Kit's coat. As he did, Kit slid her left foot behind the man's right calf and thrust her right foot into his shin. "NOW!"

Face-to-face with the man, Kit saw a look of fear burst into his eyes. At the same time she pressed his leg, Corazón propelled the two of them forward.

Everything became a jumble. Kit heard the man's head hit the floor with a vicious thud—heard, but did not see, as she was already turning sideways with the roll of the chairs with Corazón sliding off to the right.

As she turned, Kit saw the butt of the man's revolver sticking out of his belt. With the man's hand wrapped around it.

———————

"All right," Ted said to Francis Boggs. "I will talk to her. But Kit is not one to call attention to herself."

"She won't have to!" Boggs waved his hands in the air. "I will do all the attention calling."

"Mr. Boggs, may I ask you a personal question?"

"Of course, my good man."

"Do you really think that moving pictures are ever going to be an important part of modern life?"

Boggs's face beamed. "Not only do I think that, but imagine what this can mean in the affairs of men! Why, in the courts of law wherein your wife traffics. What if one could re-create a crime, as described by the witnesses, and then showed it to a jury?"

Ted nodded. "I do see that."

"In the meantime, you must let me film the two of you together. I simply will not be denied!"

Mike McGinty shook his head. "I don't see how you do it, Kit. Just when I think I've heard it all."

"I'm telling you, Mike, it's true."

They were standing in the front yard of Glenna Boswell's home, Kit still feeling the burn of the ropes on her arms.

"You say this man tied you up and you managed to take him down with your feet?"

"With Corazón's help."

McGinty cast a quick glance at Corazón, who smiled sheepishly.

"You say the man had a gun?"

"Yes."

"And he shot a hole in the ceiling?"

"I will show it to you."

"And that after you and Corazón tumbled him to the ground, he ran away?"

"I can only give you the facts, Mike."

"I'm afraid to ask for more." He removed the unlit cigar from his mouth. "Now, what do you suppose possessed him to do that after going through all the trouble to tie you up?"

"He was looking for something."

McGinty scowled. "I surmised that! Why don't you tell me what it was?"

Kit shook her head. "Can't do that."

"What? Are you playing games with me, Kit Shannon?"

"Fox."

"I don't care what your name is. I want you to level with me right now."

"If I tell you anything, you are duty bound to pass along that information to the prosecution. Surely you can understand that."

McGinty sighed. "But you want me to try and find the guy who tied you up? Come on, Kit, you're not playing fair."

"Fair it is, Mike. You have a job to do. Find the trespasser with the gun."

"What about you? You're a trespasser, too."

Kit explained to him about having Wanda's consent to enter the house. When she finished, McGinty shoved his cigar back in his mouth and said, "You can be the most frustrating woman in the world, do you know that?"

"I love you, too, Mike. Now I'd better get going. I have a case to prepare."

"Not so fast. When Mrs. Boswell returns, I am going to have to inform her of what took place in her house. Just how am I going to explain your presence?"

"You don't have to. Tell her I was here at the behest of my client. And tell her whatever you want about the man with the gun. I am sure that will give her more than enough to think about."

"You give everybody more than enough to think about. Now get out of here before I decide to take you to headquarters."

———

Finally she was at home with Ted, determined to give him her full attention. It was a pleasant evening, and Angelita served them iced tea out on the front porch overlooking the city and the Pacific Ocean off in the distance. Aunt Freddy had once called the ocean her "little pond."

"Well now," Ted said, "I have had a rather eventful day. I would like to tell you all about it."

Kit smiled and wondered just how eventful it could have been compared to her own. "Please."

"We tried out the plane. It flew beautifully! I guided it over the bluffs and down to the beach."

"The beach? That's hundreds of feet."

"I know. But it was stable and handled perfectly. Gus rigged up something that's pure genius, helped me keep in control the whole time. The only thing . . ."

"What is the only thing?"

"I had a little bit of excitement on the landing."

"Tell me! Are you all right?"

"I'm here now, am I not?"

"Ted Fox, tell me right now what happened to you."

"I landed, that's the main thing, and managed to keep the plane off the rocks—"

"The rocks!"

"And come in smooth as silk on the sand." Ted leaned forward, glass in hand. "It was a smashing success."

"Smashing!"

"That's not the right word. It was a stunning success. Not only that, I met someone."

An odd turn of phrase in the middle of his harrowing account. "Who?" Kit said.

"A motion picture maker, a fellow named Boggs. Very excitable. He was taking moving pictures down on the beach, for a motion picture version of *The Count of Monte Cristo*. He wants to put us on film, Kit."

"Us?"

"He wants to make us the most famous couple in the United States. Even more famous than Evelyn Nesbit and Harry Thaw."

Kit almost choked on her tea. "They are notorious, not famous!" Harry K. Thaw, a prominent citizen of the East, was on trial for the murder of the architect Stanford White, whom he shot because of his continued dallying with Thaw's wife, the former chorus girl, Evelyn Nesbitt. It was the scandal of the day.

"Are you all right, dear?" Ted said.

"I don't think I want such notoriety. What did you tell this man?"

"I told him I would speak to you about it. It might be good publicity for the monoplane. Perhaps that would attract investors."

"I don't need investors."

"But the nation deserves to hear more about your work. I've thought about this from God's perspective, too."

"That's good."

"Cannot you bring glory to God through people knowing about you?"

Kit thought about that a moment. "But movies. Famous couple. It all sounds like a flimflam."

"*Film* flam," Ted corrected.

Kit laughed. "Whatever it is, let us not make a decision now. In two days the preliminary hearing begins. I have enough to think about."

"Yes," Ted said. "I suppose I do, too."

19

As ALWAYS SEEMED TO HAPPEN when Kit walked into a courtroom, there was a thick crowd awaiting her in Judge Hardy's domain. Noting a press section on the left, she saw Sanford Erskine of the *San Leandro Clarion* chatting with a man seated next to him. She figured him to be Bob Barry, the reporter. He fit the description Al and Sam had given her.

She also saw some familiar faces from Los Angeles.

Tom Phelps, the *Times* reporter who had known Kit since her arrival to Los Angeles, was down to cover the proceedings, as was a man named Kell from the *Examiner* and a few others she did not recognize. But regional newspapers were springing up all the time now, and it was not a surprise to see so many here.

Along with the press were the folks who found court trials and hearings to be entertaining. That, and Kit was continuing to get front page coverage in their local paper, the *Clarion*.

Fielding Hardy opened up the prosecution case at the preliminary hearing by calling an old nemesis of Kit's.

"Doctor, would you please state your name for the record?"

"Raymond J. Smith, coroner of the County of Los Angeles."

The coroner was a smallish man with eyeglasses and a haughty bearing. Kit had grilled him on several occasions in various cases, but the one that stood out was when Smith had convened a coroner's inquest in the death of a boy, Samuel Franklin, in a trolley accident. Kit was able to show the bias of the coroner in favor of the trolley company when an accidental death occurred that involved one of their lines. It was part of her victory over Western Rail and had earned her the permanent enmity of Raymond J. Smith.

"How long have you been the coroner of Los Angeles?"

"Eight years, nearly."

"How many autopsies have you performed in that time?"

"Must be going on two hundred now."

"Did you have occasion to perform an autopsy on the body of the deceased, Chilton Boswell?"

"Yes, I did."

"When was that autopsy performed?"

"Tuesday last."

"And did you prepare an autopsy report?"

"Of course."

"Did you bring it with you?"

"Yes. Would you like to see it now?"

"I will just ask you, Doctor, if you reached a conclusion about the cause of death."

"I did. Chilton Boswell died as a result of arsenic poisoning."

"Is there any doubt in your mind about that?"

"No."

"So, in your opinion, the deceased, Chilton Boswell, was murdered by being poisoned with—"

"Objection," Kit said. "The doctor has no way of knowing whether this was a murder or suicide or an accident. All he is competent to testify about is the *cause* of death. And even that is subject to my cross-examination."

"But this is a murder case," Fielding Hardy said. "We all know that."

"We know nothing of the kind. This is a preliminary hearing on that very issue."

The judge looked at his brother. "Do you have any more questions for the coroner?"

"Yes. Dr. Smith, does arsenic poisoning usually result in some sort of convulsions in the victim?"

Smith nodded. "Yes, if the victim is conscious. If the victim is unconscious or asleep, heart failure may occur without other signs."

"I don't suppose I have more questions now, Your Honor. I'm sure, however, I'll have a number of them after Mrs. Fox gets done with her cross-examination."

"Then we'd better let her get to it." Judge Hardy looked at Kit. "Go ahead, Mrs. Fox."

Kit stood and faced the wily coroner. Raymond J. Smith had never bothered to hide his contempt for her. Be that as it may, today Kit was not out for reconciliation.

"Doctor, what training have you had, if any, in the detection of poisons?"

"Training?

"Yes."

"On the job training."

"How many cases of poisoning have you dealt with in your career?"

"I don't know how many. More than a few."

"How many more than a few?"

"I don't have those records with me at the moment, Mrs. Fox."

"How many cases of arsenic poisoning, would you say?"

"I'm not sure."

"Enough so that you are certain that you can detect arsenic in a person's body?"

"Of course I'm certain."

"Are you familiar with *Scherf's Guide to Poisons*?"

"I've seen it, sure."

"I'm asking if you are familiar with it."

"I know where to find it if I need it," Smith replied sharply.

"Did you consult this book before your autopsy of Chilton Boswell?"

"I did not have to. The evidence of arsenic poisoning was obvious."

"What did you examine to find this obvious evidence?"

"Why, the stomach of course. The lining of the stomach was

discolored with an irritant in a manner consistent with that of arsenic."

"According to *Scherf's Guide,* and quoting Professor Milton Bastos, Head of Toxicology, Medical Examiner's Office for the City of New York, arsenic cannot be detected in the stomach unless it is consumed over a very long period of time. Isn't that correct?"

"I can only tell you what I saw and what I concluded."

"But you cannot tell us why you concluded it?"

"I have told you what I know."

"Of course, Doctor, you have no way of knowing who administered the fatal dose of arsenic to Mr. Boswell, do you?"

"No."

"Nor even if the dose was self-administered."

"By the decedent?"

"Suicide, Doctor."

"I don't consider that likely."

"And why not?"

"Just seems unlikely, that's all."

"That Mr. Boswell would ingest arsenic?"

"Yes, that is what I mean."

"But isn't it true that men of Mr. Chilton's age sometimes ingest arsenic for, shall we say, reasons of personal pleasure?"

"I'm not sure what you mean by that."

"What is commonly called an aphrodisiac."

Fielding Hardy objected. "Mrs. Fox is taking us far afield, Your Honor. This line of questioning is inappropriate to the decorum of this courtroom."

"What is this line of questioning intended to prove?" the judge asked Kit.

"I would remind the court that the defense need not prove anything and that the burden rests on the prosecution. If evidence is admitted that points equally toward two different interpretations, the court is obligated to accept the interpretation most favorable to the defense. That is why the presence of arsenic in the body of the victim, in and of itself, does not point to murder. If there are other uses for arsenic that the coroner has not considered, such a thing throws more doubt upon the basis of the charge."

"We have not finished with our presentation," Fielding Hardy said.

"And I have not yet finished with this witness," Kit added. She turned to Dr. Smith once more. "You did not test the victim's blood for traces of arsenic, did you?"

"I told you I examined the stomach lining."

"You did not test any other part of the body, is that correct?"

"No."

"Isn't it true that the lining of the stomach may be affected by many things other than poison?"

"Yes."

"Such as acids created by the ingestion of certain foods?"

"That is possible."

"Did you attempt to determine what food was in the stomach of the decedent?"

"I did not."

"Why not?"

"I didn't think I needed to. I had the report from the doctor who examined the body on the ship."

"That would be Dr. Novak?"

"Yes."

"You took Dr. Novak's word, though he had not performed an autopsy or any tests?"

"He is a doctor."

Kit stepped away from the witness box and addressed the court. "Your Honor, I move that all the testimony of Dr. Smith be stricken from the record. By his own admission he relied upon the unverified report of a doctor whom he did not know and used that report to conduct a cursory autopsy of the body. Vital evidence was ignored. There is no possible basis for finding that Chilton Boswell died of anything other than natural causes."

Fielding Hardy did not bother to respond. He lifted his hands up toward his brother, the judge, throwing the decision to him.

Clarence Hardy scratched his head. "Well now, the court only has to find that there is a likelihood of a crime, enough to bind the defendant over for trial. Then the jury can make up its own mind surrounding the evidence. So I'm going to deny your motion, Mrs. Fox. Anything else?"

A fair and impartial judge would be lovely. "Not regarding this witness, Your Honor."

Looking relieved, Dr. Raymond J. Smith stepped down and hurried from the courtroom.

Fielding Hardy stood and said, "I call Lowell Sanders to the stand."

Sanders was used by Hardy to establish that Chilton Boswell had been found dead in his own stateroom. That was the point on which Kit immediately pounced in her cross-examination.

"Mr. Sanders, you do not know how Chilton Boswell got to the stateroom, do you?"

"I assume he walked in."

"Yes. You assume. You do not know."

"I saw him there on the floor."

"After he was dead, correct?"

"Well, he sure wasn't dancing a jig."

Some members of the gallery laughed, and Kit was sure she heard a loud sigh from one of the ladies in the front row. Lowell Sanders cut quite a dashing figure on the stand in his crisp brown suit and silk tie.

"But he may have danced a jig all over the room before he died, for all you know, isn't that right?" Kit asked.

"That seems unlikely."

"Why is that, sir?"

"Well, because he died."

"The coroner has already established that, sir. I am asking if you have any way of knowing what Mr. Chilton Boswell was doing immediately before he died."

Sanders shook his head. "I didn't see him."

"And therefore you don't know if he died and was dragged into the room or not, do you?"

"Nobody ever said he was dragged in."

"I am asking about what you know, sir. Please answer the question."

Fielding Hardy loudly cleared his throat. "Your Honor, I must object to the tone Mrs. Fox is taking with this witness."

"Is there any reason to badger the witness?" the judge asked her.

"I would like the witness to answer my questions directly, Your Honor, so the court may be informed as to what the witness knows. If Your Honor would like to direct the witness to answer what I ask him, we can move things along."

"Go ahead. Please, Mr. Sanders, answer as best you can."

Kit took this as a partial victory. "I will ask you again, sir. You did not see Chilton Boswell immediately before his death, did you?"

"No."

"In fact, the last time you saw him was at dinner that night, isn't that correct?"

"Yes."

"Mr. Sanders, can you tell the court where you were on the ship between the hours of seven-thirty P.M. and midnight?"

Lowell Sanders did not attempt to hide his scowl. "What's that got to do with anything?"

Judge Hardy interjected, "I was thinking the same thing, Mrs. Fox."

Kit stood her ground. "This is a prosecution witness who has testified about a very important matter. I would like to test his recollections and his capacity to observe these things."

"I'll allow only a few questions in this regard, Mrs. Fox. Mr. Sanders has already testified to a single relevant fact—that he saw the body of the deceased in the stateroom. You may question him around that fact."

"And I would like to know where Mr. Sanders was between seven-thirty and midnight on January sixth."

"The witness may answer."

Lowell Sanders did not look pleased at the judge's ruling. "I was attending to my duties, Mrs. Fox. I was on the bridge most of the time. I retired at eleven-thirty, I believe."

"Were you on any other part of the ship besides the bridge?"

"I may have been. In passing."

"Did you at any time enter the gaming room or speak to Don Raffels?"

"Why would I do that?"

"I am asking, sir."

"The answer is no. I didn't speak to anyone except other members of the crew and Captain Raleigh."

Kit paused before saying, "That's all I have for this witness, Your Honor."

20

GLENNA BOSWELL SAT IN the witness chair like a queen longing to execute a subject. Her string of pearls shone atop her black dress—a picture of stylish mourning.

"You are the mother of the deceased?" Fielding Hardy asked.

"Yes."

"Can you tell the court a little about your son?"

Kit said, "Objection, Your Honor. Irrelevant and immaterial and vague as to purpose. We are here to establish the facts surrounding Chilton Boswell's death, not the story of his life."

The witness huffed so loudly the court reporter recorded it in shorthand.

"Your Honor," Fielding Hardy said, "if you please, we wish to establish a motive for murder, and that is not possible unless we explore the so-called marriage between the victim and the defendant."

"So-called?" Wanda said from the counsel table, a catch in her voice. Corazón, sitting next to her, put a hand on her arm.

"The defendant will not speak," Judge Hardy said. "I will allow some questions regarding the background of the victim. I trust that the prosecutor will keep his questions relevant?"

"I can assure the court."

Kit thought she'd best not roll her eyes at this little dance.

"Now then, Mrs. Boswell, please tell the court what sort of a man your son was."

"A good man," Glenna said. "He was a good boy who became a good man. He had a good head on his shoulders and was well liked by those who knew him. He was marked for greatness."

"To what dreams did he aspire?"

"He thought that in Los Angeles a man could take himself as far as his wits would allow. He had a good head for business and thought he might try his hand at any number of things. The sky was the limit until . . ."

"Until what, Mrs. Boswell?"

Glenna shot a look at Wanda. "Until that woman came into his life and tried to—"

"Objection! Your Honor, must we allow this defilement of my client's character? That is not relevant here."

"Please, Mrs. Fox," the judge said. "You will have your chance to cross-examine. This proceeding will glide along faster if you just let the prosecutor do his job."

Kit plopped down in her chair, sensing Wanda's nervousness beside her. The reporters in the gallery were writing quickly, no doubt trying to capture every word of the exchange. Kit noticed a rapacious smile on Bob Barry as he scrawled.

"Mrs. Boswell," Fielding Hardy said with dollops of honey on each word, "you were about to tell the court what the defendant did that was not in the best interests of your late son."

Glenna nodded curtly. "As I was trying to say before the interruption, that woman, who is not from a prominent family but is a dancer of the sort that does not appear in polite society, used all of her feminine wiles to entice my son into marrying her. I tried to discourage the union, but he was smitten by her shameless . . . bodily . . ."

"Do you need a glass of water, Mrs. Boswell?"

"Please."

Kit seethed as Fielding Hardy took his sweet time pouring a glass of water from a pitcher on his table. He was playing for the reporters, not the judge. The judge was already in his pocket.

After Glenna's theatrical gulp, Hardy questioned her again. "Would you say that your son was distraught after his marriage to—"

"Really, Your Honor, I must object." Kit's voice was full of exasperation. "The prosecutor is leading the witness, putting words in her mouth."

"All right, Mr. Hardy," the judge said. "Rephrase that last question."

Bowing, Fielding Hardy said, "How would you characterize your son's emotional state after his marriage?"

"He was distraught," Glenna said.

The gallery broke into laughter. Even they picked up what a bizarre spectacle this preliminary hearing had become.

"Mrs. Boswell, can you tell us of any instance involving the defendant and your son that may indicate a desire to do him harm?"

"Objection, hearsay."

"Overruled," the judge said. "The prosecutor has asked for an incident, not a statement."

"Then I object for vagueness," Kit said. "We are in the realm of opinion."

"I will take that into account," the judge said, "Continue."

Glenna seemed to gain strength from the judge's words. "There was the time just before Christmas last year, when I came upon them in the study at my home. Wanda was visiting. I had been out shopping when I came in and heard Wanda shout, 'I'll see you rot in the ground for that!' Yes, I remember those words distinctly."

"Your Honor," Kit said, "those are words. I move to strike on the ground of hearsay."

"I'd remind the court," argued Fielding Hardy, "that the statements of a defendant are not subject to the hearsay rule."

Kit was stunned. He was right. He was a lot sharper in the mind than his folksy way belied. Kit was going to have to keep vigilant and brush up on her evidence code.

After the judge overruled Kit's motion to strike, Hardy decided he had enough and turned the witness over to Kit.

"On the day you heard my client, Wanda Boswell, tell your son those words, you testified that you had just returned to your house from shopping, is that correct?"

"Yes."

"Where were you shopping, Mrs. Boswell?"

"Why, at several stores along Broadway and Main."

"Which stores?"

"Which?"

"That is what I am asking."

Glenna Boswell frowned. "I think I was at the Broadway most of the time, and then at the dressmaker and the grocer."

"Did you purchase anything?"

"Of course."

"What did you purchase?"

Fielding Hardy drawled an objection. "Irrelevant and immaterial."

"I would ask the court's indulgence," Kit said, "as it has allowed the prosecutor wide latitude."

"I will overrule the objection." The judge looked like it didn't much matter anyway. Kit knew it probably would not keep Wanda from having to go to trial, but it would at least preserve Glenna's testimony for later use.

"What was it you purchased?" Kit said.

"Naturally, I cannot remember everything. I believe I purchased a linen waist and a pair of shoes. Doeskin. Yes, that was it."

"Where did you purchase these items?"

"At the Broadway."

"Do you have an account at the Broadway?"

"Of course."

"Then it would be a simple matter to confirm your purchases, would it not?"

Glenna shifted her girth on the witness chair. "I do not see the point."

"When you came home you testified you entered the house and heard my client shout something, do you recall that?"

"Of course I do. I heard her say that—"

"Say or shout?"

"I . . . I am not entirely sure. It was loud and distinct."

"You testified earlier that Wanda shouted."

"I heard her distinctly."

"Where were you standing? Just inside the door?"

"I believe . . . yes, I had just entered and was closing the door."

"And you say that Wanda and Chilton were in the study?"

"Yes."

"Where is the study in relation to the front door?"

"Down the hall, I would say a matter of ten or twelve steps."

"Was the door to the study open or closed?"

"I don't know," Glenna said brusquely. "What does it matter? I heard what I heard, whether the door was open or closed."

"Do you remember what you were wearing that day?"

"What?" Glenna seemed confused at the sudden switch in subject. "I am not entirely certain. What an odd question."

"What was your means of transportation?"

"I hired a cab, as I always do."

"An Owl?"

"I think it was."

"You think?"

"I do not see why—"

"Mrs. Boswell, you have testified with certainty about the words you say you heard uttered by my client. That is the only thing you are certain about. You cannot recall with precision anything else about that day. Your memory is rather selective. I want that noted by the court."

Glenna's face reddened.

The judge looked for a moment as if he'd been personally assaulted. "Mrs. Fox," he said, "I don't need you to tell me what to take note of. I'll consider all the evidence as it comes. I've got ears."

And Kit had a tongue, which she bit lest she say anything that might get her a contempt citation.

"Your Honor?" Glenna Boswell said.

The judge nodded to her.

"If I may bring something to your attention. I don't know if it is proper of me to do so, but it may be of some importance to you."

"By all means, Mrs. Boswell."

Glenna gave Kit a quick glance before returning to the judge. "Your Honor, I have it on good authority, from a detective of the Los Angeles Police Department, that Mrs. Fox and her assistant broke into my home while I was away and rooted about inside."

"Rooted about?"

"I cannot imagine why they did so."

Judge Hardy pointed his gavel at Kit. "Is this true, Mrs. Fox?"

"This is quite irrelevant," Kit said. "I demand that the statement of the witness be stricken from the record."

"Denied. What about it?"

"Your Honor, this has nothing to do with the preliminary hearing. I will not answer any questions about it in open court. If there is a complaint to be made, let Mrs. Boswell go to the police."

Judge Hardy let out a few labored breaths, full of angry air. "If you have meddled with evidence in this case, I—"

"That is a serious charge," Kit said, "and I deny it. And unless evidence to the contrary is brought forth, I will not give any further comment."

There was a long moment during which time Kit wondered if the judge was going to burst a blood vessel. She was in the right and had backed the judge into a corner. Any move on his part to hinder her defense would become another issue on appeal, should Wanda be convicted.

Finally the judge said, "I will take this matter under advisement and look into it myself. For the time being, I will allow the hearing to continue. But let me state, unequivocally, that if I find there has been any untoward action by the defense, I will not hesitate to bring the full force of the law down upon her head."

"So long as the same standard applies to the prosecution," Kit said, "I am in full agreement with the court."

"Ask your next question!"

"I have no further questions for Mrs. Boswell at this time."

Kit, her heart beating rapidly, sat down at the counsel table. She thought she saw Wanda smiling slightly.

Fielding Hardy asked only one question on redirect examination. "Despite what Mrs. Fox has tried to confuse you with today, are you absolutely certain that you heard those words?" He read from his notes, " 'I'll see you rot in the ground for that.' "

"Yes," Glenna said. "Absolutely certain."

Fielding Hardy rested his case.

"Your Honor," Kit said, "I will not present any witnesses at this time. It is the burden of the prosecutor to present credible evidence that clearly shows not only that a crime has been committed but that there is nexus between the crime and the accused.

"As to the first, there is nothing in the evidence to suggest that Chilton Boswell was intentionally poisoned by anyone. He may have died by his own hand. The evidence can be interpreted either way on this point and therefore must by law be interpreted in the light most favorable to the accused.

"As to the second, the only evidence that suggests a connection to my client is one statement supposedly overheard by the victim's mother. I wish to remind the court that the immediate family of a victim must be held to a high standard of credibility and that personal bias must be rooted out. Mrs. Boswell's testimony was shaky at best on the details of that day, yet when it comes to the one possibly incriminating fact—and there is doubt about that—she claims she is certain.

"Well, she was also certain about her animosity toward my client. Clearly she does not think Wanda Boswell was worthy of her son.

"The statement she claims she heard from my client cannot stand alone. What a person says must be considered in context, and the prosecution has offered no other evidence about that particular conversation. Once again, the evidence must be interpreted in my client's favor. This one statement does not establish a connection between the death of Chilton Boswell—which may not even be a crime—and my client."

Kit was satisfied that she had stated her position clearly for the record. If Wanda was bound over for trial, Kit would take an immediate appeal. She would have a good shot at a reversal.

Then Fielding Hardy stood and, looking smug, dropped his bombshell.

$$21$$

T ED PRAYED.

Alone at his desk at the Bible Institute, looking at downtown Los Angeles, he thought of Kit and felt she needed prayer. Today was the day of her preliminary hearing.

He closed his eyes. *Lord, give Kit strength and wisdom and guidance now as she defends her client. Give her . . .*

He paused, opened his eyes, looked out the window. He felt it again, the odd disquiet that welled up in him from the heart. What was going on?

Why should he not be content? At this moment in time he should have been the most contented man on earth. He had a wonderful, godly woman for a wife and prospects for his aviation projects, including the offer of someone to put it all on film. He was a Christian now, working for an enterprise that sought to put the Word of God into people's hands. The next few years looked like they'd be the best of his life.

So why the dissatisfaction?

"I have in my hand the diary of the defendant," Fielding Hardy said. "I am sure that Mrs. Fox, in consultation with her client, will not deny that this is what it purports to be—the very words of the defendant, written in her own hand."

Her breath leaving her, Kit stared at the small red leather book in the prosecutor's hand. She turned to Wanda with a questioning gaze. Wanda's mouth was slightly open. She shook her head, but not in the way of denial; it was, rather, apologetic.

"May I have a moment to consult with my client?" Kit asked.

"By all means," said the judge.

Kit leaned close to Wanda's ear. "Is that your diary?"

Wanda's voice shuddered. "It appears to be."

"Why didn't you tell me about it?"

"I forgot all about it."

"More to the point, is there anything in there that is incriminating?"

"Can he read it out loud in court?"

"He would not have produced your diary if he did not intend to read something from it. Now think."

"I can't. I put so many things in there. My most intimate thoughts. Can't you stop him from reading it?"

Kit took hold of Wanda's wrist. "I will see what I can do." Kit stood up and faced the judge. "I should like to examine what the prosecutor claims to be my client's diary."

"Your Honor," Fielding Hardy said, "must we take up the court's time?"

"She has the right to examine it," the judge said. "Hand the diary to the defense."

Fielding Hardy placed the diary in Kit's hands. Kit sat down next to Wanda and looked at the leather-bound volume with her. She opened it and saw the girlish handwriting.

Wanda closed her eyes and whispered, "It's mine."

"I request a conference in chambers," Kit said.

"What is the nature of this request?" Judge Hardy said.

"I would prefer to let you know in chambers."

"Very well. I think we need a short recess on any account."

Kit did not wait for the judge to ask for anything. As soon as he had shut the door to his chambers she said, "I want to know where the prosecutor got this personal item."

"I don't have to reveal that," Fielding Hardy said. "The only issue is whether the writing in here is relevant. And I intend to show Your Honor that it is relevant."

"This item was not on the original inventory list prepared by Detective McGinty. That means Mr. Hardy has come to it in some fashion other than the authorized investigation."

"Surely the prosecution is entitled to an ongoing investigation," said the judge.

"So long as nothing illegal takes place."

Fielding Hardy whirled around to face Kit. "Are you insinuating that this office—"

"I'm not insinuating. I'm asking. How did you come by this diary?"

Folding his arms across his chest, Fielding Hardy said, "I don't think I have to answer that."

"Your Honor," Kit said, "the fourth amendment to the Constitution of the United States provides that people have the right to be secure not only in their person and place but also their effects. Since this diary was not secured under the authority of a search warrant, I want to know how the prosecution acquired it."

Judge Hardy seemed to be taken aback. The Constitution could do that to a judge. He frowned and looked at his brother. "Mrs. Fox may have a point after all. Why don't you just tell us where you got the diary?"

Now it was Fielding Hardy who looked as if he had taken a roundhouse punch to the chin. "Clarence—I mean, Your Honor—I can't go around telling defense lawyers where I get my evidence. Especially not lawyers trained by Earl Rogers."

"Do me a favor and just tell me where you got the diary," the judge said.

For the first time Kit saw that there might be a source of conflict between the judge and the prosecutor, the judge's brother. Would the judge take his role as judicial officer as seriously as his oath suggested? If so, would the application of legal pressure force him to do the right thing, even if at the expense of insulting his own brother? Kit filed these inquiries in the back of her mind for later analysis.

Fielding Hardy sighed. "All right. The diary was taken from a hidden compartment in a jewelry box."

Kit nearly gasped. "How did you come by the jewelry box?"

"This item was left with one of our deputies by an unidentified man."

"Did your deputy get the name of this man?" Kit said.

"Unfortunately, he did not."

"I'm not surprised," Kit said. "And where are the jewels that were in the box?"

Fielding Hardy gestured with his palms up. "The box contained no jewelry."

Kit's jaw clenched. "There is something quite suspicious surrounding this evidence. I wish to put an objection on the record to the introduction of this diary and any other evidence that the prosecution has gathered that it cannot account for by legal means."

Fielding Hardy's own jaw twitched. "Are you saying my office has done something unlawful?"

"Now, counselors," said the judge, "we need not get at each other's throats. There will be plenty of time for that during the trial. It seems to me that Mrs. Fox is not in possession of any evidence to suggest the prosecution has done anything illegal. Fielding here has a diary that appears to have been written by the defendant. He says there is evidence in it that's essential to this preliminary hearing. I will give Mrs. Fox the courtesy of having this evidence presented here in chambers first. If I think it is relevant, we will put it on the record."

"Thank you, Your Honor," Fielding Hardy said. He opened the diary and flipped to a page. "I'm reading the entry on a date two days before the killing, when the defendant wrote these words: 'Sometimes I get so angry I don't know what I might do to him.'"

Kit stared at the prosecutor and tried to keep her mouth closed. This would be devastating if ever introduced at trial. She was also thinking about the harm it would do to have these words published in newspapers because of this preliminary hearing. "Your Honor, I would request that you merely take this evidence under advisement and not consider it in your final determination of probable cause."

"But, Your Honor," Fielding Hardy said, "Mrs. Fox is the one who claims there is no connection between her client and the crime. We have now produced evidence to show the defendant's state of mind with regard to the deceased. I want this on the record."

"If this statement finds its way into the newspapers," Kit said, "it may very well infect the jury pool. Your town is small, and news seems to travel fast."

The judge said, "The prosecutor is right about your bringing up the objection."

"I will stipulate that this is what the diary says and will not object to Your Honor's considering it under seal. Its admissibility is still in question, and before it becomes public record, I'm going to want a hearing on the matter."

The judge nodded. "Then I'm ready to rule. Your client is going to be bound over for trial, Mrs. Fox. For murder in the first degree."

22

KIT FOUND WANDA TWIRLING in her jail cell. Dancing? She seemed to be lost in some ecstatic spell.

"Wanda!"

Her client stopped abruptly. "Oh! Hello, Mrs. Fox."

"We need to talk about what's happened."

"I don't see the need." Her voice sounded hollow, almost ghostly. "I'm going to trial for murder, and you can't do anything about it."

Kit thought the woman needed to be brought back to earth. "I am quite displeased with you as a client. I think you are innocent, yet you are doing everything to keep me from helping you."

Wanda spun around once, gracefully, then faced Kit. "I choose to leave it in the hands of the Fates."

"Fates? What are you talking about?"

"The Fates—the gods of chance."

"Stop it, Wanda. There are no gods of chance. There is one God, and you have one lawyer. You are going to need both. And you are going to start telling the truth."

"I'm sorry, Mrs. Fox. Honest, I'm not trying to keep anything from you."

"I'm not just talking about the facts of this case. I'm talking about truth. You seem to think that truth is something to be played with. Why didn't you tell me about the diary?"

"I forget things sometimes."

"Did you forget that you wrote about such anger toward your husband that you might do something terrible? That is the implication."

Wanda looked around her cell like a bird in a cage. "I've been told I say terrible things sometimes, and sometimes I write things. I don't mean them. I was trying to be whimsical. Do you think I'm whimsical, Mrs. Fox?"

Kit was not at all sure what she thought of Wanda Boswell right now. "I want the truth from you, not whimsy."

"Then you think I'm wicked?"

"I did not say that."

"People have told me that. Even Chilton. I try not to be. That's why I dance. When I dance I feel pure."

"Where is the last place you danced, before you married Chilton?"

"The last place?" Wanda's gaze wandered a moment.

"Look back at me, Wanda. Tell me where you last danced."

"I'm trying to remember. The Morosco. Yes, that was it. I was in a chorus." Wanda did a little spin. Kit began to wonder about whether Wanda would be able to take the stand in her own defense. Would she suddenly pop out of the witness chair and twirl?

"I want your pledge that you will not hide any more facts from me, Wanda. I want you to trust me completely."

"All right," Wanda said. "I promise."

"We must get ready for trial. There are going to be witnesses to interview, as well as much preparation. Is there anything else in that diary I need to know about?"

Wanda sighed. "I think I wrote something about wanting to strangle Glenna."

Wonderful, Kit thought.

The Morosco Theatre happened to be well-known to Kit Shannon Fox. It was here that she had once held the stage against two prominent critics of the Bible—Clarence Darrow, the noted

Chicago lawyer, and Dr. Edward Lazarus, a local clergyman who was caught up in the grip of the "new criticism." In the debate, Kit argued for the full inspiration and authority of Scripture.

The debate lingered on in the churches and seminaries of America, which was one of the reasons Kit had overseen the establishment of the Los Angeles Institute of the Bible. The battle for the Bible was going to be a long one.

When not hosting debates, however, the Morosco was one of the leading vaudeville stages in California. It was also the last known employment address of Wanda Boswell.

As Kit walked toward the stage door in the alley off Third Street, she wondered briefly if she should even be here at all. Investigating the background of her client? That should not have been necessary.

But in Wanda's case, it was. Her secretiveness was troubling, and if any unseemly information was available here, Kit needed to get it before the prosecution did. That is, if they hadn't gotten it already.

It took a good two minutes of pounding on the stage door before it creaked open.

"What is it?" The annoyed stagehand—an older man with a newspaper rolled up in one hand—glowered at Kit.

"Is the stage manager in?"

"'Course he's in! This is a stage, isn't it? We got a show to get on, don't we? What do *you* want?"

"Sir, my name is Kathleen Shannon Fox. I am an attorney, here on business."

The stagehand straightened. "Kit Shannon, the lawyer?"

"Mrs. Fox now."

"I know who you are. I was behind the lights when you took on Clarence Darrow!" Now he smiled. "By thunder, that was quite a show! Come on in, Mrs. Fox."

He opened the door for her. The cool of backstage felt pleasant to Kit. A man in a ragged suit and battered derby juggled four round white balls with such effortlessness that it was astonishing. His dexterity hit her as quite a contrast to his appearance, which, frankly, resembled that of a tramp. When he saw Kit, he let the balls hit the floor and doffed his hat.

"Bewitching," he said. His voice was odd, sounding to her much like a squeaky door.

The stagehand said, "Bill, this is the lawyer Kit Shannon Fox. Mrs. Fox, our juggler for the show, Bill Dukenfield."

The juggler struck the stagehand with his derby. "Cad! Churl! The name is Fields!" He took Kit's hand. "W. C. Fields, my little prairie blossom. Tramp juggler extraordinaire."

"Happy to make your acquaintance, Mr. Fields."

"She's here to see Kingsley," the stagehand said.

"I was under no illusion, you jackanapes, you coxcomb, that a woman of such obvious attributions was here to see you!"

"Come on, Mrs. Fox, before I give him a belt in the nose."

Fields bowed, looking pleased with the exchange. He winked at her.

Kit followed the one Fields had dubbed a jackanapes to the open stage. A skinny young man at a piano plinked a tune as a line of chorus girls kicked in unison. Fascinated, Kit watched their lithe legs.

A corpulent man with a head like a melon sat at a table smoking a pipe and watching the dancers. Using glowing terms, Jackanapes introduced Kit to the man whose name was Kingsley.

"I'm in rehearsal," he said, giving Kit a terse nod.

"If I may ask you a few questions about someone who once worked here, I would greatly appreciate it," Kit said.

Kingsley looked her up and down. "You ever do any dancing?"

"No, sir."

"Mind if I look at your legs?"

"Yes. If I may—"

"I'm looking for dancers."

"I represent Wanda Boswell."

Kingsley removed the pipe from his mouth. A twisted smile snaked across his face. "What trouble is she in this time?"

"She's charged with murder."

"I ain't surprised." Kingsley looked past Kit. "Get those legs up there! Sylvia, your left is like a tree trunk!"

One of the girls shouted, "Says you!"

"We can't talk here!" Kingsley stood and motioned for Kit to follow him. He led her to a small office in the rear of the theater. It was stuffy and windowless, decorated with fading playbills and peeling paint.

Kingsley offered Kit a stool. "All right, Mrs. Fox, let's get this over with."

"Thank you. What sort of woman would you say Wanda Boswell is?"

Without hesitation, Kingsley said, "A lying, conniving spawn of Satan."

The words almost knocked Kit backward. Kingsley's face was full of rock-hard anger. Or disgust. "At least one cannot accuse you of being indirect."

"You want me to soft-pedal it? I ain't gonna do that. Not my style. If a woman is a woman like she's supposed to be—one who's innocent and trustworthy—I don't have a problem. But that ain't what Wanda Boswell was like."

"Suppose you tell me what she was like. Start by telling me how you knew her."

"She danced here, if you can call that wiggling she did dancing. I sure don't call it that. I call it temptation, part of the devil's own scheme. Anyway, that's how I knew her. And when I tried to get to know her a little better, she treated me like I was nothin'."

"Would it be fair to say, sir, that you had a romantic interest in Wanda?"

"I'm a man. I got my limits. I can only take so much before I fall, if you know what I mean. She knew what she was doing."

The interview was not going as planned. Kit didn't know exactly what she had hoped to hear. Perhaps that Wanda Boswell was an innocent young girl who wished only to express herself through art. Now she hoped the prosecutor didn't find this man and use him to locate a string of suitors.

"Mr. Kingsley, do you think Wanda Boswell is capable of murder?"

"Who knows what goes on in the brain of a woman? There are probably men who want to kill *her*."

Kit swallowed. "Are there any names that come to mind?"

Kingsley pursed his lips. "I didn't keep track."

"Was there any man you might be able to think of?"

For a moment Kingsley looked at the floor. "If I describe 'em for you, what say to having dinner with me tonight?"

"Sir, I am married."

His eyebrows bobbed. "Like I said, what say to having dinner with me tonight?"

Kit turned to go.

"Hold it!" Kingsley put his hands in the air. "You don't have to get all moral on me. I'll tell you what I know."

23

BACK AT THE OFFICE, Kit found Corazón and Raul waiting for her.

"What a pleasant surprise, Raul."

He bowed. "I have come with a request, Mrs. Fox."

"Of course."

After a quick glance at Corazón, Raul said, "We wish to be married."

Kit clapped her hands and embraced Corazón. "That is the best news I've heard in weeks."

"May we have your permission?" Raul asked.

"But of course. You not only have my permission, you have my blessing. But what makes you think you need my permission in the first place?"

"My father, he is the owner of a tavern. If his work is to be interrupted by something that is done by one of his workers, it is common courtesy for the worker to ask permission. I will be taking the hand in marriage of your assistant."

"Then I hope I shall not be losing an assistant but gaining a team."

"Team?" Raul asked.

"To help with my investigations."

Raul looked at Corazón. "Do you know what she is talking about?"

Corazón smiled, a twinkle in her eye. "I did not tell you. It was to be a surprise."

"But what are you two cooking up?"

"Corazón is essential to my practice," Kit explained. "She will continue to be my assistant, and I would like to put you both on retainer. What do you think about going into business, Raul?"

For a moment Raul looked as stunned as a Roosevelt Progressive at a Wall Street convention. Then a huge smile broke out across his face. Corazón kissed his cheek. And that was when Raul's eyes began to mist.

"What is it, my darling?" Corazón said.

"I am sorry. I have always wanted to be like my father. To work for myself and not for others. But not in a saloon. I have wondered how this would come to be. You have made me very happy, Mrs. Fox."

"And you two have made me very happy. When would you like to be married?"

"In the summer," Raul said.

"Very good," Kit said. "That gives us plenty of time to get some work done. Shall we begin now?"

Raul and Corazón sat as Kit plopped a copy of the *Times* on her desk. "Professor Faire is speaking this evening, at the University of Southern California. I've been thinking more and more about him. Tell me, what would a respected professor of philosophy be doing on a cruise to Hawaii alone? Further, why would he be snooping around Chilton Boswell's room? I don't believe his story about Chilton owing him a gambling debt. Chilton was much too clever to get caught cheating at cards."

Corazón looked briefly at the ceiling. "Perhaps the professor had business with Mr. Boswell before the trip?"

"That's what I was thinking. There is only one way to find out. We will pay a call on Professor Faire when he least expects us. Are you ready for a breath of hot air?"

Raul and Corazón looked at each other.

————————

"It was Christianity which first painted the devil on the world's wall," Professor Aiden Aloysius Faire said. "It was Christianity which first brought sin into the world. We would still be in a state of blissful innocence had it not been for the preachers and teachers of Christianity."

Kit sat with Corazón and Raul near the back of the lecture hall. The rest of the place was filled almost to capacity with young men, many of them smoking pipes in what seemed an attempt to look profound. She could see many of them growing up to be little Faires in their own right—atheistic, skeptical, haughty.

One young man sitting at Kit's left leaned over and whispered to a fellow, "Nietzsche." Kit knew the German philosopher had become the vogue in academic circles, even though the man had died a raving lunatic. What better philosopher for a skeptic like Faire to be quoting? Only he did not mention Nietzsche's name.

"The church is a city of destruction. Imprisonment. You see, egoism, not sacrifice, is the essence of a noble soul."

Kit recognized the phrase. Faire had said the same thing, or something quite similar to it, at dinner aboard the ship. He was certainly one for phrasemaking.

Corazón said quietly, "This is the hot air you spoke of?"

"Yes," said Kit.

A skinny young fellow in front of them turned around and said "Shh."

"I shall now tell you of a better way toward freedom. It comes from the freedom of the mind. It is all part of a philosophical system that I am developing for the betterment of mankind, and it will soon be published in a book. You, however, are going to get it for free."

He looked toward Kit, Corazón and Raul, who must have stuck out like peacocks at a rooster show. Although he did not acknowledge their presence, he made it clear he was aware of them.

The speech droned on for another hour. Then the professor entertained questions for another thirty minutes.

At last the event ended. Faire was approached by a few of the students at the front of the hall. Kit waited patiently in the back with Corazón and Raul until the last of them had departed. She then approached the professor.

"I was quite certain I was rid of you, Mrs. Fox," he said. "Did you enjoy the lecture?"

"Let us say I was listening carefully to your words."

"That is all I can ask. Is there something I can do for you?"

"Only a few questions, Professor. These are my assistants, Corazón Chavez and Raul Montoya."

"Mexican?"

"Citizens of Los Angeles."

"Los Angeles is changing." Quickly forcing a smile, he added, "For the better."

Kit asked him, "May I inquire as to your business in our city?"

"Why, may I ask, is that a concern of yours?"

"It is of concern only because you are to be a witness in Wanda Boswell's murder trial. Rather than asking those who are sponsoring you here in the city, would it not be better to offer your reasons to me personally?"

"I have nothing to hide."

"Then what is it that brings you here from Chicago in the first place?"

"A lecture, as you just saw. I will be doing more of them before returning."

"And a cruise to Hawaii?"

"Relaxation, of course. The life of an academic is one that can be quite taxing. When I learned of the cruise, and having never been to the Hawaiian Islands, I thought it might provide me a needed respite from the rigors of my profession."

"Did your contact with Chilton Boswell have anything to do with your decision?"

Faire blinked behind his pince-nez glasses. "I don't know what you mean."

"Miss Chavez spoke to an associate of Chilton Boswell. This man saw someone fitting your exact description in conversation with Chilton at a local saloon shortly before the Hawaiian excursion. Perhaps you can explain that."

A long pause settled between them. "I don't quite understand your interest, Mrs. Fox. A murder was committed. A man is dead. You represent the widow, who is also the suspect. If you are attempting to create reasonable doubt by implicating me, I can tell you I will not be a party to it."

"You have not answered my question about your meeting with Chilton Boswell."

"Mr. Boswell came to me about a personal matter."

"Why would Chilton Boswell seek out a professor of philosophy from Chicago?"

"Because Boswell entertained thoughts of writing a book some-day. As one who has published, he thought I might be able to offer him advice. I did so. I did not think he would later show his grati-tude by cheating me at cards."

"How did you and Chilton happen to meet?"

"As I said, I am here for some lectures. Mr. Boswell saw my name in the paper, much as you did, and found his way to one of my talks."

"I thought you said the Hawaiian trip preceded your lecture tour."

"Yes, I did say that. But I was giving a few talks independently. My sponsors were generous that way."

"Who are your sponsors?"

Faire reached for his overcoat, thrown over a chair behind the dais, and began putting it on. "I do not wish to be unfriendly, Mrs. Fox, but I should like to keep my associations private, if you don't mind. Will there be anything else?"

"You said Chilton came to one of your talks?"

Faire shrugged. "He introduced himself, said he wished to speak with me about publishing a book, so I invited him out for a drink. Now, is that so wrong?"

"Did Chilton Boswell show you a sample of his writing?"

"No. He described some of the things he hoped to write about, that was all. I took him to be a rather earnest but perhaps not a very deep young man."

"What were some of the things he described to you?"

Faire had his overcoat buttoned up now and placed his hat on his head. "I think that should be enough for you, Mrs. Fox. I believe you are thinking about me as possibly the one who killed Chilton Boswell. That is your job, I understand. But as you can see, I am open and aboveboard with you. I have nothing to hide. I must go now as I have an engagement."

"Where can I reach you?" Kit said.

"I choose not to be reached. Good day."

AT CHURCH ON SUNDAY the Reverend Miller Macauley chose as his text the passage from John about the woman caught in adultery. "'And Jesus said unto her, Neither do I condemn thee: go and sin no more.' This is the twofold nature of our Savior's work," Macauley said from the pulpit, his Scottish brogue delighting Kit. With Ted on one side and Corazón on the other, Sunday church always felt right—even if Ted did seem preoccupied today.

"On the one hand He forgives us our sins; on the other He warns us not to lead a life of sin. You cannot have only one half of Jesus."

After the service Kit and Corazón attended, as was their practice, the meeting of the Ladies' Aid Society. The agenda for the meeting was to have been a discussion of funds to be raised for the county hospital. But as soon as Kit was seated, the chair, Mrs. Faye Jefferson, announced a special guest speaker.

"I am sure you will recognize the name of Mrs. Henrietta Studdard," Mrs. Jefferson said by way of introduction. "She writes that lovely column in the *Times* that so many of us treasure. Her advice on all things woman is a godsend. I only wish the younger ladies of the city would take her comments to heart."

A round of grumbling assent swept through the room. Kit, however, was wondering how she might slip out unobtrusively. While she did not have anything against Mrs. Studdard, whose column she occasionally read, she did not have any particular affinity either.

Yet seated as she was in a middle row of the wooden chairs, Kit reckoned herself and Corazón a captive audience.

Polite applause greeted the speaker, a rather stout woman who seemed to have a smile permanently plastered on her face—the sort of smile, Kit thought, that looked like a professional duty rather than a sincere indicator of feeling.

Mrs. Studdard wore an ornate black gown with Chantilly lace and a hat that could only be described as voluminous. The brim seemed to be twice as large as any Kit had ever seen, with a sprouting of black and white plumes that suggested an overcrowded aviary. She was, in a word, substantial.

"Good morning, ladies." Henrietta Studdard stood at the polished wood podium that failed to wholly cover her. "I want to thank you so much for the gracious invitation to speak with you on the Lord's Day. I cannot think of a higher privilege than to address the cream of Los Angeles womanhood on this most sacred of days and in this lovely church."

More polite applause. The smile stayed fixed to Mrs. Studdard's face. And the room began to feel a bit stifling to Kit.

"My subject today is the place of the woman in the home. I daresay it is troubling that such an address should have to be made, but this is the age in which we live. The blurring of lines between home and work, and between husbands and wives, is threatening to tear at the fabric of our society. The woman at work is rather like the dog that walks on its hind legs—it is not to be preferred."

Now Kit really wanted to leave. Instead, she endured a lecture of nearly an hour's length. It was bearable only because Kit read a large portion of Paul's letters from the Bible on her lap.

She had the oddest feeling that, for most of the talk, Mrs. Henrietta Studdard was speaking directly to her.

The meeting finally ended, Kit endeavored to make the exit with Corazón before anyone could stop them. But the small crowd proved a hindrance, and when her shoulder was tapped, Kit somehow knew Mrs. Studdard would somehow be involved.

"Kathleen, I should like to introduce you to Mrs. Studdard," Faye Jefferson said.

"How do you do?" Kit said.

"Delighted, my dear." Mrs. Studdard's smiling lips hardly moved. "You are Kit Shannon Fox."

"Yes."

"The noted lawyer."

"I suppose so."

"So young," Mrs. Studdard said to Mrs. Jefferson. "And pretty."

"It was very nice to meet you." Kit began to turn.

"I wonder if I might ask you a favor," Mrs. Studdard said quickly. "As one prominent Angeleno to another."

"Favor?"

"You would be doing me a great service if you would take tea with me this afternoon. There is a matter of some importance I wish to take up with you."

"This afternoon? I am not certain—"

"Shall we say four o'clock? My house on Adams? I am so looking forward to it."

———

Of some importance," she had said. As Kit pulled up to the Adams Street residence of Henrietta Studdard, she wondered just what it could be that the woman wished to discuss with her. She hoped it wouldn't take long. She would have to make preparation for returning to San Leandro.

"Thank you for coming to my home." Mrs. Studdard received Kit in the parlor of her well-appointed house. A beautiful painting of a Spanish hacienda surrounded by trees hung on one wall.

"You like that?" Mrs. Studdard asked.

"It is quite lovely. Very peaceful," Kit replied.

"It is. My home in Santa Barbara. It was built by my late husband, may he rest in peace. I do love it so."

Kit nodded.

"May I show you the outside?"

Tea was served by a maid on the patio overlooking a colorful garden. A large magnolia tree, with its waxy green leaves, shaded them. It was a home fitting one of the more noted women of the city.

Kit knew only that Henrietta Studdard had been writing her column since before Kit had arrived in Los Angeles in 1903. Where she came from, or what her qualifications were, Kit knew not. But anyone who published in the *Times* had a platform of long reach.

"You mentioned that you had a matter of some importance," Kit said. "May I be of help to you?"

Mrs. Studdard placed her teacup down with an intrusive clack. "Mrs. Fox, I should like to be of help to you."

"To me?"

"Yes, dear. I am a woman of some maturity, which provides me with a bit of wisdom to pass on to the younger generation. I have also been a Christian woman my entire life. And so I should like to speak with you as someone who has earned the right to speak."

"By all means," Kit said. She was quite curious now as to the purpose of this meeting.

"I want you to understand that I realize the world is changing. So many busy streets now. The rather leisurely pace of life that I enjoyed as a little girl is no longer part of the warp and woof of life in the city, though I still sometimes yearn for those days to return. I know they shall not. But I yearn. Oh yes. Sometimes I yearn. But that is neither here nor there."

Kit was beginning to want to be anywhere but here. Even so, she nodded politely and waited for the woman to continue.

"But we must always be about the work of God, about the glory of God. That is life's purpose. And if we see that there is something which possibly besmirches the glory of God, is it not our duty to speak out on His behalf, to see if we might not right the ship, so to speak?"

Kit thought about the time she stood up at another tea, one involving many of the finest ladies of high society, and interrupted their speaker—Dr. Edward Lazarus, a minister of the Gospel who did not believe in the divinity of the Gospels. Certainly she had not been remiss in confronting the man. Truth be told, she rather delighted in it.

"By all means, Mrs. Studdard."

"I am delighted to secure your agreement. That is what makes what I'm about to say easier."

Mrs. Studdard cleared her throat, causing a shaking of the skin between her chin and chest.

"Would you not agree with the Scriptures, which tell us that a noble wife looketh well to the ways of her household?"

"Of course."

"Household, my dear."

"Yes?"

"Not to be blunt, but will there be children?"

"That is to be blunt."

Mrs. Studdard inhaled audibly. "Nevertheless."

"Nevertheless what?"

"My dear," Mrs. Studdard said in an effort to recapture the moment. "We're living in an age that challenges hearth and home. I was reading in the newspaper the other day that there are one hundred thousand lady typewriters in the working place. Can you imagine? Will they be married? What will become of their children? What will become of their husbands? All these girls wish to become Gibsonized. That awful man Gibson glamorizing the ideal hussy. Dreadful."

"I do my best not to be a hussy."

"How is it different if one acts like a hussy? My dear, I don't believe you have any ill will in mind toward your husband in your home, but this professional life that you have embarked upon is not for the married woman. When you were single and without care, perhaps God did not mind that you engaged in the pursuit of the law. But now that you are married, I feel it is incumbent upon myself as a woman of advanced years to plead with you to do what is right in the sight of God and the church, and retire from your professional duties and make a home for your husband and children."

"Do the wishes of my husband matter?"

"I should say not. The male creature is an odd amalgam, sometimes too compliant and sometimes an ogre. You must do what is right, and that means giving up selfish pursuits for the good of the home."

"I don't wish to appear ungrateful, Mrs. Studdard," Kit said carefully, "but I believe that is a decision best left to my husband and me as we submit to God in prayer. Would you not agree?"

"I should think that a word of advice would be sufficient. But there is another aspect to all of this."

Kit waited, unable to think of any other aspect.

"You are something of an example to young women in this city. I have received more than one letter, I'll have you know, which mentions your name."

"My name?"

"Young women who point to you as a model, thus calling into question the wisdom of my own words."

"Mrs. Studdard, I certainly appreciate your interest in—"

"I am not sure you completely understand." Mrs. Studdard's frozen smile had suddenly disappeared. "I must write in my column about the threats I see toward those young women in my charge. I have never written anything negative about anyone, by name that is, and I do not wish to begin now."

A threat! Kit could hardly believe her ears. "Well, I have had many things written about me already, not all of them flattering."

"I ask you to pray about this, my dear. We are women of God. Will you at least pledge to do that much?"

Kit's rising anger was mollified for the moment. She could not argue with the suggestion of prayer. Indeed, in some way that was beyond her, could it be that Mrs. Studdard had a point?

"I shall do so," Kit agreed, and meant it.

Mrs. Studdard's smile returned. "And I shall pray for you, my dear, I promise. I know you will do the right thing."

25

KIT DID NOT ATTEMPT to pray at the wheel of her Ford. But it wouldn't have mattered had she been alone in her bedroom. The steam leaking from her ears would have hindered her prayers. The idea of Mrs. Studdard taking Kit's private life upon her substantial shoulders! The nerve!

Another autoist, a man in goggles and gauntlets, nearly clipped her with his car. Or was it she who had been in the wrong? Whatever the reason, the man's epithet, ending with "Woman driver!" brought her out of her musings and somewhat dissipated her anger.

Was this just pride, pure and simple? Was it possible that this Mrs. Studdard was saying something she needed to hear?

Kit tried to clear her head of the thought. She drove to the office to see that things were in order for her return to San Leandro. Tonight she would be dining with Ted. He wanted her to meet this Boggs fellow. Until then, she had a few details to take care of.

First, she called Corazón at home. "I would like you to take a little trip up to Santa Barbara tomorrow," Kit told her. "Did you know that Mrs. Henrietta Studdard has a home there?"

"Is true?" Corazón said.

"And that was where Glenna Boswell went recently, as you determined. There may not be a connection, but I want to know more about Mrs. Studdard's background. See what you can find out."

"I will do it."

Kit spent the next few minutes going over her outline of the upcoming trial. There were still major pieces missing. As it stood, it was going to be a case of reasonable doubt. Kit would have to sow enough of it in the minds of the jurors to keep Wanda Boswell from the gallows.

She heard the shuffling of heavy feet outside her door. She opened it and found Earl Rogers and his chief assistant, Bill Jory, in the corridor, heading toward his office. Rogers was dressed in his usual impeccable style, with his cream-colored suit as crisp as a winter morning, his shoes glistening with polish.

"Hey, Kit!" Earl said with a wave.

"Hello, Earl, Bill."

"What are you doing here on a Sunday?" Rogers said. "Shouldn't you be in church?"

"Shouldn't you?"

"Don't stop trying to convert me, Kit. Someday you may actually do it."

Jory snorted. "Not likely." He turned to Kit. "How's that murder trial going? You got them rubes down in San Leandro walking the line?"

"Hardly," Kit said. "Someday I'll tell you all about it. Right now I need the advice of two of the sharpest tacks in Los Angeles."

Earl looked around the corridor. "Where are they?"

"Funny, Earl. But the situation isn't. Tell me, if I needed to find out where stolen jewelry ended up, where would I go?"

Earl folded his arms. "What have you got yourself into this time?"

"That I am not sure of. My client had a box of jewelry that went missing. It had a secret drawer where she kept her diary. The diary showed up in court but the jewelry is gone. Stolen, obviously."

"You have any idea who might have stolen them?"

"A few people spring to mind. What would they do with the jewelry if they wanted to convert it to money?"

"The person would go through a fence. Not a picket fence, but a man who traffics in stolen goods. Don't you agree, Bill?"

Bill Jory nodded. "Only fences would be right here in town."

"And if you were to select a fence to do business with," Earl asked, "who would it be?"

"No question about it," Jory said. "Bones Stackhouse."

"I agree." Earl turned to Kit. "Would you like to meet him?"

"What a grand idea," Kit said. "I was beginning to wonder how to enlarge my social circle."

———————

Bones Stackhouse operated out of one of the oldest and most dilapidated buildings in Los Angeles. Located just outside the business district, it had once been a livery stable. But with the coming of the trolley and the gas-powered automobile, livery stables were on their way out. Still, the vacant structure needed looking after, and "That's where I come in," Bones explained after Earl's introduction. "I will store your items for a modest fee."

"If it happens he doesn't sell them," Earl said, "you may even get them back."

"That's a slander, sir."

"Truth is a complete defense, I'm afraid."

"I admit only to taking from them that's got too much and won't miss the things of this world. And I never dip where friends have trod."

"We will leave the world of business now and get to the ways of the underworld."

Bones Stackhouse scowled at first, then broke into a huge smile. He nodded and led Kit and Earl to what had once been a stall but now had wooden stools and an overturned barrel for a makeshift table. The man's office. Kit almost laughed.

"My associate would like to know about the traffic in stolen jewelry," Earl said. "Have you had any such activity in the last week?"

Bones rubbed his chin, which held at least a day's stubble. "My clients trust me. They like to remain unanimous."

Kit stifled a laugh.

"Yes, you are the most ethical fence I know," Earl said with a wink. "That's why I waived my usual fee when I saved you from that robbery charge last year."

"Now are you calling in your chips?"

"Who knows when you'll be in Dutch again? Who knows who you will turn to?"

Bones looked at Kit. "He's a clever one, ain't he?"

"The cleverest," Kit said.

"All right. I did have an inquiry from a party about some jewelry. But I turned down the deal."

"Why?" Earl asked.

"One of the pieces was a fake. Trying to pass bad rocks on me. Bad for business."

"What type of piece was it?" Kit said.

"A ring with two baguettes. Not good work."

Kit said to Earl, "Wanda described a ring like that."

"Who's Wanda?" Bones said.

"My client. She's been accused of murdering her husband."

Bones shook his head. "Marriage is the antidote to love. What a mystery."

"We didn't come here for a lecture on matrimony," Earl said. "You say you turned down this proposition?"

"Most defiantly."

"Then you have no confidential relationship with the party. So come on, spill. Who was it?"

"I didn't get a name."

"Can you describe him?"

"Big fella. Beefy. Not very mannerly, if you know what I mean."

"No, I don't. Please explain."

"Kind of charged ahead without any of the graces. He was like a bull who carries his own china shop around with him. Said he was going to show me what was what."

Kit sat forward. "Did he have a big red nose?"

"He did."

"I think I may know this man. Samuelson. He was aboard the ship. But how could he have stolen the jewelry?"

Bones said, "He wasn't the one who stole 'em."

"What are you saying?"

"I told you, this fella was representing another party. That's what he said, anyway. And I got the feeling he wasn't lying."

"Did this man tell you where he could be contacted?"

"You're in luck," Bones said. "He told me exactly where he was staying."

"Well?" Earl said.

"Now, Earl, you know times is hard. I got my expenses."

Earl looked around the stall. "Yes, the decorating must have cost you a pretty penny. All right, Bones, how about a fin?"

"A lousy fin?"

"It's more than you'll make today, I wager."

Bones squinted. "A fin, and free legal advice."

"Done." Rogers slipped a five-dollar bill into Bones's hand. "Now where is this fellow?"

"Dermott Hotel. You know it?"

"What room?"

"Seven."

Earl motioned to Kit. "Let's go." He stood and turned to Bones. "Here's the legal advice."

"Huh?"

"Obey the law."

The Dermott was not one of the finer inns in the city, but neither was it a flophouse. Located near the depot, it served its purpose as a stopover for salesmen and transients and the occasional flim-flam man.

Kit recognized the desk clerk. He was a thin man with a thin mustache who had shown up in the criminal courts from time to time, though for what offense Kit was not aware. Los Angeles was still a small city of concentric circles—from the lower depths to the upper strata of society. As long as she was going to practice in the criminal courts, Kit would see many of the same faces over and over again.

Earl, of course, knew the man by name. "Steve, this is Kit Shannon Fox, and we have an appointment with one of your lodgers."

"I don't see you," Steve said.

"Thanks. You have a key to seven?"

Steve nodded, waited. Earl, whose pocket never seemed bereft of currency, handed Steve a five-dollar bill—the price of the day.

Steve gave Earl the key.

"Always best to be prepared," Earl explained as they headed down the corridor. Room seven was at the very end.

"Suppose it's not Samuelson?" Kit said.

"Then we will offer our apologies and leave."

Earl placed the key in the lock and opened the door.

The room had a yellowish tint, from the sunlight on the window shade. The bed was unkempt and smelled of sweat and beer. Earl closed the door behind them.

"Nobody home," Earl said. "Let's look around for the jewelry box."

"I do not have a good feeling about this," said Kit. "Suppose he should come in?"

"Then you and I shall talk our way out of it, like we always do."

"Juries do not carry guns, Earl. Perhaps Samuelson does."

But Earl was already busy going through the meager chest of drawers inside the room. Kit supposed she would do what she came to do and went to the closet door. She opened it.

And Edgar Samuelson's body fell to the floor.

26

"STRANGLED, IT LOOKS LIKE," Earl Rogers said.

Indeed, Samuelson's neck had an ugly, reddish-blue mark around it.

"We'll call McGinty," Rogers said. "But we'll have to get our stories straight."

Kit shook her head. "Earl, we will tell him exactly what we did. We came in and started snooping around and discovered his body."

"That's going to sound wonderful. At least let's go through his pockets."

"Earl! He's the victim of a homicide. We have to let McGinty look."

"I'll deal with McGinty." Earl knelt down—an odd sight in his resplendent white suit in the middle of a seedy hotel room—next to a bloated dead man. But with catlike precision he examined Samuelson's coat pockets. He pulled out, in order, a linen handkerchief, a wallet, a mustache brush, and, from a front pocket, the ace of spades from a deck of cards. The latter he held closer to his eyes.

"Interesting," Earl said.

"What?"

"There is a sum written at the bottom. Five hundred dollars."

"Why would that be written there?"

"It's a gambler's demand. Samuelson was into someone for that amount, and it was due."

"You must give all this to McGinty when you call him," Kit said, turning.

"And just where are you going?"

"To cash in a chip."

———

"Charmed," Don Raffels said.

Kit answered, "Samuelson is dead."

The gambling boss did not look shocked or surprised. "He was, I am afraid, a man who was in over his head."

They were in his office at the gambling house he ran just outside the county line. It had taken Kit only half an hour by auto to get here, over a well-worn road. Many a gambler had come this way from the west side of the city to this den of gaming and drink.

"He was holding a demand for payment," Kit said, "written on an ace of spades. Your ace of spades."

Raffels frowned. "How do you know it is mine?"

"The back of the card bears the design you use in your casino."

"It's not an uncommon design."

"The demand was written with a dollar sign that has a peculiar slant to it. I have seen that only once before, when you signed a check to your bartender on the ship."

Raffels smiled and shook his head. "You are a remarkable woman, Mrs. Fox. I am afraid I must own up to it. Yes, that was my demand. But you do not suppose that I had anything to do with Mr. Samuelson's demise."

"I do not know anything at the moment. By now an examiner from the coroner's office is looking at Samuelson's body to determine the time and cause of death. You can, of course, establish where you have been for the last twelve hours or so?"

"Of course. Even so, why should you be interested in who killed this man? You are not a detective."

"Samuelson was involved in a transaction that was, shall we say, not on the up-and-up. Nor was he acting alone. I thought you might be able to tell me who he might have been working with. You, perhaps?"

"I assure you I had no dealings with Mr. Edgar Samuelson."

"Other than the one in which he owed you money."

"Yes."

"Was that for a loan or a gambling debt?"

"Both. I advanced him the money to continue a hand of poker. He lost. I paid off. He owes—or rather, owed—me the money."

"Mr. Raffels, you have not been entirely truthful with me, have you?"

"I beg your pardon?"

"When I asked you aboard the ship about those who might have had a grudge against Chilton Boswell, you told me you did not know of any. Yet you sat dealing a poker game in which Samuelson, Professor Faire, and Chilton Boswell played. Why did you keep that fact from me?"

Raffels put on a smile that looked to be forced. "Why do I get the uncomfortable feeling that you are accusing me of something?"

"Of not being truthful?"

"Of murder."

"I assure you, Mr. Raffels—"

He stopped her with a raised hand. "Where I come from, Mrs. Fox, such talk can be very dangerous. If you were a man I would strictly warn you not to open your mouth again."

For a long moment nothing was said as the dark eyes of the gambling boss burned with threat. Then he smiled again. "But why should we talk so unpleasantly to each other, eh? There is an understanding now, no? And that is how I do business. Leave well enough alone, and life will continue to be a pleasant thing for the both of us."

———

"I am sorry, Mr. Boggs," Kit said. "I do not wish to be turned into a motion picture."

"But why, Mrs. Fox? I am talking about immortality!" Boggs did a hop on one leg. Ted, who had brought him here to Kit's office, put a hand on the man's shoulder.

Kit wondered what to make of Francis Boggs. He was full of

enthusiasm about Ted and the plane. Now he was just as enthralled, it appeared, with her. He was like the new breed of salesmen, too, who were full of the gospel of get-up-and-go—men who flooded into Los Angeles with dreams of striking it rich selling real estate or automobiles.

"Immortality," Kit said, "is something I leave to the good Lord."

"And if I could get Him on film, don't you think I'd do it? What wouldn't that mean to the world!"

"I wonder, Mr. Boggs, if you aren't taking the motion picture idea too far."

Boggs laughed and then scratched his chin. "How about this? If I take down on film some of this trial you're getting ready for? You just walk into the courtroom or some such . . . I will be capturing history."

Kit shook her head. "I would rather not know about it. But with that camera you are like a reporter. You are entitled by the First Amendment, I suppose, to take pictures."

"That's the ticket!" Boggs clapped Ted on the back. "I will be sly!"

Ted smiled. "You seem to have found your calling in life."

"I am filled with the possible! You will be hearing from me."

With that, Francis Boggs shot out of the office, slamming the door behind him.

As soon as he was gone, Ted looked at Kit, and the two of them started laughing simultaneously.

"You had to meet this fellow," Ted said. "He may be on to something here. Recorded history."

"I suppose." Kit flopped back into her swivel chair. "I just do not think I want to be a historical relic yet." She felt suddenly tired. Francis Boggs was the sort of man who could suck energy out of a generator. But it wasn't only that. The Wanda Boswell case was beginning to wear on her.

"Are you feeling well?" Ted asked.

"Like a relic."

"Tell me."

"It's this case. It is like gossamer. I cannot see anything solid in it. I have a client who is not completely honest with me and a brother act in San Leandro that I have no confidence in."

Ted leaned back in his chair, arms folded, contemplative. Maybe he had an idea. At this point Kit was ready for any new suggestion. Ted said nothing.

Kit got up, went to the window of her office overlooking Broadway, and opened it. The general clatter of the street scene burst in. The bang of automobiles mixed with the rush of pedestrian traffic, the latter causing almost a swishing sound, like a river. Voices occasionally broke in. A street preacher condemned the masses; a newsboy shouted a headline about President Roosevelt; a cop yelled at a drunk to get up off the sidewalk.

It all seemed in keeping with the noise in Kit's mind. "The answer is out there somewhere. Why am I not seeing it?"

"Maybe the strain is getting to you," Ted offered.

Kit turned from the window. "Do you think so?"

"How could it not? You put your entire being into a case and cause. That's what makes you a great lawyer. It's also what makes you . . ." His voice trailed off.

"What were you going to say?"

Ted breathed in deeply. "I only wonder if it is what's best, now that we are back in the city, ready to get on with our lives."

Kit sat on the edge of her desk, facing him. "If what is best?"

"This." Ted's arm swept the office. "The law. And this case, which is taking you back to San Leandro and away from your home."

A dull thud in her chest compelled Kit off her desk and back to the window. Only now she paced in front of it, not looking out. "I want to be home as much as you want me there, Ted. You know that, don't you?"

"I hope that is true."

"How can you think anything else? I am your wife."

"And I am your husband. I think I should have a say in how your life is directed."

"But you do." Kit stopped at the bookshelf, turned, and walked back toward her desk.

"Will you quit pacing and sit down?" Ted's voice was filled with annoyance. It hit Kit with the force of a blow.

"I wish to stand," she said.

Ted looked at her, surprised. "Then I will stand up."

He did. It was a gesture that gave Kit a hollow feeling in her middle. Like something had been taken out, leaving a hole.

"Kit, if I am to be the head of a household, and not just a flier who is married to a lawyer, I must be able to have some say in what you are doing."

"You always have."

"Have I? We were on our honeymoon, if you recall, and you couldn't help meddling in a case."

"Meddling?" The word shot out of Kit like a bullet. "Wanda Boswell came to me for help!"

"But you didn't have to take her on as a client, did you?"

"No, but I thought she needed my help."

"Just like that prostitute who needed help right after our wedding. Kit, someone is always going to need your help."

"Isn't that why I have been called to practice law?"

"Are you so sure about that now? Called? By God? Or is there another call you're not hearing?"

Stunned, Kit stepped backward toward the window. "I don't know . . . what to say."

"Isn't that a first."

She stiffened.

"I want you to think long and hard about this," Ted said. "I want you to pray about it. I want you to search the Scriptures and your heart. And I want to be part of your decision because I want to be part of your life. And not the smallest part."

"But you are never—"

"Will you hand this trial over to someone else? Earl Rogers perhaps?"

"Ted, I'm in the middle of—"

"The trial hasn't started yet, you can do it."

"No, it wouldn't be right."

"According to whom? Kit Shannon?"

"Fox," she said softly.

Ted's face hardened. "Think about what I've said. Give me at least that courtesy." He started for the door.

"Ted, wait."

"I will see you at home," he said. "That is, if you get your work done." And then he was gone.

The clamor of the street suddenly seemed louder to Kit, making thoughts about anything a nearly impossible task. Kit closed the window and sat down, determined to pray.

She had to fight herself to do it. Her mind was whirling. This was something she was not used to. Almost always she could, by force of will, whip her thoughts into line. But they were not lining up now.

What was happening? And why was this happening in the middle of a case?

What was God trying to tell her?

Part Two

27

THERE WAS NOT AN EMPTY SPACE in the entire court-room. The gallery had been stuffed with as many chairs as could be accommodated without turning it into a solid sea of wood. A small ribbon of floor across the back was enough for at least ten people to stand and watch, so long as they did not lean too far forward. A narrow aisle down the middle had been rendered even smaller by the addition of other chairs, so that the bailiffs or anyone else would have to walk almost sideways to get to the rail that divided the gallery from the lawyers.

Once again Kit Shannon Fox was going to trial.

Even with the window open and sea air wafting in, the court-room had become quite hot, especially for February. Kit was glad she had worn her summer suit—pale blue linen trimmed with cream lace. Under the circumstances she felt relatively comfortable, more comfortable than the eager newsmen who seemed to sweat with every swipe of their pencils.

Wanda looked pale in her beige cotton skirt and shirtwaist, which Kit had brought to her the night before fresh from the laundress. Her expression was flushed and her eyes heavy-lidded. Kit put a hand on Wanda's arm, trying to be reassuring. But how much assurance could she give to a client who had been such a burden? Kit wondered what the jury was going to think of Wanda Boswell;

her dazed look would engender either sympathy or disquiet among the men in the jury box.

Corazón, sitting in the third chair at the counsel table as Kit's investigator, was the only one who seemed at all serene.

Over the course of the last several days Kit and Corazón had spent long hours preparing the law and the facts of the case. The problem was that the facts were lean, with virtually everything pointing toward Wanda Boswell, thus leaving Kit feeling less confident than at any other time since her first courtroom battle.

For one thing, Kit did not know if she could put Wanda on the stand to testify on her own behalf. She would be confronted by Fielding Hardy—who had her diary in hand, though the judge had not yet ruled on its admissibility—and perhaps a witness or two about something shocking Wanda had failed to reveal to Kit.

In the face of all the evidence, the jury would want to hear her side of things. But Kit was not confident in Wanda's ability to tell the straight truth.

This case was going to come down to a matter of reasonable doubt. In several past cases Kit had been able to produce evidence exonerating her client; this time she would have to convince the jury to take seriously the presumption of evidence, the burden of proof, and the concept of reasonable doubt.

And she would begin the process of educating the jury immediately. Jury selection was about to begin.

Hovering over all of this was a veil that seemed to have been hung between her and Ted. They had not been explicit about her continuing to represent Wanda; it was more like an agreement of silence. Ted had not pressed the subject of her leaving the case, and she had not brought it up.

It was only a few days ago that they had said anything to each other about the trial, and even then their words were terse, as though both of them were afraid a single wrong sentiment might tear the delicate fabric of their marriage.

Kit had not so much made a decision to stay on as Wanda's lawyer as she had let the status remain. Each day closer to trial seemed to her a sign, almost, that she was to continue.

She made every effort to be the dutiful wife at home, seeing to household matters and accounts as best she could while at the same time preparing for the trial.

Two days ago she stopped short and wondered if she was fooling herself. Was it possible that remaining on this case and being the sort of wife Ted wanted were two desires that could never merge into one?

Then, when it became clear the trial would begin with Kit still involved, Ted told her to do what she thought was best. He tried hard to sound supportive, but there was still a coolness to his words that Kit felt and yet chose to ignore.

But now the judge was on the bench, causing Kit to bring herself back to the present. For she had a small bombshell of her own.

"If Your Honor please," Kit said as soon as the judge called the case of *The People of the State of California versus Wanda Boswell.* "I would like to make a motion that the prosecution be removed from this case."

A dull murmur rippled through the courtroom. Judge Clarence Hardy sat up indignantly. "On what grounds?"

"On the ground of misconduct in an attempt to influence potential jurors."

Fielding Hardy slammed his hand on the counsel table so hard that the contents of a glass of water sloshed over, wetting some papers. "That is an outrageous accusation!"

"You had better have some facts to back up this claim," the judge said.

"I do, Your Honor. I should like to call a witness."

"I object," Fielding Hardy said. "You can't allow this, Your Honor."

"Approach the bench, the both of you."

Apparently what the judge wanted to say next he didn't want the reporters, or anyone else, to hear. He waved away the court reporter. This was going to be off the record.

"Now see here, Mrs. Fox," the judge said with barely concealed ire. "What sort of stunt is this?"

"I do not conduct stunts in court, Your Honor. I am in earnest."

"This man has a reputation. Are you out to ruin it?"

"I am trying to get at the truth here."

"I flatly deny any wrongdoing. Clarence, call this off right now—"

The judge motioned for silence. "I want you to select a jury and get on with the trial. At this late date—"

"Your Honor, I have made a motion on the record. I am entitled under the code to make an offer of proof. I am prepared to do so. If I am denied, that is grounds for reversal. You know that."

"I know no such thing."

"Besides, you would not want the newspapers to get the impression that you are protecting a family member, would you? That kind of small-town intrigue is frowned upon these days, especially by those who are searching for a new port of Los Angeles."

As she expected, both judge and prosecutor were momentarily stunned. Kit saw the judge's cheeks turn rosy. "You two get back to counsel table."

When they did, the judge said, "Back on the record now. I deny your motion, Mrs. Fox. Will there be anything else?"

"Exception," Kit said.

"Noted for the record," Judge Hardy said. "Is there—"

"I move for Your Honor to recuse himself. Conflict of interest with the prosecution."

Judge Hardy's face was aflame. "Denied!"

"Exception."

"Noted!"

"I am ready to select a jury, Your Honor."

"That is a relief!" Judge Hardy said, to the sound of laughter in the court.

———

Fielding Hardy questioned the first twelve men called to the witness box. Three of these men knew him personally. Even so, he asked them if they could be fair and impartial, and of course they answered in the affirmative.

When Kit asked that the judge dismiss the three for cause, he refused. That meant Kit would have to use three of her peremptory challenges—which enabled a lawyer to excuse jurors without any cause other than that the lawyer wanted them gone—if she wanted to clear the jury box of friends of the prosecutor.

Next it was Kit's turn to question the potential jurors. She went straight to the law. She did it by selecting individual jurors to serve as sounding boards, enabling her to instruct them in the law before the case began.

To potential juror number seven, she asked, "Sir, do you believe in the presumption of innocence as guaranteed every single accused person in our system of justice?"

The older man, who was a local merchant, nodded. "Yep, I do, ma'am."

"As you look at my client, Wanda Boswell, right now sitting here in court, is she guilty or innocent as far as you're concerned?"

"Why, I don't know that yet. I won't know it until I hear the evidence."

"Ah, but, sir, the answer is that she's *innocent.* Right now, she is presumed to be innocent of any crime whatsoever. Even though someone is arrested and placed on trial, that person remains innocent until proven guilty beyond a reasonable doubt. Do you agree that that's the law?"

The merchant squinted and seemed to be getting the concept. "Well, I guess that is the law."

"Will you then pledge to follow the law when you go to deliberate a verdict?"

"Sure I will."

Kit turned to another juror, number three, a shoemaker. "Sir, will you pledge, if you are a juror in this case, to hold the prosecutor to his burden of proof?"

The man nodded.

"And when the judge tells you that the law says the burden must be overcome by proof 'beyond a reasonable doubt and to a moral certainty,' will you hold to that standard?"

Again he nodded.

"If you go back into that jury room and there is a doubt in your mind about the guilt of my client, even if the other eleven jurors are against you, will you pledge to hold your ground?"

The man looked uncertain.

"What I mean, sir, is that we demand a unanimous verdict from our juries, to protect the accused. And no one juror is any more or less important than another. So if you truly have a reasonable doubt, you are duty bound to hold to it, no matter what the pressure brought to bear."

At this point Fielding Hardy, who had been laudably silent up to now, stood to offer an objection. "I believe that Mrs. Fox is now taking on the role that Your Honor fulfills, with her instructing on the law rather than questioning these men as to their objectivity."

"If Your Honor believes I have said anything at all in error," Kit said carefully, "please set these gentlemen straight."

Fielding Hardy flushed a bit at that, and the judge did not immediately speak. Kit thought the two of them had just been backed into a nice little corner.

"Of course I cannot do that, Mrs. Fox," the judge said. "You have not misstated the law. However, I must ask that you allow me to instruct them on the law at the end of the testimony."

"I would not have it any other way," Kit said. "Now, if I can get the assurance of these men that they will follow Your Honor's instructions, I will be satisfied."

And she did get a pledge—from every juror left in the jury box. Between them, Kit and Fielding Hardy excused ten jurors.

It was time for opening statements.

"Gentlemen of the jury, the evidence in this case will show that on the night of January sixth, aboard the cruiser *Majestic,* a young man of great promise named Chilton Boswell was deliberately taken from this sphere of life by the hand of a murderess, the one who sits at yonder table, Wanda Boswell."

Fielding Hardy pointed a trembling finger at Wanda, as if his prosecutorial hand shook with the collective outrage of all mankind. Hardy was nothing if not a showman.

"The evidence will show that on the night in question, Mrs. Boswell poisoned a bottle of champagne, lacing it with arsenic, allowing her new husband to drink his own death where he sought only to celebrate his wedding."

Kit stood up, reluctant to object during an opening statement, but feeling she had to say something now. "Your Honor, there can be no evidence as to what was in the mind of the deceased. We do not know, and we will never know, what was in Chilton Boswell's mind at the time of his death. I would ask that the court instruct the prosecutor to stay within the bounds of admissible evidence."

"The prosecutor is doing just fine, Mrs. Fox. I am sure that the jury will do as they have been instructed and listen only to the evidence that is admitted."

Kit nodded and sat down. At least she had served notice that she was not going to let Fielding Hardy stray too far from proper argument.

Hardy continued for another fifteen minutes, at times gesticulating wildly with theatrical indignation. When he sat down he was sweating profusely and mopped his brow with a handkerchief.

Though Kit did not have to make an opening statement at this point, she decided to do it anyway. She stood and faced the jury with the resolve to make her statement brief and to the point.

"Gentlemen, you have all sworn under the law to do your duty as jurors and listen to the evidence with an open mind. Your duty to follow the law means that you cannot convict unless you are convinced beyond a reasonable doubt and to a moral certainty that my client is guilty. The evidence that the prosecutor will be presenting to the court will not overcome his burden of proof. Therefore, when you go to deliberate, your duty will be to return a verdict of not guilty. Thank you."

28

DR. EMIL NOVAK WAS the first witness for the prosecution.

"You were the ship's doctor aboard the *Majestic* during the fated voyage, is that correct?" Fielding Hardy asked.

"Yes."

"And on the morning of January seventh, were you summoned by Captain Raleigh to a certain stateroom?"

"I was."

"Please tell the jury why."

The doctor looked at the jurors. "I was told by a steward that there was an urgent matter and that the captain wished to see me in stateroom A-204. I went immediately. Inside I was greeted by the captain and Mrs. Fox. Oh, and a body on the floor."

"Whose body was lying on the floor?"

"Mr. Chilton Boswell, a guest."

"Then what did you do?"

"I made an examination of the body."

"Did you reach any conclusion as to cause of death?"

"I only ventured an opinion that the man had been poisoned. The condition of his esophagus and skin were two of the things I relied upon. But I knew also that an autopsy would be the only sure way to make a determination."

"Thank you, Doctor."

Hardy sat down.

"Doctor," Kit said, "did you tell anyone aboard the ship that you thought Chilton Boswell was poisoned?"

"Why, no. That would have been a breach of my ethical duties."

"Thank you."

Kit took her seat, leaving Fielding Hardy to call his next witness.

Her name was Ada Dimble, and she looked like everyone's favorite grandmother. As the old, neatly dressed woman made her way to the stand, Kit felt Wanda's hand on her arm.

"She looks familiar," Wanda whispered.

Fielding Hardy placed his thumbs under his suspenders and began questioning the witness as if welcoming a family member to the old cracker barrel. "Mrs. Dimble, would you kindly tell the jury how it is you found yourself aboard the *Majestic* on this cruise to the Hawaiian Islands?"

"I would be happy to." Mrs. Dimble nodded toward the twelve jurors. They looked back at her with benign expressions. She might have been the kindly mother to a few of them, and grandmother to a few others. "It was my daughter, Fiona, who urged the trip on me. She said I had not been on a trip since my dear husband passed. Mr. Dimble and I were married nearly fifty years, you know. Would have celebrated our golden anniversary just last year, June the twenty-fourth. I was a June bride, you know. We thought that June would be a lovely month because my flowers . . . I garden, you know—"

"Mrs. Dimble."

"Yes?"

"Your daughter urged you to take the cruise and that is what you did?"

"Oh yes, yes. And it was a glorious trip. Except for the unpleasantness, of course."

"By which you are referring to the murder of Chilton Boswell?"

"Objection," Kit said. "Your Honor, Mr. Hardy is assuming as fact the very issue in this case. We know only that Chilton Boswell was found dead aboard the ship. Whether he was murdered or not is a question for the jury to decide, not the prosecutor."

Judge Hardy said, "All right, I will sustain the objection. The prosecutor will choose his words more carefully for the time being."

And Kit thought, *For the time being? So he may be less careful in the future?*

"Let me rephrase the question for you, Mrs. Dimble. When you mentioned the unpleasantness aboard the *Majestic,* to what were you referring?"

"Why, the murder."

The courtroom burst into laughter. The jury seemed to enjoy the moment as well. Kit waited for the judge to gavel the chamber into order before moving to strike the answer.

Judge Hardy shook his head. "The witness gave her answer and I'll let it stand. As you say, Mrs. Fox, the jury can sort this out."

Fielding Hardy and the judge both looked pleased. The prosecutor continued his examination as if the entire episode had been scripted for the theater. "Let us return to the, as you said, unpleasantness. You had a stateroom on the first-class deck, is that correct?"

"My daughter insisted that I travel in the first-class compartments, you see. I argued with her at the time. I'm a modest woman by nature and not given to ostentation. Perhaps that is because I was brought up on a farm, in Iowa you see—"

"Mrs. Dimble."

"—where we got by on very little. Yes?"

"Can you tell us where your room was located, in relation to the *unpleasantness?*"

"Oh yes. I was next door to the young man and the murderess."

Kit shot to her feet. "If Your Honor please! I move that the witness's answer be stricken and the jury instructed to disregard it." She knew full well the jury would not be able to forget what she was now calling attention to. The proverbial cat was out of the bag. But at least she could argue, by way of the objection, that the witness and prosecution were biased. Maybe the jury would begin to understand that.

To her surprise, Judge Hardy sustained the objection. "I will remind the gentlemen of the jury that the issue of murder is for you to decide when all of the evidence has come in. And Mrs. Dimble, please refrain from using the term *murder* when referring to the incident in question, or to the defendant. Is that clear?"

"Why, what should I say? That young man was murdered, wasn't he?"

Kit tried to control her emotions. This would have been comical had it not been a trial involving a young woman's life. "Your Honor, perhaps we should recess in order for you to instruct the witness regarding what the law requires of her. She continues to prejudice this jury and—"

"I don't need a lecture, Mrs. Fox."

Oh, but you do. A long one. "I assure the court I am only trying to keep this trial from turning into a sideshow."

"Now that's a loaded word if I ever heard one!" Fielding Hardy slapped his sides.

The judge put his hands up. "Now, now. Let us try to get through this witness in good order. Mr. Prosecutor, you will keep your questions short and to the point. And, Mrs. Dimble, please try to answer only the questions you are asked."

Ada Dimble looked consternated. "That is why I am here, isn't it? I was told that I was to stick to the story."

Fielding Hardy cleared his throat. "If I may, Mrs. Dimble. Please tell us what you know. You were next door to the defendant and Mr. Boswell?"

"Yes, I was."

"Did you have any conversations with them?"

"I did not. I believe they were on their honeymoon, and you know how young people in love prefer things, don't you?" Ada Dimble smiled and cocked her head at Fielding Hardy. "Yet I was not certain how this couple regarded each other."

"Why do you say that, Mrs. Dimble?"

"Because of the arguments."

"You heard the defendant and Mr. Boswell argue?"

"My, yes. Voices raised. Such words."

"Can you describe what was said? Were you able to hear clearly?"

"Quite clearly. My sense of hearing is something the good Lord gave to me, and it is still working to this day."

"I see. Now then, what was said, as best as you can remember?"

"Oh, I remember the young woman over there"—Mrs. Dimble pointed at Wanda—"shouting that her husband should stop his gambling. And he answered her that he would do as he pleased, because that was his right to. And I heard the young woman shout at him that she could get even angrier and he would not like that one bit."

"Did you hear anything else?"

"I heard the young man say that his wife was a dangerous woman."

Wanda leaned over to Kit and whispered, "This is all lies."

Kit patted Wanda's hand, not sure whom to believe. Wanda, she knew now, was not prone to tell the whole truth herself.

"Was it your impression, Mrs. Dimble, that Chilton Boswell was somewhat afraid of what his wife might do?"

"Objection. That question asks for an opinion only. Irrelevant and immaterial."

"Overruled."

Fielding Hardy said, "You may answer."

"Yes, he did seem to be afraid of her. Judging by what happened he had good cause, did he not?"

Kit could only shake her head.

"On the night Mr. Boswell met his demise, do you recall hearing anything in the adjoining room?"

"It seems to me that Mr. Boswell entered rather late in the evening."

"How did you know it was Mr. Boswell?"

"I heard the door close rather abruptly, and then I heard him clear his throat."

"Did you hear anything else?"

"I heard the sound of glass against glass, as if one were pouring spirits from a bottle into a drinking glass. It makes a rather familiar sound."

"I see. Did you hear anything after that?"

"Why, no. All seemed quiet after that."

"Deathly quiet?"

"Oh yes."

With that, Fielding Hardy turned Mrs. Dimble over to Kit.

KIT KNEW SHE WOULD HAVE to tread carefully. Earl Rogers had told her that the two most difficult witnesses to cross-examine were children and older women. The jury did not like to see such witnesses badgered.

She approached Ada Dimble slowly and began asking her questions in a soft, deferential voice. This was also the best way to get information from an opposing witness, answers that could be brought up later in closing argument. Kit had seen Earl Rogers skewer witnesses before, but some of his best results were obtained when witnesses fell under his spell and were coaxed into seemingly innocuous admissions. Only when Rogers wove them into the tapestry of his closing argument did their devastating effect on the prosecutor's case become clear.

So it would be here, that is, if Kit did her job.

"Mrs. Dimble, do you recall the judge instructing you to answer only the questions the prosecutor asked?"

"Why, yes. That was only a few moments ago, wasn't it?"

"That is for you to answer."

"Yes."

"Your Honor, I would like to have the court reporter refer back to that exchange and read Your Honor's admonition, and also the reply of the witness. May we hear it?"

The judge nodded to the court reporter, a young man in a

brown suit and bow tie. He flipped back through his shorthand pad until he found the passage. "Question: 'Now, now. Let us try to get through this witness in good order. Mr. Prosecutor, you will keep your questions short and to the point. And, Mrs. Dimble, please try to answer only the questions you are asked.' Answer: 'That is why I am here, isn't it? I was told that I was to stick to the story.'" The reporter readied his pad once again.

"Do you recall giving that answer?" Kit asked the witness.

"Of course I do. I was sitting right here, you know."

"Who was it who told you to 'stick to the story'?"

"Why, that nice Mr. Hardy."

A ripple of laughter issued from the gallery.

"The prosecutor?"

"Yes."

"You met with him before testifying?"

Fielding Hardy objected. "This is all privileged information, Your Honor."

"On the contrary," Kit said. "The prosecution does not enjoy any legal privilege with a witness. What was discussed before Mrs. Dimble's testimony is relevant to this whole issue of bias."

"Then I object on the grounds of hearsay, Your Honor."

Kit shook her head. "The hearsay rule does not apply when the statements are introduced in an effort to understand the witness's state of mind. I want to know what Mrs. Dimble thought when the prosecutor told her to stick to the story. What story was she told? Why didn't the prosecutor tell her to stick to the *facts*?"

"Isn't this a quibble?" Judge Hardy asked. "Story? Facts? All the same."

"Words matter, Your Honor. I should like to ask the witness to explain why she used the word *story*." In the lull that followed, Kit quickly added, "I would like to know if the prosecutor tried to influence this witness by telling her what the story was supposed—"

"That is enough, Mrs. Fox. I am going to sustain the objection."

"Then I will ask the witness this way. Did you meet with the prosecutor before today to discuss your testimony?"

"Same objection, Your Honor."

"I am not asking for the words used," Kit said. "Surely the jury should know if there was a meeting between the prosecutor and a key witness."

"I sustain the objection," Judge Hardy said sharply. "And the jury is to disregard the comments of the counsel for the defense. You are not to draw any conclusions one way or the other."

Kit knew they would anyway. It was time to move on.

"You mentioned your reasons for taking this cruise. Your daughter, I believe, encouraged you?"

"Yes, that is correct."

"And you had recently lost your husband?"

Mrs. Dimble nodded forlornly. "My dear, departed Felix."

"Married for nearly fifty years?"

"Oh yes, glorious years they were, too. We met in the great state of Michigan, you know—"

"Excuse me, Mrs. Dimble. May I ask, was there ever a cross word in your marriage?"

"Why, of course, dear. Aren't you married?"

The courtroom became an echo chamber of laughter once again. Kit did not mind. The exchange seemed to give Fielding Hardy some satisfaction, which was probably why he did not object.

"So Mr. Dimble and you, on occasion, had words?"

"Oh yes, we did. Mr. Dimble could shout something fierce. It was like a force of nature. Have you ever been in a tornado?"

"But you were never afraid of him, were you?"

"Oh, there may have been times—"

"Never to the point of fearing for your life, however."

"Oh my, no."

Kit nodded. "Now, on the night you say you heard someone enter the Boswell stateroom, with a door closing abruptly, with a man clearing his throat, you do not know who that man was, do you?"

"Why, it was the nice young man who was murdered."

Kit pursed her lips but decided not to ask the judge to admonish the witness again. She had a more important path to trod. And part of that was a path in front of the jury box.

"You did not see him, did you?"

"How could I, young woman? I was in my own room."

"Precisely. You assumed it was Chilton Boswell."

"Who else would it be?"

"You did not hear his voice, did you?"

"No, I—"

"So you do not know if this was a steward or someone else who may have entered the room, do you?"

"But I heard the pouring of champagne."

Kit stopped pacing in front of the jury box. She could feel the eyes of twelve men on her. "You did not mention that it was champagne in your direct testimony."

"Didn't I?"

"Shall I have the reporter read back the testimony?"

"That will not be necessary," Fielding Hardy said. "The witness may have heard about the champagne bottle by reading about it in the papers. It is not necessary to our case that she know what it was being poured, only that she heard the sound."

"I thank my learned counsel for his closing argument." Kit stared at the judge. "But it would be more proper if he lodged an objection."

"Continue your questioning, Mrs. Fox." The judge was beginning to look impatient.

"Mrs. Dimble, you say that you heard the clinking of glass and the pouring of a drink?"

"Yes, of that I am certain."

"Because of your God-given sense of hearing?"

"Oh yes."

"Even through the wall of your stateroom?"

"Why, I . . . that is, yes, I heard it, and that's all I know."

"Might you have had occasion to put your ear to the wall?"

Mrs. Dimble was not good at hiding her secrets. Kit, who was using a soft voice for her questions, was content to let the jury see the change in Mrs. Dimble's countenance. The elderly woman blinked several times and put her hand to her mouth. She seemed to be thinking, *How did you know that?*

"Is that so wrong?" she said finally.

"Not at all. I merely want the jury to be assured that you truly heard what was going on in the stateroom next to your own. You have told us you have good hearing and that you were close to the wall."

"I heard everything most clearly."

"Thank you. No further questions."

30

"THE PROSECUTION CALLS Professor Aiden Aloysius Faire."

Faire came forward, regal in his bearing, haughty. He was trying to portray an air of extreme confidence. He could have been striding into a hall full of anxious freshmen, all eager to hear his every word. A witness with such confidence could inspire the jury—which was why Kit had prepared a little surprise for Hardy and the professor.

Faire took his stance before the witness stand as the clerk approached him with a Bible. "Place your left hand on the Bible, raise your right hand and—"

"Objection," Kit said.

The judge almost fell off his chair. "Objection to what? The witness has not been sworn."

"Precisely. This witness is an avowed atheist, Your Honor. When he takes the stand you may ask him yourself. His swearing on the Bible and upon an oath before God would be misleading this jury."

The stunned silence in the courtroom was like a tightened fist. Fielding Hardy was speechless, looking to his brother for a favorable ruling of some sort, yet not offering any reason.

"But you cannot—" Judge Hardy stopped himself. "Can you?"

"If Your Honor please, the rules of evidence allow a witness to forgo the traditional oath and merely affirm to tell the truth, the whole truth, and nothing but the truth. I submit that this *requires* a witness affirm to tell the truth if such witness holds to atheism. Perhaps you ought to ask the witness if he believes in the Bible and the oath before God. If he does not, then he must not be allowed the traditional oath."

That brought a quick look of panic to the judge's face. "I shall put it to the witness. Professor, what is your view, sir?"

Faire glared at Kit. "I am a truthful man, and I will so affirm, Your Honor."

"Very well. You may take the stand."

He did, and as Fielding Hardy approached it seemed to Kit both men were seething. A good thing, as anger dulled the mind. Perhaps she could get something near to the truth out of the professor in spite of his resistance.

Fielding Hardy let the anger explode from his voice. "Despite what the clever counsel for the defense has attempted here, you are not an untruthful man, are you?"

"No, I am not. I am a professor of philosophy and ethics. I believe in moral behavior, and telling the truth is moral."

"As we all understand." Hardy nodded with self-satisfaction toward Kit. "Now, sir, you are a professor of philosophy?"

"At the University of Chicago, yes."

"A fine university."

"One of the very best in the country."

"And how long have you been so employed?"

"Ten years."

"And you teach ethics?"

"Yes. That is one of my areas of specialty." He quickly added, "Which includes telling the truth."

"Defense counsel has announced that you are not a theist. Can you explain this to our jury so there will not be any misunderstanding?"

"Of course. While I do not devalue those who hold to religious views, I have strived to establish a basis for ethics that is not dependent upon traditional religion. I believe that the Greeks and others have taught us that human beings may be moral creatures without the aid of religion. It is my desire to teach this to young people so that when they go out into the world, should they not embrace religion, they will be ethical citizens nonetheless."

"A laudable goal, Professor. I'm sure we would all agree."

Not all, Kit thought.

"What brought you out to our neck of the woods?"

"I came to deliver a series of lectures."

"And how did you come to the *Majestic* and the cruise to Hawaii?"

"I thought it would be a capital way to relax after an arduous trip out here, and in between my series. I had been working hard on a new book before coming out here and thought the rest would do me good. I had never been to Hawaii."

"Did you have a meeting with Chilton Boswell before the trip?"

Faire looked at Kit as he answered. "The young man, a nice young chap I might add, sought me out after a lecture. He wished to talk to me about writing a book of his own. Many young people these days wish to write. They see it as a glamorous pursuit. It is hard work, I may assure you."

"When did this meeting take place, Professor?"

"Oh, I would say two or three days before the trip."

"And where did you meet?"

"At a watering hole in Los Angeles, somewhere on Main Street I believe it was. Yes."

"So did you offer advice to Mr. Boswell?"

"Indeed I did. I told him that writing was hard work and that he should be careful to give it his best effort. I also warned him it was not the quick way to riches. I rather had the impression he wished to make money in order to satisfy the demands of his new wife."

"What gave you that impression?"

"I must object, Your Honor." Kit stood. "This trial should be about the facts and not the impressions of a witness. His speculations about my client are irrelevant and immaterial."

"Overruled."

Kit was beginning to burn inside. "I take exception."

"Noted for the record," the judge said curtly. "Continue the examination."

"You may answer," Fielding Hardy said.

"Mr. Boswell was quite open with me about his new wife's demand for money and the finer things in life. He felt a bit of pressure to please her, though I also got the impression she was not easily pleased."

"Now, I'm certain that the learned counsel for the defense would like to ask you about a certain incident aboard the ship on the way back from Hawaii. I refer to your being found in the Boswell stateroom after the murder. Would you like to explain that to the jury?"

"Certainly. As I told Captain Raleigh and Mrs. Fox herself at the time, Mr. Boswell owed me a sum of money that arose out of a session of poker aboard the ship. While I do not condone my actions entirely, I removed nothing from the room and indeed have cooperated with the authorities on the investigation into the murder."

"Thank you for your forthrightness. I am sure not even a Christian can say that she is without sin." Fielding Hardy smirked at Kit. To the witness he said, "Did you have any animosity toward Mr. Boswell?"

"Not at all. He seemed a man with everything to live for, cut down in the bloom of life."

Fielding Hardy turned to Kit. "Your witness."

Kit was on her feet in an instant. She did not want to give Faire time to breathe, and she wanted the jury to know she meant business.

"When did you decide to take this cruise to Hawaii, Professor Faire?"

"When?"

"What day?"

"I would have to think about that."

"Please do."

"All right." Faire looked up slightly as he cogitated. "Just after I arrived in Los Angeles, previous to my first lecture at the University of Southern California, which was December fourteenth. I saw an advertisement in the paper."

"Which paper was that, do you recall?"

"I believe it was the *Examiner*."

"I see. And you booked passage shortly thereafter?"

"Within days, yes."

"Is it fair to say that it was at least before December twentieth?"

"Oh yes."

"And your meeting with Chilton Boswell, the one where he sought you out for writerly advice, was only two or three days before the trip?"

"Yes."

"Don't you find it quite a coincidence, Professor, that the man who sought you out in Los Angeles just before your passage was also booked on the same cruise to Hawaii?"

Faire paused before answering. "Life, I have come to see, is full of coincidences. Some happy, some sad. That is what the world is like."

"A world without God?"

"Precisely."

"Let us talk a bit about your teaching, sir. You have stated that you are a professor of philosophy at the University of Chicago, is that correct?"

"Correct."

"Is that a full professorship?"

"Of course."

"My assistant, Corazón Chavez, who is sitting at the counsel table, contacted the University of Chicago. Is it not true that for the last two years you have taught only an introduction to philosophy to the freshman class?"

Faire raised his imposing eyebrows. "What of it?"

"Should not a full professor of philosophy be teaching more classes and at a higher level?"

"Young woman, you have no idea what intrigue there is on occasion at the university level. That I have a dispute with some within the academia is not relevant to our task here, is it?"

"I must agree," Fielding Hardy said. "Your Honor, I find this entire line of questioning to be irrelevant."

"I will show the relevance," Kit said. "Professor Faire has testified about certain matters, which, if they are shown to be less than factually presented, will reflect upon this witness's credibility."

"My credibility is unquestioned!"

"How many books have you written?"

Judge Hardy rapped his gavel on the bench. "I have not made a ruling, Mrs. Fox. Of what relevance is it regarding how many books the professor has written?"

"He testified that he was hard at work on a new book when he came to Los Angeles. I would like to know how many other books he has written."

"I can see no harm in answering that one question," the judge said.

But Professor Faire looked as if it were a hard question indeed. He pulled at the knot of his tie.

"You may answer," Kit said.

"I merely said I was at work upon a new book. It will be my first book—that makes it new."

"Is it unusual for a full professor of ten years not to have written a book?"

"Not if his teaching duties demand most of his time."

"Is the teaching of a freshmen class a heavy demand upon one's time?"

"That depends upon the freshmen." Professor Faire was pleased when his line garnered some laughs.

Kit suddenly felt a little light-headed. The courtroom was stuffy, no doubt about that. What was immediately troubling to Kit was the thought that Faire was doing very well under cross-examination. She needed to be at her very best with him. There was something in his story that did not ring true, and she was sure she could find the weaknesses if she were able to continue.

"Do you have another question for the witness?" Judge Hardy's voice broke in.

Kit was not sure how long she had been standing there, silent.

"Your Honor, I will cease questioning at this time but would request that you make this witness subject to recall."

The judge nodded. "Professor, you are subject to recall during the defense case. I admonish you not to discuss your testimony with any other witness."

"You mean I must come back here?"

"That is what I mean, sir."

"Quite inconvenient!"

With a sniff, the judge said, "The law is often inconvenient." He looked at Kit in a way that made her feel she was an inconvenience to the judge—but that he was giving her more favorable rulings because he knew she would appeal.

As Faire stepped down, grumbling something to himself, Kit edged back to the defense table. She needed a drink of water.

"Call Mrs. Glenna Boswell," Fielding Hardy said.

31

GLENNA BOSWELL WAS SURELY GOING to be one of the keys to this trial. Since the preliminary hearing, she would have been thoroughly prepared by Fielding Hardy for her testimony in trial.

Hardy called her to the stand as his next witness. As in the preliminary hearing, Mrs. Boswell had dressed herself for show. Her hat was enormous—black mohair felt with six white, uncurled ostrich feathers emerging from a velvet ornament in the front. Her gown of black crepe voile with scalloped collar was sweeping in its majesty even as it gave a silent testimony to her mourning. Kit wondered if some of the men in the jury box would be reaching for their handkerchiefs soon. She would have to tread carefully when she cross-examined.

"Are you quite comfortable, Mrs. Boswell?" Fielding Hardy said to her after she had taken the oath and was seated in the witness chair.

"As comfortable as a mother grieving can be, I suppose."

"As it is rather warm today, if you need to take a short pause or would like a glass of water, do not hesitate to request it."

"Thank you." She looked at the prosecutor with large and grateful eyes.

"You are the mother of the deceased, Chilton Boswell?"

"Yes, I am."

"Will you please tell the jury about your son?"

Kit decided not to object as she knew the judge would allow this line of questioning as he had during the preliminary hearing. She would wait until cross-examination to suggest gently that Mrs. Boswell was not the most objective of witnesses when it came to her son.

Glenna Boswell proceeded to repeat much of the same information she had recounted in the preliminary hearing, adding several sniffles and a few tears as she did so. Kit could almost feel the heat coming from Wanda. She hoped the jury would not see her client's seething anger.

"It was not your desire to see your son married to the defendant, was it?" Fielding Hardy said when he resumed questioning.

"It was not."

"Please tell us why."

"I don't believe she loved my son. I believe she saw him as a way to gain money and influence. She is, after all, only a dancer of the most disreputable sort."

"Your Honor, I must object." Kit could take it no longer. "What the witness believed has no bearing upon this case. What my client does in the arts or any other human endeavor has nothing to do with the facts that the jury must find in order to return a verdict—"

"Mrs. Fox," the judge began, "you may state your grounds without—"

"—and I must ask Your Honor to keep this trial from becoming a carnival of inadmissible statements and speculations—"

"—making any speeches."

"—that will prevent my client from receiving a fair trial."

The judge banged his gavel on the bench. "That will be enough, Mrs. Fox."

Not nearly enough, Kit thought. She would be making more speeches like this if the trial continued in the same way. She might receive a contempt citation, but that was a risk she would take to keep the Hardy brothers from running roughshod over her client and the Constitution.

She was also playing to the newspapermen, who were anxiously recording as much of this exchange as they could. The judges at the appellate level would be reading about what went on here and getting a bit of a different account than the raw record might reveal.

Perhaps aware of what she was up to, Judge Hardy said, "Let us try to conduct this trial with all of the professional decorum the law requires. I'm going to direct the reporter to strike the last answer of the witness and instruct the prosecutor to ask only questions about the facts. I will, of course, allow a grieving mother to express herself on occasion. The court is not without a heart."

Clever. The judge was implying to the jury that Kit was the one without a heart. The Hardy brothers were a formidable team indeed.

"Very well," Fielding Hardy said. "Will you please tell the jury what you heard the defendant, Wanda Boswell, say to your son, the deceased Chilton Boswell, on the afternoon of December twentieth of last year?"

"I most certainly will."

Glenna Boswell turned to face the jury. No doubt Fielding Hardy had told her to do so. It was an effective tactic. Almost all witnesses looked at the lawyer as they answered questions. Her turning to the jury gave Glenna Boswell a sympathetic position.

"I had returned home from a hard day of shopping. I was therefore not thinking too clearly as I was tired. As a matter of fact I cannot recall what I was wearing that day, nor even what I bought."

Even more clever. Knowing what Kit had shown during the preliminary hearing about Glenna Boswell's selective memory, Fielding Hardy had coached the witness on how to respond to anticipate Kit's cross-examination.

"However, I do remember as clearly as I remember my own name what I heard as I came through the door. The words that Wanda spoke to Chilton were so startling that they are burned into my memory forever. She said, 'I'll see you rot in the ground for that.'"

"Those were her exact words?"

"Exact words."

"Did you have the occasion to confront the defendant about this?"

"I most certainly did. I made my presence known. I walked right into that room and told her there would be no such talk in my house."

"And what was the defendant's reaction?"

"She attacked me."

"That's a lie!" Wanda's words cut through the courtroom like an ax.

Kit's heart almost exploded. Not merely because Wanda's voice had come so unexpectedly beside her, but because Wanda's defense was also about to explode. Even before the judge began his tirade, Kit was trying to get Wanda to sit back down. Her client had jumped to her feet and was practically on top of the counsel table.

"The defendant will be quiet immediately!" the judge shouted, his face red. "Mrs. Fox, you will instruct your client not to speak in this courtroom again unless she is under oath or I speak to her directly. Is that understood?"

"Understood, Your Honor."

"But it is a lie," Wanda repeated to Kit, loud enough for everyone to hear her.

Kit's world began to spin as she gripped Wanda's arm and said, "Be quiet. We will have our chance to cross-examine."

Wanda did not look like she believed Kit. Her eyes began to tear up, and she shook her head. "She wants to bury me."

"I said, be quiet!" Judge Hardy rapped on the bench so loudly with his gavel that it sounded like a rifle shot.

Corazón reached over and tried to calm Wanda down.

Kit addressed the court. "Your Honor, I apologize on behalf of my client, who is distraught. I assure the court this will not happen again."

"I certainly hope not. All right, Mr. Prosecutor. You may resume your questioning."

Fielding Hardy said, "I apologize to you as well, Mrs. Boswell. I know this is most disconcerting for you considering your loss. Are you able to continue?"

"I think so." Glenna Boswell delicately touched her throat.

I am watching Sarah Bernhardt, Kit thought. *This should be captured on film and shown to actresses around the world.*

"Before the interruption," Fielding Hardy said, "you spoke of an attack by the defendant upon your person, is that correct?"

"Yes. I was scared for my very life."

"Did the defendant touch you?"

"Oh yes. Her hands were around my neck and her nails dug into my flesh. I tried to scream but the pressure on my throat did not allow for it."

"And what happened then?"

"Chilton saved my life."

"Thank you, Mrs. Boswell. I know this has been hard for you. I will turn the witness over to Mrs. Fox, and I request that she tread lightly."

Tread lightly indeed. A grieving mother was not a prime witness for strong cross-examination. Kit would have to show gentle inconsistencies that she could open up into large gaps during closing argument.

As she stood, Kit felt as if a huge weight were upon her shoulders, with a vise grip on her head. Was it the way Glenna Boswell was looking at her? With such contempt and resoluteness. Maybe Kit would have to take the velvet glove off after all.

She stopped in the middle of the courtroom. A white light behind her eyes shot down through her body, expanding and then retracting, leaving her weak and nearly senseless.

She fought against it. The room became a blur. She had to stay on her feet, question the witness. The case was in the balance. . . .

Kit turned, unaware of her direction, and the last thing she saw before losing consciousness was the face of Fielding Hardy, not making any move to help her.

32

TED LOOKED UP FROM his ledger. He was almost finished with entering the month's expenses for the Bible Institute, preparing to go home and enjoy a long and leisurely dinner with his wife, when he saw he had an unexpected visitor, brought in on the arm of Reverend Macauley.

"Ted, I would like you to meet Mrs. Henrietta Studdard," Macauley said.

Ted stood and bowed before the woman, whose hat had barely cleared the doorway. Studdard. He had heard that name before.

"You may know that Mrs. Studdard writes a highly regarded column for the *Times*," Macauley explained.

"I know of it," Ted said, "though I must confess I have not kept up on my newspaper reading."

"No matter, dear boy," Mrs. Studdard said. "I write for the young women of the city. In that regard, I see that you do not qualify."

Ted chuckled good-naturedly, wondering why she had come to meet him. Then he found out.

With a Scottish grin, Macauley said, "Mrs. Studdard has become interested in our work and wishes to discuss a donation. As the financial officer, you are the one in a position to help her with the matter."

"Of course," Ted said.

"Then I will leave you to it," Macauley said, bowing out as quickly as a mouse darting into a hole.

"Please have a chair," Ted said.

Mrs. Studdard settled herself into a chair opposite Ted's desk. "I have had the pleasure of making your wife's acquaintance," she said. "We had tea, in fact."

"Tea with my wife? How pleasant."

"I wish I could say it was entirely pleasant." Mrs. Studdard extracted a fan from her handbag and began waving it in front of her face. "Not that she isn't a fetching creature. She is quite lovely."

"Thank you."

"A bit stubborn perhaps, what with that auburn hair and Irish background."

"That is what makes her a good lawyer."

"And that is what I have come to talk with you about."

"I'm sorry," Ted said. "I thought you came to discuss a donation."

"Oh, that." Mrs. Studdard waved the fan dismissively. "Of course. But you must understand my position. You see, I believe that the Lord must be honored by where I place, as a gift, a portion of what he has blessed me with."

Ted nodded. "We at the Institute would not have it any other way."

"I am so glad to hear you say that, which brings me back to the matter of your wife."

"I am afraid I don't understand."

"I shall endeavor to explain. I believe it is in the best interest of the home and society that domestic roles are clearly defined in the eyes of God. God ordained that the family should consist of a wife and mother at home and a man earning the money to till the soil, as it were. And if you should be blessed with children, then they deserve to have all of these things provided them."

Ted leaned back in his chair, which creaked loudly. "I'm not entirely in disagreement with that sentiment, Mrs. Studdard, but Kit and I share a rather unique view. Both of us feel that God has called us to unique pursuits. Kit to the law and myself to the air."

"What about children?"

"I suppose that is a bridge we will cross when we come to it."

Mrs. Studdard snapped her fan closed and slapped it on her lap. "These things must be thought of now. Are you going to assume the role of head of the family?"

"Of course, I—"

"If so, are you going to sit your wife down and instruct her that it would be better for her to give up the law now rather than to wait until such time as the two of you begin the godly work of raising a family?"

"I hadn't thought—"

"I well know that, dear boy. Youth does not think much these days. After all, it is 1907, not 1807. The young are restless. But as the voice of experience in these matters, I must say it is imperative to cling to the old ways."

"I will certainly talk this over with Ki—"

"I wish that you would prevail upon her, I do. As someone who has high hopes for the work of the Institute here, I would not want anything to cause my hesitation in giving."

Now Ted was on the verge of being, if not insulted, at least defensive. Not so much for the Institute, but for Kit. "No one wants you to feel uncomfortable, Mrs. Studdard, of course—"

"It is more than that." She sniffed suddenly. "I simply hate to see this happen to you, dear boy. Believe me, you will feel much better when this decision is reached. Mutually, if need be, for I do advise you to persuade her. It is for your good, and that is what concerns me most."

"As I said, I shall speak with Kit."

"I would be delighted to write about the Institute's support of biblical principles," Mrs. Studdard added.

"That is quite generous. Now, you wished to discuss the specifics of a donation?"

Mrs. Studdard, still smiling, said, "I suppose now I should wait until you have spoken to your wife. That seems the prudent thing to do, does it not?"

San Leandro Clarion

KIT SHANNON FOX SUCCUMBS TO HEAT!
Or was it the pressure of a trial that looks increasingly dire?

Yesterday, in the courtroom of Judge Clarence Hardy, where the murder trial of Wanda Boswell is under way, counsel for the defense, Kit Shannon Fox of Los Angeles, fainted dead away just as she was about to cross-examine a witness. Mrs. Fox was removed from the courtroom on a stretcher and, by order of the judge, taken to the office of Dr. Miles Layton, where she was revived.

Some observers mentioned that it was very hot in the courtroom yesterday. Others, however, noted that the trial had not been progressing well for Mrs. Fox's client. The mother of the decedent, Chilton Boswell, had just completed a compelling and moving direct testimony which all of the jurors seemed to favor. One man even suggested that Mrs. Fox may have engineered or at least welcomed her fainting spell in order to have time to think about what to do at this stage of the trial.

Unavailable for comment, Mrs. Fox is recovering at her home in Los Angeles. The judge ordered all participants to return in two days to his courtroom.

Kit sat up in bed. This was absurd. She had fainted—that was all, and now she was fine. Wasn't she?

The events of the last fifteen hours were a jumble in her mind, and only now was a picture forming of what had happened.

She recalled being revived and helped to a carriage. Still woozy, but with faithful Corazón by her side, she was assisted to the office of a local San Leandro doctor. She thought his name might be Layton. He examined her, and she remembered almost having fainted again, only this time from the thick smell of his cologne.

Perhaps he had noted Kit's reaction and so released her to Corazón's care. The two had taken the train back to Los Angeles and hired a cab to take them to the house, where Kit had managed to get a little sleep.

Now she was feeling fine. Fine! She needed to get back to San Leandro.

It was late morning and she was hungry. Ravenous, in fact. She threw off the covers, got up, and immediately felt light-headed. How long had it been since she'd eaten? And where was Corazón?

Kit ambled toward the door, which opened the moment she reached it.

"Back in bed with you!" Corazón ordered. Someone stood behind Corazón. A man.

"We have to get to work," Kit protested. "We have a trial—"

The man stepped around Corazón and took Kit by the arm. "I do not care about your trial, young woman. You are to get back in that bed this instant."

It was Layton, the doctor. Why was he here?

The room began to spin. It was not a help that the doctor's cologne was just as she had remembered it. Kit sat down. Where was Ted? She needed to talk to him so he wouldn't worry.

"You mustn't be up and about." The doctor helped Kit back to her bed, began smoothing the sheets behind her, fluffing the pillow.

"Doctor, why did you come up to Los Angeles? I have a doctor."

"I wanted to check up on you. Besides, my sister lives nearby. I thought I'd make a day of it. And I thought it important to tell you about your delicate condition."

Kit lay back. "What condition?"

With a broad smile the doctor said, "Why, a baby of course."

The room began spinning even faster now.

The doctor was a nice enough man, but his cologne . . . or was it the baby he just mentioned that was making her feel nauseous? "Baby?" Kit swallowed a gulp of air.

Corazón, beaming like a light, nodded her head vigorously. *"Un bebé! Un día feliz! Un regalo de Dios!"*

Kit felt even dizzier. The news was stunning to her—a surprise, a joyous shock. "Where is Ted?" she asked.

"He is coming," Corazón said.

Kit started to sit up. "I've got to—"

The doctor gently pushed her back down. "I am going to demand that you immediately cease all strenuous activity and remain here at home."

"You don't understand, Doctor. I am in the middle of a trial."

"I am well aware of that, Mrs. Fox. I read the *Clarion.*"

"*Clarion*?"

"You were on the front page this morning."

Kit shook her head. "They don't miss a trick, do they?"

"You are the biggest news to hit San Leandro since the Busby brothers tried to steal a ship back in '89."

Wonderful, Kit thought. *Another rogue for the rogue's gallery.* "But the trial," she said.

"I forbid it," Layton said. "You must understand that you cannot place yourself in that arena of conflict. It simply cannot be done. Not only must you stay off your feet as much as possible, you must avoid the stresses and strains of modern life. We live in an age of rush, rush, rush. A baby cannot be rushed."

"But I am not far along, am I?"

"It does not matter. The situation is fraught with peril."

With a dry throat Kit said, "Might I lose the baby if I continue the trial?"

"Yes. You have taken on an occupation that is more suited to the male of the species. Regardless, any working woman who is with child should cease all efforts and rest. That is what is best. Do you understand me, young woman?"

"But I have a client," Kit said weakly. "In jail."

"I'm sure Judge Hardy will see that a new lawyer is appointed."

"That's what I am afraid of." *A baby. Wonderful news. Right?* Her jaw clenched. *This is wonderful news. Yes, it is.*

Where is Ted?

Lord, what do I do now?

———

Ted lifted Kit's feet and placed them on the ottoman, gently massaging them. It felt good and relieved the tension. The fire in the fireplace was comforting. Outside, the Los Angeles night was peaceful and yet it seemed to hold the threat of rain. Things were cloudy, to be sure, inside as well as out.

Ted was behaving like a mother hen and had been from the time he'd come home. "There. Are you comfortable?"

Kit smiled. "Quite comfortable."

"Angelita is making tea. And I'm here to fulfill your every wish."

Kit thought a moment, then said quite seriously, "Will you run down to Schneider's and bring me back some knockwurst and onions? And some ice cream?"

Without missing a beat, Ted said, "Which one would you like first?"

"Just throw it all in a big bowl together," Kit said, this time only half serious.

"Why don't we start with the tea and make sure you're sane before we do anything else?"

Kit laughed, and it felt good to do so. Yet part of her could not relax, for there were many issues to be resolved within the next two days. The judge was going to want her answer, whether she was going to continue with the trial. She couldn't. The doctor was quite adamant. Even her own doctor had concurred, though with some hedging.

Suddenly, without her even having a chance to give it much thought, it looked as if her legal career might be over. Certainly she was going to fulfill her wifely duties now; certainly she was thrilled to be bringing a new life into the world. It was just so new, the whole train of thought.

The thought troubled her, and she did not like that it did.

But at least she was at home, with Ted. He was glowing with happiness. The news of the baby agreed with him. It seemed to have washed away a whole crust of concerns that had been building around him for the past several weeks.

Ted continued to rub Kit's feet. A delicious feeling, and Kit did not want him to stop.

"What shall we name him?" Ted asked.

"What makes you think we're going to have a boy?"

"I don't know. It just came to me. Any objections?"

"None whatsoever."

"Henry?"

Kit pondered. "Solid, but I'm not quite sure."

"Edward?"

"Edward Fox. That does sound solid."

"George?"

"Solid as well."

Ted looked at the ceiling, his thumbs bringing pure pleasure to Kit's right foot. "I'm not sold on any of those. There are many Henrys and Edwards and Georges. How about Maximilian?"

Kit giggled. "So regal! Is he to be president someday?"

"Of course! But we must be careful not to outweigh our last name. Maximilian Fox. Max Fox. Too many Xs."

"What if, just on the off chance, we have a daughter?"

"Then she will be the prettiest and smartest girl in all of Los Angeles. And we will name her appropriately."

Kit nodded. "Anna? Ruth? Alice?"

Ted paused. "Our daughter is going to be named something that speaks volumes."

"So we are having a daughter after all?"

"You know what? I believe I will let God make the decision."

"He already has."

"Have I told you how happy I am?"

"You don't have to tell me. I can see it."

"That you are now going to be home all the time, resting, and . . ."

He paused, and Kit caught herself in a frown.

At that moment, Angelita entered with the tea. She looked as pleased as Ted did. She was part of the family, of course, and the news of the baby seemed to spark wonderful memories and hopes within her.

"And where is Corazón tonight?" Kit asked Angelita.

"She is with the man she will marry, I think."

"Raul Montoya. The family is getting bigger by the moment, eh?"

Angelita curtsied with a smile and exited the study.

Ted poured tea for the two of them, handed a cup to Kit. After a sip, Ted put his cup down with a startling, or perhaps nervous, *clank*. "Have you thought about who will take over for you?"

There it was, the subject both of them had been avoiding. Kit held her teacup in both hands, feeling the warmth, and not knowing exactly what she was going to say because she herself did not know how she felt about giving up the trial. Finally she said, "There is much to think about."

"What is there to think about, other than who will take over?"

Kit did not have a ready answer for that. What she wanted, what she had been waiting for, for weeks now, was a sign from God. A clear, unambiguous communication, something neither she nor Ted could mistake. If only God used the telephone.

"Ted, I know we have not discussed my future in the law or my continuing this trial. Now is the time. Speak plainly and I will listen."

"Plainly?"

"Please."

Ted stood, somewhat unsteadily at first, as if the weight of what he was about to say was causing him an imbalance. He recovered and leaned on the mantel, a serious look on his face. "Kit, I love you and I'm happy that you are my wife. No, it's more than that. Exceedingly happy in a way that I can hardly express. But I must confess that I do not like what you do. I don't want you to be a lawyer anymore."

She had suspected this was on his mind, but the shock was no less potent.

"You told me to speak plainly," he added quickly.

"But I—"

"Did not mean it?"

Her neck began to tingle, something that happened whenever she became agitated enough. Anger or disquiet, it happened just the same. She wasn't sure which she was yet, only that the conversation was getting heated.

"Ted, you know I mean what I say."

"I know that very well." He laced and unlaced his fingers. "I also know that you have a stubborn streak."

Kit sat up, stiffly, in her chair. "Convictions can seem like stubbornness."

"Convictions can also mislead if they are not firmly checked. You are going to have a baby, Kit. Our baby. That changes everything. That baby will need a mother. You can't think of working outside the home. And to be going to court while you're expecting—"

She heard a knock at the front door. "Who could be coming to see us at this hour?"

Presently, Angelita appeared in the study doorway and announced that Mrs. Studdard wished to call on Kit.

"Show her in," Ted said.

Kit quickly put on her slippers. "What on earth might she want?"

"I think it would be good for you to hear what she has to say. I was speaking to her the other day and—"

"Did you ask her to come here?"

"Ah, children!" Mrs. Studdard waddled into the room, smiling and holding out her gloved hand to Ted. The feathers on her hat trembled. Then she approached Kit with her hands in the air. "Please do not get up, Mrs. Fox. It is well that you are comfortable and in your own home."

"Thank you very much for coming to see me, Mrs. Studdard. Would you like some tea?"

"Delighted." Mrs. Studdard wedged her girth into a chair next to the fire. Ted asked Angelita to bring another cup. "How wonderful it is that you are home at last with your husband by your side. Hearth and home and husband. Are there three more wonderful words for any woman?"

"Not that begin with the letter *H*," Kit said.

"I beg your pardon?"

Kit saw Ted's look of consternation and quickly added, "Yes, I am glad that I am here tonight."

"And here to stay," Mrs. Studdard said. It sounded almost like a command.

"Ted and I were just discussing that."

"Discussing?"

"Yes. Discussing what is best for all concerned."

"Simply that you should be at home now, I am certain of it."

"That seems to be the consensus." Kit looked at Ted, who was looking a little sheepish as he leaned on the mantel.

Mrs. Studdard addressed herself to Ted in an imperial fashion. "I wonder if you would mind leaving us to our girl talk, hmm? There's a dear."

A bit flustered, Ted said, "Yes, of course. May I offer you anything else before I go?"

"No, no. I won't be staying long," Mrs. Studdard said curtly, and with that Ted left the room.

Mrs. Studdard heaved a sigh as she turned toward Kit. "Now, my dear, you cannot have been truly considering continuing with this awful murder trial. Being in the family way and especially after you fainted right in open court."

"Oh, did that news reach Los Angeles already?"

Mrs. Studdard ignored the question. Kit wondered if Mrs. Studdard missed the edge in her voice.

"You are quite inexperienced in these matters, my dear," Mrs. Studdard said. "That is why I consider it my duty to help guide you through this most difficult time."

"I do thank you, though I do not foresee the difficulty—"

"Of course you ought not to lift any heavy objects, but also do not raise your arms too high for any reason. You should not bolt down any stairs or steps, jarring yourself. And you must stay indoors as much as possible. Public show is not a good idea. Also, sleep as much as you possibly can. As for diet—"

"Mrs. Studdard, I—"

"Mind that you do not overindulge on any item, although I can well remember certain urges which overcame me during those times I carried a child."

"May I—"

"Kippers, I recall. Oh yes."

"If I might—"

"Do you like fish, my dear? I should like to know if that is something common among—"

"Mrs. Studdard." Kit stood, causing a look of upset to come upon Mrs. Studdard's face. "I wonder if you would mind terribly if I don't discuss this matter any further at this time. I feel tired and—"

"No, no, I quite understand. I simply wanted to pay my respects and assure you that I will be available to help you, my dear."

More likely to see that I don't do anything you wouldn't approve of. "Thank you, Mrs. Studdard," Kit said. "I shall call on you if I need you."

The older woman set down her teacup, her eyes growing suddenly hard. "See that you do." She stood up. "We all want what is best in the eyes of God, now, don't we?"

Kit's jaw locked down into a polite smile. Her Irish tongue quivered inside her mouth, but Kit held it. "Good evening," was all she said.

33

THE FOLLOWING AFTERNOON, without speaking to any doctors, or even Ted, Kit took the train back to San Leandro. She wanted Wanda to hear the news from her. She owed her that much. And Kit also wanted to make sure that any lawyer who took the case was someone she could trust.

But when she arrived at the jail and got to Wanda's cell, it was Wanda who spoke first.

"Please, Mrs. Fox, don't leave me to no one else!"

Wanda Boswell's eyes were filled with fright and desperation.

"What have you heard?" Kit said.

"The prosecutor—he came in here and told me I was to get another lawyer."

"Fielding Hardy spoke to you?"

Wanda nodded.

"That is absolutely a violation of ethics and the law."

"He said you were going to have a baby. Is that true, Mrs. Fox?"

"Yes."

"That's good news," Wanda said with a downcast face.

"Wanda, there are many fine lawyers who can take your case," Kit said. "I will see to it that, whoever it is, you can depend on that person. I will also see that their fee is taken care of, until such time as you can—"

"I don't want another lawyer! I want you. You are the only one who understands me."

Kit looked at the ground and felt pressure in her chest. Wanda Boswell had not been a good client, but Kit had never dropped out of a case once she'd started. Furthermore, it was not ethical for her to withdraw just because a client proved difficult.

In truth, she did not want to give up this case. Everything inside her was telling her to continue—except that part of her that knew she had to honor her husband's wishes. She also knew that no other lawyer knew this case as thoroughly as she did. Even Earl Rogers said the secret to his success was preparation. Any lawyer would need a great deal of preparation to continue the trial, and Judge Hardy was not likely to grant the time needed.

All that aside, Kit had come here to tell Wanda that she couldn't continue on as her lawyer.

"Mrs. Fox, I've been praying," Wanda said. "I know that God wants you to be my lawyer."

Praying? Wanda?

"Will you trust me?" Kit said.

"Yes," Wanda answered, quickly adding, "if you will stay my lawyer."

"Just trust me in this. I will continue to consider this matter. If you have truly been praying, keep on it."

Wanda nodded. "All right, I will. But I'm going to pray that God tells you to stay!"

———

In her now familiar room at the San Leandro Hotel, Kit prayed. At the open window, looking out at the darkening ocean just beyond the piers, she inquired of God.

Lord, what should I do? I know your holy Word commands that I should honor my husband, that there is no higher calling than to raise up children in the way they should go. I wish to honor you with all of my life. I have tried to do that in the practice of law. I know I have fallen short. But I also know that justice has been done because of

*where you have placed me. All the glory goes to you, my Lord and my
God.*

*I am torn. Please tell me what I should do. I will listen to your
voice and will do your will to the best of my ability. May my life be
one that honors you. I submit myself to you and believe that you will
direct my steps.*

When she had finished her prayer, Kit's cheeks were streaked
with tears. And yet she felt cleansed. She had done what her papa
always said to do: place the burden in the hands of the Lord and
leave it there. He was fond of quoting from the book of James. *"If
any of you lack wisdom, let him ask of God, that giveth to all men
liberally, and upbraideth not; and it shall be given him."* Kit uttered
the next words out loud. " 'But let him ask in faith, nothing waver-
ing. For he that wavereth is like a wave of the sea driven with the
wind and tossed.' "

She would not doubt. When she fell asleep, it was peacefully, as
a little girl in the arms of her father.

And then the dream.

It was 1903 again, and Kit Shannon was fresh off the train at
the Los Angeles depot, new to the law, new to the city, half afraid
of the world she was entering but holding her father's Bible in her
hands as if it were the key to everything.

Aunt Freddy greeted her, took her home. "I know the finest eli-
gible gentlemen in the city, my dear. We will ascertain those of good
breeding and old eastern fortunes, from those of new money and
more ostentatious circumstances. You shall meet them all. And I
daresay, with your looks and my help, you shall have your pick!"

Kit, in the dream, tried to speak but found she couldn't.

"Marriage is the foundation of our civilization, and as pretty as
you are, my dear, still you're no spring chicken. A few more years
of spinsterhood and you'll be expected to dress in black."

But I am marrying Ted Fox! She wanted to scream it in her
dream, but no sound came.

She saw Ted then, the way she first saw him, sitting as he was
on the stairs in Aunt Freddy's house during the introductory party
she'd thrown for Kit.

"We will marry," she said in the dream.

But he ran from the house. Kit followed, running after him in the night, her feet bare, the ground hard and rocky.

He was a shadow racing away from her, faster and faster, until she could not see him anymore.

Then the plane. The monoplane. She saw it up in the night sky, Ted guiding it. But just as quickly, in the way of dreams, it was gone.

Kit tried to cry out but had no voice. She heard the sound of broken wood and wire and knew Ted's plane had crashed.

She ran through the nightscape of her dream and found the wreckage. She tried to call out Ted's name. Then she saw a body. Dead or alive?

Alive. Turning. But not the body of Ted Fox.

The bruised and broken body of Wanda Boswell.

Her eyes were accusing.

And that was when Kit woke up to the dark morning of San Leandro, gasping for air.

Kit was jittery as she got out of bed, yet her morning bath and time spent reading her father's Bible brought her to equilibrium. She had an hour to prepare for another journey back to Los Angeles. Her valise was nearly packed when she heard a tap at her window. Then another.

She went to the window and saw the boys, Al and Sam, tossing pebbles. She waved and opened the window.

"Need to talk," Al said in a whispery voice. Sam nodded eagerly next to him.

"I'll be right down," Kit said.

She met them at the side of the hotel, where they could not be seen from the street.

"We heard something," Al said.

"Yep," Sam added.

"What was it?" Kit said.

"It was like this, see," Al began. "Me and Sam were in the

broom closet, that's one of our hidin' spots because old Mr. Rattray don't come in and sweep up till late, after everyone goes."

"And there's two doors, so we can get in and out," Sam said.

Al clipped him on the shoulder. "She ain't interested in that."

"Maybe she is," Sam said.

"Are you, Mrs. Fox?"

Kit said, "Why don't you just tell me what you heard."

Al nodded curtly at Sam. "See?"

"Just tell her, then," Sam said.

"Well, we were listening and heard Bob Barry on the phone. He was talking to that Mr. Hardy."

"Which Mr. Hardy, could you tell?"

"The prosecutin' Mr. Hardy," Al said. "Ain't he the one named Fielding?"

"Yes."

"That's what Bob called him, Fielding."

Kit said, "Go on."

"And he was sayin' could he feed him more dope. That's the word he used, *dope*. Could he feed him more dope on the trial, and especially on you."

"Me?"

"He said *Mrs. Fox*. And then he sounded angry and hung up."

Kit felt gears meshing in her head.

"Did we do good?" Sam asked.

"Real good," Kit said.

The boys beamed.

34

THE TRIP BACK TO LOS ANGELES was delayed by a dead cow on the rails. That seemed somehow fitting to Kit. There was something dead somewhere on the tracks of her own life, and it had to be removed.

Lacking a sense of peace, she had decided that any obstacle between herself and Ted, any at all, was not worth it. She would tell him that. That was the one thing she was bursting to say.

If he still wanted her off the case, she would drop it. If he still firmly believed that her giving up the law was the proper course, she would do that as well.

The train started up again. Kit looked out at the landscape—the orange groves and farmlands and horse ranches, and the smaller towns that were growing quickly as a result of being near Los Angeles. People were flooding into the city and needed places to live. Many ended up in suburbs like Willos and Dominguez Junction, Watts and Ascot Park. Each had its own personality and also its own secrets.

Like everyone involved in the Wanda Boswell case.

Kit jolted up in her seat. She couldn't stop thinking about the case. *But I must,* she thought, *I must.*

What were they hiding, all of them? What was Prosecutor Hardy holding back? And the judge, and . . . *Stop!* she told herself.

The train pulled into the depot. Corazón met her with the Ford.

"Mr. Fox is waiting for you," Corazón said.

It sounded to Kit like she was being summoned to see the schoolmaster. That had happened more than once at St. Catherine's, where Kit had learned the art of getting to the point quickly.

So when she saw Ted, waiting for her in the library, she closed the doors behind her and said, "Ted, I have something I wish to say."

"And I have something as well. Let me go first. If I don't, I just might explode."

"Me too!"

Ted smiled. "Then lest Angelita have to clean up the mess, I will make it fast. Please, sit."

"I don't think I can. My feet want to move."

"All right. Have it your way." He took his Bible from the table and opened it. "I was seeking God's will on something. I was praying and reading Scripture, and my eyes fell upon the following passage from the book of Romans: 'I commend unto you Phoebe our sister, which is a servant of the church which is at Cenchrea: That ye receive her in the Lord, as becometh saints, and that ye assist her in whatsoever business she hath need of you: for she hath been a succourer of many, and of myself also.'"

Kit tried to fill in the blanks. The blanks remained.

"Those words stopped me. It was suddenly as clear as day to me."

"What? What was clear?"

"That God has work for you to do, that it brings aid and comfort, and that it is through the law, and that I'm not to stand in the way."

"Ted, wait—"

"Let me finish. I'm just getting warmed up. You are carrying our child, and I have tried to think of a reason for you to drop out of the trial. The only reason I could come up with is that it would not be good for your health or the health of our baby. Certainly Mrs. Studdard has her views on that."

Kit nodded, unable to speak, choked with emotion.

"But then I thought, is Mrs. Studdard the authority? The final word? If I were a patient and she a doctor, wouldn't I want a second opinion? Then I wondered, where can I get a real expert to help me on this? And I had a masterful idea! I amaze myself sometimes."

Nearly bursting, Kit said, "Tell me!"

Ted walked to the door of the library, opened it, and called for Angelita. Presently, Corazón's mother entered the library, wiping her hands on her apron and smiling.

Ted said, "I wanted you to hear something. Angelita, will you please tell Mrs. Fox what you told me?"

The housekeeper nodded. "Mr. Fox, he is asking me about my children. Are five, as is known to you. And I am having all of them as I work. Sometimes in the fields. God is giving them to me . . . how you say, *sano*?"

"Healthy," Kit said.

"*Sí.*"

"And you? How did you feel?"

"Strong."

"Angelita also has something to make you feel better, an Aztec remedy passed down in her family."

"*Té aztec*," Angelita said, "*con raíz del jengibre.*"

Kit looked at Ted. "But the doctor. Mrs. Studdard."

"I talked to our doctor this morning," Ted said. "He agrees with Angelita. He wants you to see him, and if all is well, he will allow you to continue. I will explain things to Mrs. Studdard."

Kit could hardly believe what she was hearing.

"And now," Ted said, "what was it you wish to say to me?"

She took Ted's hands in her own. "Here is what I wish to say. If we have a boy, I want him to be named Theodore Fox Jr."

San Leandro Clarion

KATHLEEN SHANNON FOX TO CONTINUE!
After succumbing to heat and discovering a delicate condition, Los Angeles attorney won't quit.

The colorful Los Angeles lawyer, Kathleen Shannon Fox,

may now be termed controversial as well. After fainting in the courtroom of Judge Clarence Hardy during a tense moment in the Wanda Boswell murder case, Mrs. Fox was taken to the office of Dr. Miles Layton, where she recovered.

Ordered to the hospital for further examination, it was discovered that Mrs. Fox bears happy news for Mr. Fox. The aviator, Theodore Fox of Los Angeles, is going to become a father.

Judge Hardy had already been making plans to secure another attorney for Wanda Boswell. Yesterday, however, he received the rather shocking news that Mrs. Fox has decided to continue with the defense.

This is an unprecedented development in the annals of American law. Only lately have the gentler sex been admitted to the practice, and very few to trial work. Mrs. Fox is perhaps the most notable example of this type of new woman. But never has an expectant mother, so far as this paper can determine, engaged in a trial before a jury or judge.

Is this a scandal? One might rightly ask. Is it proper for a woman on the cusp of motherhood to be engaged in a battle that tests even the strongest of men?

"It simply should not be done," says Mrs. Henrietta Studdard of Los Angeles, a noted society matron. "Motherhood is a higher calling than the law. Women should respect the home and the God-given order of things."

35

OUTSIDE THE PRESENCE of the jury, Kit objected to the introduction of Wanda's diary. "It is hearsay," she argued to the judge, "and unless my client takes the stand, it cannot be introduced."

She was feeling wonderful at the moment, having just had some of Angelita's marvelous Aztec ginger-root tea, prepared by Corazón at the San Leandro Hotel before the two of them came to court. More than that, she was energized with purpose. Arguing the law always did that to her.

Fielding Hardy was ready with a reply. "The hearsay rule does not apply to the admissions of a party. What is in this diary is directly relevant to the issues of the case. All that is required is that I be able to have someone authenticate that it is indeed the handwriting of Wanda Boswell. I am prepared to do that with a witness."

"Who is the witness?" the judge asked.

"Glenna Boswell."

Kit's throat clenched. "Glenna Boswell is not an expert in handwriting analysis," she said.

"But as my learned opponent no doubt knows, such is not required under our rules." Hardy took up a sheet of paper from his table. "If I may read from a recent Supreme Court decision. 'Any person who himself can write may testify to the style of another's handwriting, if he has observed it. An expert is not required.'"

The judge looked at Kit. "Have you a response to that?"

She shook her head.

"All right. Let's have the jury back."

As soon as the men were seated in the box, Fielding Hardy called Glenna Boswell back to the stand. He showed her the open diary.

"Do you recognize the writing?" he asked.

"I do," Glenna said without hesitation.

"And how do you recognize it?"

"Because I have seen it many times, in letters and notes."

"To whom does the writing belong?"

"Wanda Boswell, my daughter-in-law."

This brought a hum of anticipation from the gallery, and Fielding Hardy paused to let them hum.

"If you will look at the entry for December 12, 1906."

Glenna flipped to the page.

"Please read for the record what is written there."

Holding her lorgnette before her eyes, Glenna Boswell read, "'Chilton has behaved wretchedly today. He seems to be wanting to put off the wedding. And he does not care about my feelings. He has told me that he may have been rash in proposing and that freedom is what a man wants most of all. Sometimes I get so angry I don't know what I might do to him.'"

"Thank you, Mrs. Boswell. I have no further questions. Your witness, Mrs. Fox."

Poised, Kit began slowly. "You claim that this is the handwriting of Wanda Boswell?"

"I do. I know her hand. It is most certainly Wanda's."

"And you claim to know this because of letters and notes Wanda wrote to you?"

"Yes."

"Do you have any of those letters or notes with you today?"

"I was not asked to bring them."

"Isn't it true that you have looked into this diary before, without Wanda's consent?"

Glenda looked momentarily stunned but quickly recovered. "I did no such thing."

"But surely you do not think that the contents of a diary are any indication of anything but the private musings of the person who owns the diary?"

Fielding Hardy objected. "What the contents of the diary indicate is a question for the jury, and not for this witness."

"Sustained," said the judge.

Kit walked to the counsel table and took a folded paper from Corazón. She walked back to the witness stand, unfolded the paper, and placed it in front of Glenna Boswell. "Would you kindly look at this and tell us what it is?"

Again Glenna placed her lorgnette in front of her eyes. She gasped and said, "Where did you get this?"

"Please identify it for the court," Kit said.

Glenna looked at the judge pleadingly. "Must I?"

To Kit the judge said, "What does this purport to be?"

"It is a letter, Your Honor, written by Glenna Boswell herself."

"Where did you get this letter?"

"It was written to my client, Wanda Boswell."

The judge scratched his chin as he addressed Glenna. "Well? Is that a letter, written by you to Wanda Boswell?"

Glenna looked at the letter again as if trying to get it to disappear. "It appears to be."

"You were certainly sure about the handwriting of Wanda Boswell," Kit said. "Why then are you unsure about your own?"

Snapping her lorgnette to her lap, Glenna fairly shouted, "You have no right to bring this in."

"Your Honor," Kit said, "the prosecution has introduced the private writing of my client into this proceeding in an effort to show something like motive. Your Honor has deemed it is relevant evidence. I should like to introduce relevant evidence of my own, which can be found in this letter. I would like Your Honor to rule on this motion."

The judge looked nervously out at the gallery, toward the reporters. "This court is concerned with relevant evidence, but be advised I will not allow the proceedings to go off on a wild tangent. Approach the bench with the letter."

Kit and Fielding Hardy stepped over to the judge. "What is it you wish to introduce?" he asked Kit.

"This portion, Your Honor."

"Let me see," Fielding Hardy said.

"I have it," the judge barked.

Fielding Hardy shrank back. The judge read what Kit showed him, then handed the letter to the prosecutor, who read the same thing.

"I object," Fielding Hardy said.

"I thought you would." Judge Hardy shook his head. "What do you think will happen if I deny it and then the newspapers get wind? Fielding, I have been your brother for a long time. You're going to have to win this case on your own."

Fielding Hardy's jaw nearly hit the bench. "But . . ."

"You may introduce this portion of the letter, Mrs. Fox. And that's all."

It seemed to Kit that Fielding Hardy nearly fainted on his way back to his counsel table. Kit, on the other hand, felt full of new energy.

"I would request the witness to read one paragraph." Kit raised the letter as she handed it to Glenna. "Please read from here, Mrs. Boswell," she said, pointing to the beginning of the paragraph.

"Must I?" Glenna Boswell asked the judge.

"Please," Judge Hardy replied.

With a defeated sigh, Glenna Boswell took up the letter. She looked at the paper for a long time before setting it down. "I cannot!"

"With Your Honor's permission, I will read the paragraph," Kit said.

"Granted."

Kit turned toward the jury, the letter in front of her. "The paragraph reads, 'I know what sort of woman you are. But Chilton tells me he loves you, and I am willing to overlook it. If any trouble should follow, however, I will have you know I can mete out punishment.' Mrs. Boswell, did you write that?"

Glenna looked downward. "Yes."

"You threatened Wanda, didn't you?"

"It was a warning only, because of my care for Chilton."

"No more questions," Kit said.

Fielding Hardy, looking somewhat shaken, stood up. "The prosecution rests."

36

KIT'S FIRST WITNESS was Don Raffels. When sworn, he stated his name as "Big Don Raffels" and then sat down.

"What is your *real* name, sir?" the judge demanded.

"I am Dante Alfonzo Filibert Guglielmi Raffaelo, born in Castellaneta, Italy. Now I am Don Raffels, and I do not mind being called Big Don. What I have now I have worked hard for."

"You may question," Judge Hardy said to Kit.

Kit looked into Raffels's dark eyes, which smoldered back at her. She had not forgotten his threat to do her harm. She had called him to the witness stand anyway.

"Sir, you were in charge of the gaming room aboard the *Majestic,* is that correct?"

"Yes, and was pleased by your presence."

"Sir, you will confine your answers to the questions I ask. Now, for the sake of the jury, my presence, as you call it, was when I came to question you, not to gamble, isn't that right?"

"Of course. Though you would have been welcomed at any of my tables."

"Was Chilton Boswell welcomed at your tables?"

"Yes. Mr. Boswell was with us each night of the cruise."

"Was Professor Aiden Aloysius Faire also present?"

"The good professor visited one or two times."

"Isn't it a fact, sir, that you were the dealer in a poker game that included both Professor Faire and Chilton Boswell?"

"Indeed. But that was not uncommon for me."

"Isn't it also true that in that game was a man by the name of Edgar Samuelson?"

Raffels nodded. "Mr. Samuelson was a regular."

"How would you describe Edgar Samuelson?"

"A rather blunt fellow."

"Did he drink much alcohol while gambling?"

"As I recall, Mr. Samuelson did like to drink."

"And do you recall him assaulting a woman in your gaming room?"

Raffels smiled. "I do indeed. He took hold of your arm."

Fielding Hardy objected. "What relevance is this line of testimony? Edgar Samuelson, whoever he is, is not on trial here today."

"Your Honor," Kit said, "the defense is going to show that there were other people with both the motive and opportunity to kill Chilton Boswell."

"Continue, Mrs. Fox," the judge said. "But I will not allow a wild-goose chase."

"Thank you, Your Honor. Mr. Raffels, during the course of the poker game, did you observe an argument occur between Chilton Boswell and Professor Faire?"

"No, I did not."

"Are you aware that they argued?"

"No."

"Is that because you had left the table?"

"That is right. I gave the cards to one of my dealers."

"Although you did observe Professor Faire leave the table and the gaming room, did you not?"

"I saw him go, yes."

"Would you say he left in anger?"

"I couldn't tell that."

"Was Professor Faire winning or losing when you dealt the cards?"

"He wasn't winning, that's for certain."

"Are you aware that Professor Faire accused Chilton Boswell of cheating?"

"Objection!" Fielding Hardy was up like a shot. "There hasn't been any such evidence presented in court. Mrs. Fox is trying to mislead this jury."

"I merely asked the question, Your Honor. If the prosecutor would allow the answer, perhaps the jury can decide for itself who is misleading whom."

"Stop," Judge Hardy said. "That's quite enough out of both of you. Mrs. Fox, you must have a basis for asking such a question."

"I do, and I shall call another witness to corroborate it."

"Then the witness can answer, if he knows."

Don Raffels shrugged. "I don't know. Maybe, maybe not."

"No further questions," Kit said. "I should now like to call to the stand Mr. Bob Barry, reporter for the *San Leandro Clarion*."

It was as if a cannon had been fired in court. The look of shock on the faces of the reporters in the courtroom was almost comical. Unlike the look on Bob Barry's face. He seemed both outraged and embarrassed. And he did not move from his chair.

"Bob," the judge said, then started again, "Mr. Barry, you will please come forward to be sworn in."

"Go get 'er, Bob," a man's voice called out from the middle of the gallery. This was met by laughter from the rest of the audience.

"Do I have to, Judge?" Barry said.

"This won't take long, I'm sure." Judge Hardy glared at Kit. "Will it, Mrs. Fox?"

"That all depends on what the witness says, Your Honor. I can assure you, however, that my questions will be brief and to the point."

"Mr. Barry, take the stand."

The reluctant reporter, glancing around at his fellows, slowly came through the swinging gate. He shook his head contemptuously at Kit as he passed by her, almost forgetting that he had to take the oath before sitting in the chair.

"Mr. Barry, you are the city reporter for the *San Leandro Clarion*?" Kit asked.

"Everybody knows that."

"You were a reporter on January seventh?"

"Of course I was."

"And you filed a story, didn't you, which was then printed in the January eighth edition?"

"I file lots of stories."

"This one was headlined *Murder on the High Seas.* I can show it to you if you like."

"I remember the story."

"Do you recall the details of the story?"

"Sure."

"Was I mentioned by name in that story?"

"You know you were."

"So on January eighth, one day after the death of Chilton Boswell out at sea, you had a story in the paper about it, down to the detail of my representation of Wanda Boswell."

"What's wrong with that? There's nothing false in that story, if that's what you're fishing for."

"I am not fishing for anything, Mr. Barry. What I want to know is how you got your information."

"I'm a good reporter."

"So good that you were able to find out what happened aboard a ship at sea within twenty-four hours of the occurrence?"

"Like I said, there isn't anything untruthful in the story. When the ship docked they took your client to jail, and by then everyone knew you were her lawyer. I got the story done and in the paper."

"But the truth is, you did not *get* the information yourself. Rather, someone gave it to you. Who was it?"

Bob Barry swallowed hard. "I don't know what you're talking about."

"The name of the person who fed you the information about the murder aboard the *Majestic.* According to the story you wrote, 'For Mr. Boswell, an enjoyable evening of cards and conviviality on what was supposed to be a pleasant honeymoon trip ended in his death.' That Chilton Boswell played cards that night is an item of information that had not been revealed when you wrote the story.

It could only have come from the ship. So I demand that you tell us who got the information to you."

"I can't reveal who . . ." Barry's eyes widened. "I mean, I—"

"So someone *did* reveal the news to you."

"I don't . . ."

"Who was it?"

"I'm not going to tell you!"

"Wasn't it the district attorney, Mr. Fielding Hardy?"

Bob Barry shook his head, not in denial but in perplexity. That gave Fielding Hardy the chance to jump up and stomp around. "I object! I object! I object!"

"I heard you," Judge Hardy said.

"If Mrs. Fox cannot offer evidence to back up this wild assertion, she should be held in contempt!"

"I am trying to offer the testimony of this witness," Kit said.

"He does not have to answer," the prosecutor argued.

"Are you afraid of his answer?" Kit could not help herself.

"Afraid! Clarence . . . Judge, do something! This is absurd!"

Judge Hardy banged his gavel. "That will do. Everyone take a deep breath."

Still on the witness stand, Bob Barry sighed loudly. It sounded like the hiss of an automobile tire with the air being let out of it.

The judge said, "Mrs. Fox, do you have any other evidence to offer this court, other than the testimony of this witness?"

"I would like to recall to the stand Professor Aiden Aloysius Faire."

The professor did not look pleased. Good. Consternated witnesses often proved to be more pliable.

Bob Barry stalked back to his chair in the gallery while Professor Faire came forward to be sworn in.

Kit began, "Professor Faire, you testified that you purchased a ticket for the Hawaiian cruise a few weeks in advance, is that correct?"

"Yes, that is correct." Faire's tone was clipped.

"In fact, you stated that you saw an advertisement for this cruise in the newspaper, isn't that right?"

"That is what I said and that is what happened."

Kit moved to the counsel table and motioned for Corazón to hand her that which was in a box under the table. Corazón placed a stack of newspapers into Kit's hands.

"I have here every issue of the *Los Angeles Times* between December fourteenth and December thirty-first. I would move that these be marked and placed into evidence. I will assert to the court that there is no advertisement for a Hawaiian cruise in any part of these newspapers."

"That is because I saw the advertisement in the *Examiner,*" Professor Faire said smugly. "It appears you have been barking up the wrong tree."

The judge said, "In view of the witness's statement that he saw the advertisement in the *Examiner,* I find that the *Los Angeles Times* newspapers presented by Mrs. Fox be marked as irrelevant and inadmissible."

Kit nodded, walked back to the counsel table, and held out her hand. Corazón gave another stack of newspapers to Kit. "Then I would move to admit these issues of the *Los Angeles Examiner,* dated from December fourteenth through December thirty-first."

Professor Faire's self-satisfied expression melted into a look of confusion. "Well, I am not at all sure that it was the *Examiner* either. It—"

"No question has been asked, sir." Kit snapped her remark toward the judge.

"That is correct," the judge said. "Therefore, I will reserve for a ruling on this evidence until you question the witness further, Mrs. Fox."

"Professor, did you not just state unequivocally that the advertisement for the cruise was something you saw in the *Los Angeles Examiner?*"

"I may have been mistaken."

"You are saying to this jury, then, that you saw the advertisement in some other place?"

"It is entirely possible."

"Isn't it also quite possible, sir, that you are lying?"

"No."

"Isn't it true that you did not purchase your ticket a week or two before the cruise, but in fact purchased it only one day before?"

"That is not true."

"Are you absolutely sure about this? No confusion this time?"

"I'm telling you the truth."

"Are you aware that the cruise line keeps a record of when tickets are purchased, and that such purchases are noted by date and name of the purchaser?"

This was true; Kit had determined the fact through her investigation. What Kit had not procured, however, was the list with the professor's name on it. She had only seen it. She hoped her bluff would be enough to get what she needed out of Faire.

It was. "You are making this out to be something sinister," the professor said. "What does it matter if I bought my ticket well ahead of time or just before departure? I don't see how it is any of your affair."

"But the reasons you took this cruise when you did are the affair of this trial."

Judge Hardy interrupted. "I shall be the one to decide what is relevant to the trial, Mrs. Fox. And as I see we are late on a Friday afternoon, I am going to recess until Monday morning. That is, unless you can wrap up your questioning of this witness soon."

Kit, who did not have anything more for Professor Faire at this moment in time, said, "I will continue with this witness on Monday, Your Honor."

She only hoped she could come up with something more. For Wanda's sake.

Which was why later she said to Corazón, "Follow him. I want to know where he goes and who he sees. I think there's more going on here than we think."

"I will do it," Corazón said.

Exhausted from the cross-examination, Kit tried to avoid the questions shouted at her by the various reporters outside the courtroom.

"Do you have anything on Faire?"

"What are you holding back, Kit?"

"What are you gonna do on Monday?"

She mouthed, "No comment, no comment," as she made for a horse-drawn cab that was parked along the street. She just wanted to get back to the hotel and rest. That was before Francis Boggs fairly leaped in front of her.

"Mrs. Fox! May I take some pictures?"

"Not now, Mr. Boggs, I'm quite weary."

"Please, Mrs. Fox. In front of the courthouse. It will be magnificent!"

"I'm sorry but no." She tried to enter the cab.

"Are you ill?" Boggs said. "Your condition?"

"I must go," she said brusquely, then climbed into the carriage and ordered the driver to move along, quickly.

37

EARLY SATURDAY MORNING Kit found herself on yet another train ride back to Los Angeles. She had grown thoroughly tired of the constant back and forth. No sooner had she settled in her seat when Tom Phelps plopped into the seat next to her.

"You have a scoop for me?" he asked.

"Did you follow me?" Kit said, exasperated. Tom Phelps was nothing if not dogged in his reporting.

"Can I help it if we took the same train?"

"Yes."

"Fine. But now that I'm here . . ."

"I have nothing for you. I can't reveal anything. I'm in the middle of trial and—"

"The betting is that you're bluffing with Faire."

"I don't care what the betting is."

"I'm the only one who didn't take the bet. I told the fellas, 'You watch, Kit Fox will pull a rabbit out of her hat.'"

"Thanks for the vote of confidence."

"Where's the rabbit?"

Kit wondered. It was certainly not in her hat. Not at the moment. She didn't even know if one existed. "Sorry, Tom."

The reporter sat back with a heavy sigh. "I'm going to miss covering you."

"Miss? What does that mean?"

"You'll be retiring, I expect. Because you're expecting." He smiled at his word mongering.

"I have not made any announcement to that effect."

"But according—" He stopped himself, like a witness suddenly aware of mangling his story.

"According to whom?" Kit turned on him. "Now you tell me what you are hiding."

"I didn't say anything out of school."

"You haven't even completed your thought. Who told you . . ." Suddenly she knew. "Your colleague at the paper, Mrs. Studdard— she wouldn't be your source on this, would she?"

"Why, no."

"You are a terrible liar, Tom."

He looked at the floor and said, "You always could see through me. Well . . . is it true, Kit? Are you leaving the law?"

Leaving the law. Would she? She had not thought past this present case. But she had never had a child either. When she did, she knew that her life would take on a new dedication, to train up that child in the way he—or she—should go. God was leading her in small steps where she should go, too.

"When I know the answer, Tom, I'll give it to you. That'll be your scoop."

"Deal," he said.

When the train pulled into the depot, Corazón was waiting. She had taken the late train on Friday, as had one Professor Aiden Aloysius Faire.

"The professor, he visited a house," she told Kit. "In Boyle Heights. He did not stay. I heard shouting."

"What happened after that?"

"He went back to his hotel."

"Good. Let's go to the house. I need to find a rabbit."

"Rabbit?"

"Come along."

———

A familiar face answered the door. At first the woman seemed not to know Kit, but a sudden recognition formed on her face, mixed with shock and fear.

"Mrs. Ferrell," Kit said. "Nice to see you again."

"What are you doing here?" she replied in a whisper.

"I should like to ask you some questions. May I come in?"

The woman whom Kit had questioned on the *Majestic* shook her head. "No. Please. My husband . . ."

"Mrs. Ferrell, this may be a matter of legal significance. If I were to summon the police—"

"Please! Come in if you must, but do not stay long."

Just how long was a matter yet to be determined. In a small parlor, Mrs. Barton Ferrell sat like a quivering . . . rabbit. That is exactly what she looked like to Kit, and why Kit knew she was on the right trail.

"You had a visitor yesterday—Professor Faire," Kit said.

Mrs. Ferrell's nervous eyes looked at Corazón, then back at Kit.

"He is a witness on the stand in a murder trial," Kit said. "He is under oath and may not discuss the testimony in the meantime. And anyone who might try to influence his testimony would be subject to a criminal indictment."

"No. Please."

"Mrs. Ferrell, I want to know why he was here."

"I cannot . . . my husband . . ."

"You and your husband may be in deep waters. I am in a position to help you."

Mrs. Ferrell became short of breath. She put her hand to her chest. "I told Barton not to get involved in all this."

"What happened?"

"I didn't want him to take it."

"Take what, Mrs. Ferrell?"

"The manuscript."

Kit could see the pieces connecting. "Are you referring to Chilton's manuscript?"

Mrs. Ferrell shook her head. "Mr. Blair's."

"Blair? Who is—"

A door slammed, like a gunshot. A moment later Barton Ferrell charged into the room. "What goes on here?" he shouted.

"Barton!" Mrs. Ferrell said with a mixture of fright and relief.

The man looked defiantly at Kit. "What are you doing in my house?"

"Seeking information."

"What have you told them?" Barton Ferrell demanded of his wife. She looked at him with an open mouth from which came no words.

"Who is Blair?" Kit said.

Barton Ferrell's eyes widened madly. He then struck his wife, hard across the cheek with the back of his hand. The blow sent the woman off her chair to the floor.

Barton Ferrell stepped over her, his hand upraised.

Kit's reaction came instantaneously. She charged forward, grabbed his hand and arm, and bent them downward in one of the holds Mr. Hancock, her jiu-jitsu instructor, had taught her. Barton Ferrell cried out in pain and fell to one knee. Kit held him there.

"You crazy woman!" Ferrell screamed. Kit did not know to which woman he was referring.

"Act civilized, Mr. Ferrell," Kit said, "and I shall let you up."

"How dare you! I'll show you—"

Kit bent the arm a little farther.

"Stop!" the man cried. "I promise—I'll be civilized."

Kit released him. Barton Ferrell's cheeks were decidedly flushed. He rubbed his arm. "You are dangerous!" he said.

"Not so dangerous as the law is to lawbreakers," Kit said. "And that is what you are."

He looked at her incredulously.

"Withholding evidence relevant to a murder trial," Kit explained. "Attempting to influence a witness. You could go to prison."

"Barton, tell her!" Mrs. Ferrell said.

"You—" He looked at his wife angrily but then relented when he glanced back at Kit. He rubbed his arm again. "I don't have to tell you anything."

"Oh, but you do," said Kit. "Right now. Otherwise I will get

Detective Mike McGinty over to question you himself."

"The police?"

"That is the agency that deals with lawbreakers."

Barton Ferrell paused. "And if I tell you what I know, what then?"

"I might be convinced to keep this conversation private," Kit said. "But I want some answers and I want them immediately. Let us begin with this manuscript. Do you have it?"

After a long moment, Barton Ferrell nodded.

"Then tell me everything," Kit said.

Barton Ferrell began to talk.

38

"I WILL NOT ALLOW YOU to speculate about anyone else committing this crime," Judge Hardy said.

It was Monday morning, and Kit stood ready to question Professor Faire once again. More than ready. But now the judge was pulling the rug out from under her. And, she knew now, her entire case.

"Speculation is based on thin air," Kit said. "And I—"

"Agreed. So, unless you can present the court with evidence to the effect that someone else may have committed this crime, there is no use continuing with this witness."

"I have shown the witness to be less than credible."

"His credibility is not at issue. His connection to a crime is."

"I'm prepared to present the court with such evidence."

The judge looked exceedingly surprised. "What form does this evidence take?"

"The form of motive, Your Honor."

Judge Hardy looked at Kit like a gambler calling a bluff. "Mrs. Fox, this had better not be a fishing expedition. I will not allow you to spin a tale out of spider webs."

"I assure Your Honor it will be no mere tale."

After a moment's reflection, Judge Hardy told the bailiff to bring in the jury. When the twelve were seated, Kit said, "Your Honor, please recall to the stand Professor Aiden Aloysius Faire."

A sputtering issued from the professor, who was seated in the middle of the gallery. He puffed his cheeks a couple of times in indignation.

"The witness will come forward," said the judge. "I remind you, Professor, you are still under oath."

With a curt nod, Faire took the witness chair.

Kit wasted no time, for she had none. The judge was glaring at her. "Professor Faire, you gave a lecture to the students at the University of Southern California recently, did you not?"

"Yes, and they were a wonderfully attentive group of young men."

"And what was the subject of your talk?"

"I spoke on the roots of religious thought."

"Was your lecture reprinted in the newspapers?"

"No."

"I do not necessarily refer to the major newspapers. Is there not a modest newspaper published at the University of Southern California?"

Scowling, Professor Faire said, "Of that I am not aware."

Kit walked to the counsel table. Corazón handed her a copy of the University of Southern California student newspaper.

"I would like the court to note that I hold the February second edition of the *Daily Trojan,* newspaper of the University of Southern California."

Kit placed the newspaper on the bench in front of Judge Hardy, who said, "It appears to be as counsel suggests. Nevertheless, we will need it to be authenticated before it can be admitted into evidence."

"I do not seek to admit it into evidence, Your Honor. I only seek to question the professor about what is reported in the newspaper regarding his lecture. If he disputes anything about it, we can take it a step further."

"All right," the judge said. "You may proceed with the examination."

"Reading from the report on your lecture, is it true that you said to the audience the following: 'It was Christianity which first painted the devil on the world's wall.' Did you say that, sir?"

Fielding Hardy jumped to his feet. "Objection! Incompetent, irrelevant, and immaterial! Mrs. Fox is trying to besmirch this witness's character."

"If the professor uttered these words," Kit said, "then it is clear he does not believe they besmirch his character. Perhaps we should ask the witness if he wishes to deny these words and his entire philosophical system."

"I do not deny them." Professor Faire sat up straight. "I stand by those words."

"Then I will overrule the objection," said Judge Hardy. "You may continue with the witness, Mrs. Fox."

"According to the *Daily Trojan,* during this same lecture you said, 'It was Christianity which first brought sin into the world. We would still be in a state of blissful innocence had it not been for the preachers and teachers of Christianity.' Did you indeed say that, Professor?"

"I did, and if you would like me to expand upon the thought, I would be happy to."

"I am not interested in the content of your philosophy at the moment, sir. I only wish to note what you said in the lecture. Now, did you also say that 'The church is a city of destruction. Imprisonment. You see, egoism, not sacrifice, is the essence of a noble soul'?"

"Yes."

"And that Christianity contains 'fool's gold principles to benefit mankind. It looks good on the surface, but for the most part the Christian religion has visited upon the world a dark record of bloodshed and violence'?"

"I said that, yes."

"'The stifling of man's ego by religion is the largest impediment to progress in the world.'"

"Yes."

The foundation was now laid, the net cast over the head and body of Professor Faire. It was only a matter of gathering him in.

"Sir, did you have a student at the University of Chicago by the name of James Blair?"

As Kit had expected, the professor's face changed perceptibly with the color seeming to drain out of it. Before he could open his mouth to deny it, Kit said, "I can produce a roster of your students as provided by the university if it will help to refresh your recollection."

"There will be no need of that." The professor took a deep breath and tried to compose himself. "I cannot remember all of my students by name. But his name does sound familiar, and if you say so, I will accept that he was once my student."

"In fact, he was your most brilliant student, was he not?"

"Once again, I have had many brilliant students over the years."

"Though not many who showed themselves to be both a brilliant mind and a skilled writer."

More color drained from the face of the witness. "Again, I cannot recall with certainty all of the wonderful and hopeful minds who have crossed my path over the years."

"Are you aware, sir, that James Blair has gone missing?"

Faire shook his head, his mouth opening and closing slightly.

"You must answer aloud for the record," Kit demanded.

"No, I was not aware—"

"Are you aware that James Blair was a close friend of Mr. Chilton Boswell?"

"No."

"And that before he disappeared he gave to Chilton Boswell a manuscript of a book he was writing?"

"I don't know what you are . . . speaking of."

Once more Kit went to the counsel table, returning with the manuscript Corazón handed her.

"This manuscript," Kit said. "I would like to read for the record, before placing this into evidence, the following excerpts. From page ten: 'It was Christianity which first brought sin into the world. We would all be in a state of blissful innocence had it not been for the preachers and teachers of Christianity.' I do not need to point out that only one word is different here than in Professor Faire's talk. The word 'still' is substituted for 'all.' Professor, do you deny that you have ever seen or possessed this manuscript?"

Faire took a handkerchief from his breast pocket and dabbed his forehead. "You are trying to confuse me."

"How about this, from page thirty-seven: 'Christianity is rather like fool's gold. It looks good on the surface. But underneath is a dark record of bloodshed and violence.' Now do you deny seeing this manuscript?"

"Your Honor . . ." Faire looked at the judge in desperation.

"Answer the question, Professor," the judge said.

"I don't know the answer."

"Then I will suggest one," Kit said. "Isn't it true that you became so enamored of this manuscript's ideas and expressions that you wanted them for yourself? And that you were going to publish this as your own work?"

"No," Faire said, but weakly.

"Is it not true that Mr. Blair had hand-copied a second manuscript, which he gave to Chilton Boswell for safekeeping?"

"I know nothing of that."

"Do you deny that Chilton Boswell was attempting to blackmail you? That he was going to expose you as a plagiarist?"

"This is all lies!"

"A practice with which you are quite familiar, Professor Faire. When you were found in Chilton Boswell's stateroom after the murder, you were not looking for money, were you, sir? You were looking for this manuscript."

Professor Aiden Aloysius Faire seemed to be deflating, his head dropping down to his chest. "Chilton Boswell was a blackmailer and a bad man." Faire looked up, scared. "Regardless, I did not kill him. You have to believe me, I did not kill him."

"You had the motive and you had the opportunity," Kit said.

"No, I did not do it! You cannot suggest that. You are going to ruin me."

"You did that yourself, Professor, when you took what was not yours. No further questions."

"You are a vindictive woman! Have you no scruples?"

Judge Hardy gaveled for order. "The witness will be silent."

"Kit, you never cease to amaze me," Mike McGinty said. "The way you wrapped that professor up in knots. Case is gonna be hard for the prosecutor to win now."

"I'm glad you could make it, Mike." They were in the lobby of the San Leandro Hotel. McGinty had come down from Los Angeles, at Kit's invitation, to watch the cross-examination of Professor Faire.

"Did you ask me down just to see more of your brilliance?" McGinty said. "I can see that anytime up in the city."

"Far from it, Mike. I just wanted you to hear Faire's testimony, and watch him."

"But why?"

"Put a tail on him."

"He's of no interest to me. I only helped on this case because—"

"It's not about this case; it's about a case in your jurisdiction."

McGinty scowled and shook his head in confusion.

"You'll recall one Edgar Samuelson was murdered in the Dermott Hotel."

"You called me on that one. You suspect the gambler."

"Raffels."

"But we haven't been able to—"

"It was Faire," Kit said. "I'm sure of it. I believe that Samuelson found Faire rooting about in Chilton Boswell's affairs and threatened blackmail. Faire took Wanda's jewels and gave them to Samuelson but killed him later to get the money. He may have planted the ace of spades in Samuelson's pocket."

McGinty scratched his head. "You think the professor just got in too deep?"

Kit nodded. "He is enamored of the philosophy of self-will. Eventually that will bury any man."

"You almost make me want to go to church again," McGinty said.

"You're invited," said Kit.

"One more question," McGinty said. "When you and Corazón

got tied up in Glenna Boswell's house. Who was the man who did it?"

"You have my description of him. My guess is if you send a man around to the Southern California Life Insurance Company, you'll find someone answering that description. I will be happy to help with the identification."

"What was he doing?"

"Looking for the same thing I was—the life insurance policy Wanda had on Chilton. I don't think they want to pay her, Mike."

"If she's found guilty, they don't have to pay."

"And if she's found not guilty, they do. So as part of your investigation into the breaking and entering, and the false imprisonment Corazón and I suffered, I'd like to swear out a *subpoena duces tecum.* I want you to seize the company file on Wanda."

McGinty nodded. "Your wish is my command."

"Truly? Then I wish to see you in church next Sunday."

"Don't press your luck, Kit. You're going to need all of it for your closing argument."

39

ONCE AGAIN THE COURTROOM was stuffed with spectators, as the case of *The People vs. Wanda Boswell* had reached the most dramatic stage—the closing arguments.

Judging from the newspaper reports, Kit thought that the odds were about even at this point. There was grudging recognition in the *Clarion* that Kit had questioned the prosecution witnesses with brilliance, with the most explosive evidence being the revelation of Faire's plagiarism.

But that did not mean he murdered Chilton Boswell.

Fielding Hardy, under the law, got to address the jury first. After his argument, Kit would have her chance. Then Hardy would get one more shot at Kit's case, delivering a rebuttal.

As Kit expected, Hardy ticked off the most favorable items of evidence against Wanda and kept it short. He would save his best for last, after she spoke.

When she rose to address the jury, Kit felt more uncertain about herself than at any time in the past. Now was the time to reach more deeply into what she believed about the law.

"Gentlemen, in just a little while, the judge will be giving you instructions on the law, which you have all sworn to follow. And our law says that no one is guilty unless you are persuaded beyond a reasonable doubt and to a moral certainty of guilt. This means, gentlemen, that if you merely think my client is guilty of the charges you must vote not guilty.

"If you are pretty sure my client is guilty of the charges against her, you must vote not guilty.

"If you are nearly certain that the evidence points to guilt, you must still vote not guilty.

"You may only vote for guilt by being persuaded beyond a reasonable doubt and to a moral certainty.

"Furthermore, the judge is going to tell you that if an item of evidence can be interpreted either for or against the defendant—that is, it can be looked at in either way equally—you must give the benefit to the defendant.

"Nor does the defendant bear the burden of proof of her innocence. Wanda Boswell does not have to prove anything to you. The judge will tell you that it is the burden of the prosecution to present enough evidence to convince you.

"If you look at the prosecution's table, I want you to imagine a large boulder sitting on it. That is the burden of proof. Mr. Hardy cannot remove that boulder simply by chipping away at it. He must remove it completely. The only way he can hope to do so is through the testimony of the witnesses. And yet that is precisely the testimony that defeats him."

Kit paused, her introduction complete. Now came the crucial part of the argument. In the past she had been able, in most cases, to prove the innocence of her clients. No such proof had been available here. The case would have to be made by shooting holes in the testimony of those witnesses speaking against Wanda.

She had kept Wanda Boswell from taking the stand. Had Wanda testified and lied under oath, Kit would have had to report this to the judge. And one lie caught by the prosecutor might be enough to sway the jury to return with a verdict of guilty.

The problem lay in the fact that juries did not like it when a defendant didn't take the stand. Earl Rogers had told her this many times. Now the case would be won or lost based upon the next hour or so.

Kit reviewed carefully all of the witnesses who had testified for the prosecution. Methodically, she went through the contradictions she was able to bring out on cross-examination. She tried to read the faces of the men in the jury box but had no sense of what they were thinking. At times she thought she was talking to the wall, only the wall would have been friendlier than the men in the box.

An hour swept by almost without her noticing it. She felt in herself a lack of passion for justice that had been hers in every trial before this one. Even as she spoke, she listened to herself and looked inward, doubting that she was doing the best job possible for her client. She voiced a prayer in her mind, asking God to help her at this very moment.

God answered. When it came time to finish her argument, she felt the words coming out of her mouth were as deeply felt as any she had ever uttered in court.

"Gentlemen, there is a reasonable doubt as to the facts. That is all you can conclude from what has been presented. It is always so with facts. But in a court of law there is a certain truth, and it is this. That law comes from God, and therefrom our notion of justice. From the moment Prince John signed the Magna Carta, down through the ages, our courts of law have been seeking to do justice on behalf of mankind.

"And long ago we decided that no one should have their liberty or life taken from them unless the highest standard of proof was met. It has not been met in this case. Your verdict, under the law, must be not guilty."

"Well, I am not surprised by the eloquence of my learned colleague," Fielding Hardy said on rebuttal. "She has made quite a reputation for herself as a courtroom magician. And I think she'd like to weave the spell around you, gentlemen, and make you forget what you heard as sworn testimony on that witness stand.

"Oh, sure, Mrs. Fox can poke at one or two things a witness may have said, make them look silly. That's her job as a lawyer. Yet in all of the essential points, the witnesses have agreed. Their agreement can mean only one thing—a guilty verdict in this case."

Hardy went over the evidence, hitting on point after point in his favor. This was, of course, the prosecutor's privilege. Under the law, because of the burden of proof, the prosecutor got the last word with the jury.

"Finally, gentlemen," Hardy concluded, "I leave this decision in your capable hands. A man has been murdered. The only person with motive, means, and opportunity is the defendant, Wanda Boswell. I ask that you return a verdict of guilty."

There was silence in the courtroom for a moment, the sort that follows the end of a trial, especially a murder trial. It seemed to Kit that it always happened this way; a collective breath was taken in as everyone realized there was only one more step—the deliberation of the jury.

Judge Hardy spent the next half hour explaining the law to the jury. Afterward he dismissed them to the jury room. It was four-thirty in the afternoon.

And no telling when they might return.

40

"YOUR CLOSING ARGUMENT today was magnificent," Earl Rogers said. He had ordered a private room in San Leandro's finest restaurant for the evening so he could "fete the finest trial lawyer in Los Angeles." He'd told her this with a wink, of course. If there was anything Earl Rogers was sure of, it was that there was no better lawyer in the country than himself—and he'd even venture to say the world.

Kit, feeling drained, was enjoying the comfort of her companions. Corazón and Raul, Earl and Bill Jory, his chief assistant, and of course Ted, who had dragged Gus along, no doubt to Gus's insistent protests.

Earl, who was on good behavior and not indulging in alcohol, raised a glass of iced tea to Kit. "I salute your efforts, because today you have become a true lawyer."

"Only today?" she joked.

"Allow me to claim the privilege of my senior status and say the following. A true lawyer is one who believes in the law, who will bring to bear all of his training and skill to the upholding of it. There are those who say that the lawyer's job is merely to overwhelm the other side, no matter the truth. I have been so accused on occasion."

Kit smiled, knowing the many slurs that frustrated opponents—

especially Los Angeles prosecutors—had thrown at Earl Rogers over the years.

"Yet I resounding reject the canards. I have always believed in the law. And in the right of every accused to be protected from the mighty talons of the state, unless and until the case is made to twelve men, beyond a reasonable doubt. That is what you argued today, Kit Shannon Fox, and I could see in your eyes you believed it."

Kit nodded. "I realized as I was arguing that I do."

"Further, to be a great trial lawyer, one must be able to use our language to persuade as a skilled craftsman uses a delicate tool. One must have sympathy, tact, and courtesy and must know men and their ways. By study and experience and intuition, the great trial lawyer must acquire a sense of the significance and force of evidence, and the correct order of its presentation. He—or she—must be able to control her temper, maintain poise under trying conditions, and even keep a sense of humor at the ready for the proper time. And, finally, she must know the law."

Once more Earl Rogers raised his glass. "All this is you, Kit."

"Hear, hear," Ted said. All of the guests drank an iced-tea toast to Kit.

"Speech," Earl said. Other voices joined in assent.

Kit laughed. "What can I say to such an overstatement?"

"Come on, Kit, you owe us a word or two," Earl said.

With a bit of reluctance, Kit stood. "All right. Let me say only this. I would not have made it to this position in my life without the help of the people in this room, and a few people who are not here with us. When I arrived in Los Angeles, knowing nothing, as unripe as a green orange, I literally bumped into a man coming out of the courthouse. He said his name was Earl Rogers and that he practiced law. Earl, I cannot begin to thank you for all you have done for me."

Her former boss nodded graciously.

"And what can I say about everyone else? Corazón, without you I could not do half the work I must. Yet you are my best friend in the world, too. Raul, you have helped me so much, and I cannot express enough the gladness I feel that you and Corazón shall be wed."

Kit now turned to her husband. "Ted, to you I owe my happiness. In every way, you have made my life complete."

She paused, unable to come up with more words to express the feelings inside her. And then she heard a throat clearing. Gus Willingham was almost in a corner of the room, his arms folded across his chest.

"I have not forgotten about you, Gus. You are part of the family. I cannot imagine Ted continuing his work on the monoplane without you."

With a grunt, Gus said, "You got that right." He looked at Ted and seemed to get a message. "But I guess Ted wouldn't be working on anything if it weren't for you. He keeps naming planes after you. That must mean something."

"It means everything," Ted said. He stood up and put his arms around Kit, sweeping one hand gently across Kit's stomach. "Everything, and more."

———

There was no verdict the next day. Nor the next.

At four o'clock on the third day, Kit visited the jail. Wanda looked haggard, as if she had not slept in a long while. She'd been losing weight as well. Jail food was known to do that to a person.

Her spirit seemed broken as Kit sat in the cell with her, holding her hand. The skin of her hand looked as white as paper, and Kit could see the muted colors of blood vessels running across the back.

"I am sure we will have a verdict soon," Kit told her, trying hard to make her voice sound encouraging. It was only a half-successful effort.

Wanda looked down at the cement floor of the cell. "Maybe it would be best if I were found guilty."

"Wanda!"

"Why not, Mrs. Fox? What kind of life is waiting for me out there? I have no money, no job. Glenna, she won't let me have any of the insurance money. The rich, they always win."

"You mustn't talk like that. You are not guilty of murder."

"How do you know?"

Suddenly Wanda's eyes took on a cold challenge. It chilled Kit to the center of her now uncertain spirit. "The prosecution did not make its case."

"That doesn't mean I'm innocent, does it? What would you do if you found out I really did kill Chilton?"

Kit did not want to answer or even contemplate the question. But there it was, hanging between them in the cell, and it was not going away.

"Did you, Wanda? Did you kill your husband?"

Instead of answering, Wanda stood up and twirled once in the middle of the cell.

"Stop it!" It wasn't so much anger as the feeling of being a prize sap that filled Kit. Had Wanda merely used her? She stood and faced her client. "Tell me now."

Wanda gave Kit a half smile and said, "Don't like it, do you? Not knowing for sure."

"Why are you doing this? Do you hold me in such contempt?"

For a moment neither one said anything. Then Wanda put her head in her hands and started sobbing.

She's like a little girl, Kit thought. Kit pulled her close and held her, then gently sat her back down on the edge of her cot. "Wanda, please, tell me everything," she said gently.

"I'm sorry, Mrs. Fox." Wanda gulped for breath, steadying herself. "I just have never been a good girl. My papa told me so. He was unkind . . . he was . . . I was afraid of him. He made me . . . I was afraid . . ."

Sobs interrupted her speech. Kit embraced her again.

"I had to find out if I could make men do what I wanted," Wanda said. "Control them. Even Chilton. I made him marry me. I told him I was going to have a baby. I'm a bad girl that way. I'm no good for anybody."

"You're right." Kit felt a shudder run through Wanda's body, like a jolt of electricity hitting her, shocking the system.

Wanda sat up, her sobs gone. "What did you say?"

"That you are no good for anybody."

Wanda's eyes got big. "How can you—"

"None of us is any good on our own," Kit explained. "That's called being a sinner. And there is only one way out. It is not dancing, or law, or courts. It is Christ. You know that, don't you?"

"I don't know how."

"You make a pledge. Like you did when you got married. Only this time you mean it. You pledge to follow Christ. And life will change for you."

Wanda turned and walked to the cell door. "I don't believe that."

"Isn't there a part of you that wants to believe it?"

Wanda was silent.

That was when the jailer entered. "Mrs. Fox?"

"Yes."

"The jury's ready."

Kit held Wanda's hand as they waited for the judge and jury to enter the courtroom. Wanda was shaking, gripping Kit's hand as if it were a life preserver in the open sea.

Reporters were still rushing into the room, which was filling up quickly as word had apparently spread around town that a verdict had been decided. Kit watched the courthouse door for a moment and saw two deputy sheriffs try to hold back the influx. She thought she saw a familiar face in the mob. Yes. It was Francis Boggs, gesticulating wildly, still trying to record history, she guessed. But he was not allowed in.

Fielding Hardy sat at his counsel table. He stared straight ahead, not acknowledging the presence of anyone else.

Finally the judge entered. Everyone stood as court was called to order. Without delay, Judge Hardy called for the jury.

The clerk opened the door to the jury room, and the jurymen marched in. Again Kit tried to read their faces, but they remained passive. The deliberations must have been difficult. What that meant, Kit did not know.

After all were seated, the judge said, "Gentlemen, have you reached a verdict?"

The juror closest to the witness box stood up. He was the foreman. "Your Honor, I regret to say we are unable to reach a verdict."

Something like a *whoosh* came from the gallery, as if all in the courtroom had breathed out at the same time. Kit's stomach tightened. A divided jury! That was both good news and bad. Good in that there was no conviction; bad in that another trial would follow—unless the prosecutor could be convinced to drop the case.

"Are you absolutely certain you cannot reach a verdict?" Judge Hardy said.

"Absolutely," the foreman answered. "We been at it for days."

"Without telling me which way the chips fall, what is the vote as it stands now?"

"Seven to five."

"If I were to send you back to the jury room, is there any chance that you can reach a unanimous decision?"

The foreman looked behind him and was met with hard looks and some adamant shakes of the head.

"No, Your Honor. We'd probably end up killing each other."

After a wave of laughter from the crowd, Judge Hardy banged his gavel. "Well, I guess I've got no choice but to declare a mistrial."

Wanda squeezed Kit's hand. "What's that mean? Am I free?"

Kit stood up. "Your Honor, at this time I would request that this case be dismissed and my client freed immediately."

"I oppose that," Fielding Hardy said. "We want a new trial."

"Counsel," the judge said, "I want everybody back here tomorrow morning. I'll hear arguments then. Court is adjourned."

As the judge rushed out, Wanda said, "Am I going back to jail?"

Her answer was the deputy sheriff walking over and motioning for Wanda to come with him.

"Please, Mrs. Fox! Don't let them take me back!"

"I will come see you."

"I can't take another night in that jail!"

Kit watched as her desperate client was almost dragged out the back door.

Reporters rushed to the rail, shouting questions at Kit. She put her hands up, waving them away. "No questions now, please."

That didn't stop them. Their voices clamored and melted into an indecipherable noise in Kit's head.

Until one voice rang out, louder and more insistent than all the others. She knew that voice. Boggs!

"Mrs. Fox! I've got to show you! Mrs. Fox!"

Kit sighed. If only Boggs and his silly magic lantern would go away for good.

A THICK FOG ENGULFED San Leandro the next morning. It was as if the sea, weary of the February sun, had reacted in self-defense, throwing a shroud over the little town that sought to be a major port city.

The fog added to the darkened mood inside Judge Hardy's courtroom. No one looked pleased to be back here. Only Wanda Boswell had a hint of relief on her face, mostly because of being allowed out of her cell.

Sitting by Kit at the defense table, Wanda turned and said, "I prayed last night. I prayed to God."

Kit nodded, and Wanda smiled. It was the first sincere look Kit could recall coming from her client. "Keep praying," Kit whispered.

Judge Hardy entered and settled heavily into his chair. "We are back on the record to consider whether charges should be dismissed or whether there should be another trial in the case of *The People versus Wanda Boswell.* What does the prosecution have to say?"

Fielding Hardy stood. "We wish to retry the case, Your Honor."

"I was afraid you might say that. Mrs. Fox?"

Kit moved from her chair to the center of the courtroom. "Your Honor, in the interest of justice, I would ask the court to consider new evidence, which will also help the prosecution to make a more informed decision."

"I must protest," the prosecutor said.

"Don't you want to be informed, Fielding?" The judge smirked. "I will answer that. Yes. What is your evidence, Mrs. Fox?"

"With the court's permission, I have subpoenaed a witness. Miss Delia Patton."

An angry Delia Patton came forward, dressed in black and appearing as though she wanted to kill someone. Kit Shannon Fox, in particular.

Kit ignored the knives coming out of Delia Patton's eyes as she took the stand.

Kit approached. "Miss Patton, on the eighteenth of February, did you visit one Dr. Miles Layton?"

"Doctor?"

"Yes. Miles Layton, of San Leandro."

"No. I am in perfect health. Why would I be visiting a doctor?"

"Do you deny that you saw Dr. Layton?"

Delia took a deep breath. "Of course I deny it. I have never been to a doctor named Layton, and I don't see what it would mean if I had."

Kit stepped back. "Your Honor, with your permission I should like to call another witness at this time for the introduction of evidence intended to impeach this witness."

Judge Hardy exhaled audibly. "We've come this far, haven't we? All right, Mrs. Fox. I will allow it. The witness is instructed to stand down, subject to recall."

A confused Delia Patton stepped away from the witness stand, eyeing Kit with a mixture of hatred and suspicion.

"I would like to call to the stand Mr. Francis Boggs." Kit nodded to the deputy at the back of the courtroom. He opened the door and in walked Boggs, dressed all in white, looking quite pleased to be part of a grand performance. He had a large canvas bag with him, affixed to his shoulder by a strap.

He took the oath and sat down on the witness chair.

"What is your occupation, Mr. Boggs?"

"I am a maker of motion pictures."

"For what company do you work?"

"Selig Pictures, out of Chicago."

"What sort of motion pictures do you make, sir?"

"Any and all kinds. I just completed the ocean scenes for *The Count of Monte Cristo*. I also record history in the making. And now I do some work for the law."

"In what regard?"

"I set up my camera across the road from the office of a doctor named Miles Layton."

"Can you tell me why, sir?"

Sheepishly, Boggs said, "Well, I was trying to get some pictures of you, Mrs. Fox."

"Why there?"

"I thought you were going to see this doctor, this Layton fellow, because he was the one who said you were . . . who decided you were going . . . well, you know, he's a doctor."

"Was it because you thought I was seeing him because I am to have a child?"

"That's it exactly! Well said, Mrs. Fox."

"Yes, and did you in fact record a motion picture?"

"I did, from the bushes across the street. It was masterful, if I do say so myself. You see, I first took my camera and placed it—"

"Thank you, Mr. Boggs. You can tell us now if you have the reel you produced with you."

"Of course! That is why I am here. But do you know that there are only two laboratories in all of Southern California that can develop motion picture film?" He reached into his canvas bag and withdrew a reel. "Here it is."

"Your Honor, may we show this to the court?"

"A motion picture?" Judge Hardy sounded almost flattered. "I'm afraid we haven't a projection machine."

Boggs snapped his fingers. "Call Mr. Ignatz Pine into the court-room!"

Judge Hardy pounded the bench with his gavel. "I call the wit-nesses, sir!"

Boggs, duly chastened, sank lower in his chair.

"Call Mr. Pine," the judge said.

The court deputy stepped out into the hall and returned a

moment later with a man pushing a large black box on a dolly into the courtroom.

"May I assist?" Boggs asked the judge.

Looking as curious as everyone else, Judge Hardy nodded. In the next few minutes the courtroom was transformed into a motion picture house. The windows were shuttered, the lights switched off, and the projector attached to the courtroom's electrical outlet box. The blank wall above the jury box became the screen. The gallery full of reporters and onlookers became a movie audience.

The projector whirred under the hand of Pine, and images appeared on the wall.

Kit narrated for the court. "This is the office of Dr. Miles Layton. You can read his name on the door there. Mr. Boggs will testify that he began his filming as he saw a woman with a parasol approaching from the right."

The figure of a woman, whose face was obscured by an open parasol, came into the picture.

"Believing it was I," Kit continued, "Mr. Boggs kept his camera trained upon the spot. But keep watching."

The woman in the picture turned, revealing a clear image of Delia Patton. Then the figure of a man entered the frame. He took Delia Patton by the arm and led her through the door of the office.

The reel of film ran out.

The lights were turned back on, and Kit asked that Delia Patton be ordered back to the stand.

"Do you still deny that you visited Dr. Layton's office?" Kit said.

"How can I?"

"Was it because you are expecting a child?"

The stunned silence in the courtroom was palpable.

Finally Delia Patton managed to say, "What of it?"

"And the man in the film—do you deny that is Lowell Sanders?"

Delia looked at Judge Hardy like a child in trouble looks at a father. "Must I answer?"

"I am afraid so, Miss Patton."

"All right . . ." she said as tears began to pour down her face. "All right."

For a long moment Delia Patton's sobs echoed in the court-room.

Fielding Hardy chose this moment to stand and speak. "A dra-matic point, but tell me, how does this have any relevance to the case at hand?"

Kit looked at the prosecutor. "I believe Miss Patton can answer that."

"Are you suggesting she had something to do with the murder of Chilton Boswell?" Fielding Hardy said.

"Only incidentally. You see, Miss Patton wished to protect her lover, Lowell Sanders, and so lied about who had made her preg-nant."

"Lied? To whom?"

Kit looked back at Delia Patton, who had her head in her hands. "To her father, Captain Wendell Raleigh."

Turning to the gallery, Kit saw Raleigh jump to his feet. His face was red with anger. "You good for nothing. . . !" he shouted at Delia Patton. "You were never any good! I should never have taken you back!"

"You made me that way!" Delia shouted to Raleigh. "You poi-soned the wrong man, didn't you?"

Suddenly Raleigh looked like a cornered animal. "That is pre-posterous!"

"No one heard the sound of a champagne cork being popped in the Boswells' stateroom," Kit said. "Not Wanda, not Mrs. Dimble next door. But someone with a passkey could have entered the Bos-wells' room after Wanda had gone to bed, removed the bottle, poured in the poison, and returned it."

Raleigh said nothing, though one of his eyelids started twitch-ing.

"It should be easy enough to reconstruct who had access to master keys that night," Kit said. "Captain Raleigh, can you tell us where you were between the hours of ten and twelve on the night of the murder?"

"I won't stand for this." Raleigh turned toward the courtroom doors.

"Stop him," Judge Hardy said. The deputy stepped in front of Raleigh. "Place him under arrest."

"You can't possibly!" Raleigh cried.

"I am going to get to the bottom of *something* around here," Hardy said.

As Wendell Raleigh was led from the courtroom, Kit quickly addressed the judge. "Your Honor, as the prosecutor is investigating the crime anew, will you dismiss the charge against my client and order her immediate release?"

Judge Hardy gave a look to his brother, then pounded the gavel. "So ordered," he said.

BEFORE LEAVING THE COURTROOM, a free woman, Wanda Boswell embraced Kit. She buried her head in Kit's shoulder and wept.

"I don't know what to do now," she said finally, her voice cracking. "I thought I was going to go to prison. I thought Glenna would see to it."

"No prison for you, Wanda," Kit said gently. "But a new life instead."

Wanda looked at Kit, eyes red but hopeful.

"You will have your life insurance," Kit added. "I will make sure the company pays you. That will provide you some earthly security."

Nodding, Wanda said, "I don't know how to thank you, Mrs. Fox."

Kit took her hand. "Corazón will get you situated in the Westminster Hotel in Los Angeles. When you are settled, we shall have tea together."

"You would associate with me?"

"Why not?"

"I am . . . notorious."

Kit smiled. "Believe me, Wanda, I know all about that. We'll be two notorious women at tea. How's that sound?"

Wanda chuckled. And then she pirouetted, gracefully, like the dancer she was.

Kit noticed Fielding Hardy glaring at her from across the courtroom. He motioned to her as if he wished to talk.

"Congratulations," Hardy said when she reached him. "You are as clever as they say."

"Mr. Hardy, with all respect, the facts were not in your favor."

"You know what you've done, don't you? You've made us look like vigilantes down here. We could lose the Los Angeles port on account of you! Do you know what that will do to our city?"

"I was hired to defend a client, that's all. She was innocent."

"I could very much dislike you if you gave me the chance," Fielding Hardy said.

"Then," Kit said, "I will not give you the chance. I don't think I'll be returning to San Leandro."

"Good." Fielding Hardy stalked off toward his brother's chambers.

Corazón joined Kit, a sly smile on her face. "You have not made a friend," she said.

"I do not think I am destined for friendships with prosecutors," Kit said. "Besides, I have you."

"Now we may go home. I may file one more case away."

"Not quite yet."

Corazón cocked her head.

"There is one more interview I need to conduct," Kit said.

———

The office that the *Times* provided Mrs. Studdard was painted in pale shades of pink and had a copious window to let in the sunlight. In contrast to the rough and tumble of the city room, with its smoky air and clattering typewriters, Mrs. Studdard's office seemed like a garden spot, with plenty of fresh-cut flowers in vases placed about.

"I should like to say that this is a pleasant surprise," Mrs. Studdard said, "yet I would be stating an untruth were I to do so."

"I will not take up much of your time," Kit said.

"If you are here to discuss my reasons for withdrawing my support of the Institute, I will only say that the reasons should be apparent to you."

"They are. No, I'm here to ask that you write nothing negative about the Institute in your column. I would also request you do not write any stories about me. I request this only because it may reflect negatively on the Institute, and I do not want to see its work hindered."

"My dear, you should have thought of that before going against my counsel. You ought to have considered all of this before behaving so impetuously and taking an ill-advised action. We must all live with the consequences of our decisions, and you shall live with yours."

"Yes, I suppose we must *all* learn to live with consequences."

Mrs. Studdard studied Kit's face as if trying to discern what she was thinking. "I agree wholeheartedly."

"Even the foolish decisions of our youth may come back to haunt us."

"Mrs. Fox, I would greatly appreciate it if you would get to the point. I have a column to produce."

"Perhaps you should consider a column on the vice of interfering with justice."

Her eyelids fluttering, Mrs. Studdard said, "Please, Mrs. Fox, what is your point?"

"I wondered why you should take such an interest in my professional and home life," Kit said.

"I told you. I thought you would be a good example to the young women of this city."

"To keep them on the straight and narrow?"

"Yes."

"Or was it to get me off the case so I would not discover the truth?"

"I don't know what you mean."

"You maintain your home in Santa Barbara, do you not?"

A flash of consternation swept across Mrs. Studdard's face. "I believe I told you as much when you came to my Los Angeles home."

"But you did not tell me this is where you received Mrs. Glenna Boswell. I suspect you wished to help her get me off the case."

"Why, I've never heard anything so outrageous."

"Although it still seemed strange to me—your interest in my dropping out of the trial. My assistant, Corazón Chavez, went up to Santa Barbara and discovered that you began your writing career there, with a column for the local paper, the *Enterprise.*"

"That is a matter of public record."

"You were not married at the time. You were writing under your maiden name, Essex."

Mrs. Studdard seemed to have difficulty swallowing. Her familiar smile had disappeared.

Kit reached into her briefcase and produced a yellowing newspaper. "Corazón visited the *Enterprise* morgue and found this. The illustrator captured you well, don't you think?"

Mrs. Studdard took the newspaper in her hands and looked at the drawing of her younger self, with the caption, *Miss Essex Commences Her Column Today.* She sighed and seemed to float back through time. "I loved that picture. I was so young. So—"

"Beautiful. I agree. Just as your daughter is beautiful."

Mrs. Studdard jerked her head up, her eyes wide.

"Delia Patton looks just like you," Kit said. "But she has her father's eyes."

Mrs. Studdard's countenance fell. She sat in frozen uncertainty. And then, as if a weight were lifted from her shoulders, Mrs. Studdard spoke. Her voice was quiet, the words clear. "Wendell was so dashing in his uniform. What woman could have resisted him? When he refused to marry me, I was crushed. But I resolved to do all I could for my daughter, make her into a woman of distinction. I suppose I was too harsh. I never wanted her to . . ."

"Repeat your mistake?"

Mrs. Studdard nodded. "She ran away from me when she was a mere fourteen years old. Some time ago, I don't know exactly when or how, she found out who her father was. Wendell wrote to me about it and said he was going to watch out for her. He was kind enough to keep me informed, but naturally, with my position in society, my reputation, I could not let our relationship become known."

She began to sob.

"Mrs. Studdard," Kit said, "there is no reason for me to reveal any of this to anyone. Regardless of that, your daughter has lost a father to the law and is going to have a child of her own. Perhaps it is time to put reputation aside, put the past behind you, and look to the future now."

"How?"

"With God's help, and mine."

"Yours?"

"Our Institute has rooms for women just like Delia. If she would consent to be housed there, receive good instruction, we can arrange for discreet meetings. After all, someone of your stature helping the Institute, why, it would be natural that you would come by often."

Before Mrs. Studdard could reply, there was a quick knock on the door. Tom Phelps opened it and stuck his head in.

"Thought I saw you come in here," he said.

"Hello, Tom," said Kit.

"Mrs. Studdard." Tom nodded at the columnist. "Sorry for the intrusion, but I thought Kit would like to know that McGinty's arrested Professor Faire for murder. Some guy named Samuelson, a fellow who was a passenger on your ship, Kit. Isn't that an incredible thing?"

"I BEGAN TO SUSPECT Professor Faire was not all he pretended to be the night we all had dinner together aboard the ship."

Kit paced in front of Ted in the library as she would have done were she analyzing a case in her office. This time, though, she was at home with Ted, and he'd asked her about the different pieces that had made up the case.

"You remember when the professor and I engaged in a small debate over philosophy and religion on the ship? The professor offered what he termed the argument of Polemarchus from Plato's *Republic*. Only this was the argument of Thrasymachus, not Polemarchus. Would a professor who specialized in the Greeks, and Plato, have made such a mistake?"

"Not likely," Ted said.

"I had Corazón find out about his teaching schedule at the University of Chicago. What she found was more than enough to show us that he was a professor somewhat in disgrace."

"And then you came up with the manuscript."

"The one Faire was in the process of plagiarizing. Written by a brilliant student named James Blair, who disappeared mysteriously not long before Faire came out west."

"How did you figure that one?"

"Blair's name shows up in Wanda's diary. I didn't make much of it, until the name was repeated by Mrs. Barton Ferrell. He was someone Chilton talked of as a friend, a student at the University of Chicago who was going to make them both a lot of money."

"Money?"

"Blair sent Chilton a handwritten copy of his manuscript. Chilton was a gambler and so knew how to get big stakes. When Chilton heard about Blair's disappearance, no doubt he contacted Faire and began the proceedings."

"A little blackmail?"

"Of a plagiarizer and a murderer. That will be one for the Chicago police."

"Then Faire did have a motive to kill Chilton Boswell."

"Which is what I wanted to show the jury. All I was trying to do was raise a reasonable doubt, demonstrating there was another person with both motive and opportunity."

Ted nodded. "And some of the jurors agreed."

"Then Francis Boggs came to me with his reel of film—Delia Patton going into Layton's office with Lowell Sanders. She is with child, and Lowell Sanders is the father. Delia's own father, Wendell Raleigh, found out about her pregnancy. I don't exactly know how. Maybe Delia told him. Maybe he confronted her with some piece of information. In any event, she lied about who the father was, to protect Sanders."

"So Raleigh murdered Chilton?"

"His wayward daughter had been taken advantage of, by a man who was a gambler and a blackmailer."

Ted shook his head. "God gave you a mind for this sort of thing."

Kit kissed him. "For this sort of thing, too—loving my husband till death do us part."

EPILOGUE

"I'm sorry but you cannot go in," the large nurse said.

Ted was frantic. "You don't understand! She's had a baby, my baby. I'm her husband and—"

"I well understand. I have done this before. You may see your wife and child when the doctor says it is permissible."

Only two hours before, Ted had been up in the sky. The monoplane had performed magnificently, to the cheers of Francis Boggs and Gus Willingham. It would only be a matter of time before Ted's name would be associated with the history of flight—that was what Mr. Boggs told him anyway.

It had been nearly six months now since the trial of Wanda Boswell. Ted had rushed home to tell Kit about the plane and was informed by Angelita that Kit had been taken to the hospital earlier to deliver their child. His trip to the hospital had been delayed when Kit's own Ford automobile had sputtered to a stop halfway down from Angeleno Heights. Had he had two good legs, Ted would have run the rest of the way. Instead, he had to depend on the trolley system and was only now arriving to the hospital and the news that Kit had had the baby—a girl!

"Then get the doctor!" Ted pleaded with both voice and hands. "I want to go in."

"If I go to fetch him, do I have your word you will not enter?" the nurse said.

Ted looked at her. "No."

The nurse's mouth opened.

"I didn't want to lie to you," he said.

"All right. I suppose it wouldn't hurt if you just saw them for a moment."

"May I?"

"But you have to remain calm. She needs her rest. The baby's with her right now, probably sleeping."

"I'll be quiet as a church mouse," Ted promised.

The nurse opened the door.

Kit held a small bundle on her chest. When she saw Ted, her smile was incandescent. "Come and see your daughter," she said.

Ted approached with all the wonder of the world swirling around inside him. Kit looked radiant, even with her hair undone and a look of exhaustion about her face.

Then she revealed the small head and closed eyes of their baby.

Ted was amazed. "Look at her. And that red hair. She is going to be just like her mother."

"Do you think this city can take two of us?"

"There are not enough of you to go around." Ted leaned over, kissed Kit's forehead, and then pulled back for another look at the living gift in her arms.

"Ted, what shall we name her?"

"I have been thinking about that. We've talked about a number of names, but none of them seems to fit, especially now that I see her. But I do have an idea."

"Tell me."

"Shannon Frederica Fox. Your family name, Shannon, to remember your mother and father, who raised you to fear the Lord. Frederica for Aunt Freddie, who took such good care of you when you arrived in Los Angeles. And our name, Fox. How does that sound?"

Tears filled Kit's eyes. "It's the perfect name for her."

"And a perfect name for a lawyer."

"Lawyer?"

Ted smiled, his blue eyes dancing. "Who knows? Maybe one day she will be named to the United States Supreme Court."

"A woman on the Supreme Court?"

"Why not? God brought us together, didn't He? I do believe He can do anything."

Ted looked at his child again.

Shannon Frederica Fox opened her eyes.

Author's Note

The history of manned flight began taking shape in 1907 and had garnered the interest of no less a man of prominence than Alexander Graham Bell, inventor of the telephone.

In the novel, Gus Willingham suggests the use of wing flaps, controlled by the pilot through a yoke harness, to stabilize the plane in its lateral motions. In fact, this innovation was an actuality at the time. The flaps were called *ailerons,* the French word for "little wings." And they became the subject of heated dispute in the race to conquer the air. The Wright brothers, Wilbur and Orville, sued the team assembled by Bell, which was led by aviator Glenn Curtiss. This flap over the flaps—and a number of other issues—demonstrates just how competitive the aviation race was. Evidence seems to suggest that the idea for ailerons came as early as 1868 from a British inventor, but it was little noted. Bell claimed the idea came to him independently as he observed birds. He wrote in a letter to his design team, "I have often seen birds suddenly reef their wings, so to speak, during a sudden squall, thus diminishing the supporting areas of their wings." See *Unlocking the Sky* by Seth Shulman (HarperCollins, 2002, p. 136).

There was no thriving film industry in Los Angeles in 1907. Most film production was done in the East in the form of one-reel films that used technology patented by Edison Laboratories. However, a man named Francis Boggs really did come out to Los Angeles to finish photography for *The Count of Monte Cristo.* Later, William Selig, Boggs's boss and the head of his own studio, decided to establish a permanent operation in Los Angeles because of the favorable weather. He did so in early 1908 when he shot the first full-length feature film ever made in Los Angeles, *In the Sultan's Power.*

Selig had another reason to opt for Los Angeles as a base of operations: He was better able to avoid the process servers hired by Edison Laboratories. Selig, it seems, was not always up on his licensing fees, another reason why the film industry grew up in Los Angeles and not in what was probably the more preferable location—San Francisco. The city to the north boasted a culture much like the East, with actors and a theatrical tradition readily available. But that city also had numerous lawyers connected with Eastern firms. Filmmakers in Los Angeles could more easily slip south of the border into Mexico should Edison attorneys come sniffing around.

Even so, between 1907 and 1913, no film company made a permanent commitment to Los Angeles, always maintaining operations in Chicago or New York or New Jersey. Until one man began to exploit Los Angeles as a film location more than any other. His name was D. W. Griffith, and he would become the first cinematic genius.

Francis Boggs died in October 1911, when a janitor at the West Coast studio burst in on Boggs and Selig during a meeting and shot Boggs four times. "Mr. Boggs was my best friend," the man said upon his arrest. "He was always very nice to me. But a man told me he was evil and had to die." This was only the first of many bizarre "Hollywood murders" to occur over the next thirty years.

The philosophy of Friedrich Nietzsche (1844–1900) was finding its way into America about this time. Nietzsche did not believe that human beings could truly know anything. All that exists is chaos. The only thing a man can do is to impose his will upon the existence. He called this the will to power, a forcing of reality to submit to one's own creative expression. Eventually he came to embrace the death of God and something called eternal recurrence. Not many people know exactly what he meant by that. Nietzsche's philosophy really turns upon itself in a way that is almost incomprehensible. So it is with any philosophy that does not recognize the source of truth. Ultimately one gets the feeling that Nietzsche was simply an enemy of God who wanted to destroy the influence of the church and Christianity. He went insane. Later, his ideas had a big influence on the emerging Nazi party in Germany.

W. C. Fields, who makes a brief appearance in the novel, was born William Claude Dukenfield in 1880. He ran away from home at age eleven, seeking fame on the stage, and became one of the premiere jugglers of his time. He billed himself as the "Tramp Juggler" and gained wide notice when he signed with the famous stage impresario, Florenz Ziegfeld. But his greatest fame would come much later, in the movies. Those wishing to see a bit of Fields's juggling genius should watch the 1934 film *The Old-Fashioned Way*.

Unbeatable Historical Fiction From Lynn Austin and Tracie Peterson!

An Unforgettable Look at the Civil War

Candle in the Darkness, Lynn Austin's first novel in her REFINER'S FIRE series, was honored with the 2003 Christy Award for North American Historical Fiction. *Fire by Night* follows with another compelling story of the Civil War, told from the perspective of characters you won't forget.

REFINER'S FIRE by Lynn Austin
Candle in the Darkness
Fire by Night

Bestselling Author Tracie Peterson's Unforgettable New Saga

From her own Big Sky home, Tracie Peterson paints a one-of-a-kind

portrait of 1860s Montana and the strong, spirited men and women who dared to call it home.

Dianne Chadwick is one of those homesteaders, but she has no idea what to expect—or even if she'll make it through the arduous wagon ride west. Protecting her is Cole Selby, a guide who acts as though his heart is as hard as the mountains. Can Dianne prove otherwise?

Land of My Heart by Tracie Peterson